talespinning

To Toni!

Welcome to my
Nightmares!

Best Wis

Dan...

xx

talespinning

David J Howe

First published in the UK in 2011 by
Telos Publishing Ltd
17 Pendre Avenue, Prestatyn, Denbighshire, LL19 9SH
www.telos.co.uk

Telos Publishing Ltd values feedback. Please e-mail us with any
comments you may have about this book to: feedback@telos.co.uk

ISBN: 978-1-84583-058-8 (paperback)

Editor: Sam Stone

Typesetting by Arnold T Blumberg
www.atbpublishing.com

Printed by Good News Press

British Library Cataloguing in Publication Data.
A catalogue record for this book is available from the British
Library.

àáâãäæçèéêëìíîïñôõöùúûü

Contents

Introduction

Welcome to my mind.

That might seem like a strange way to greet you, dear reader, but it's probably the closest to the truth. This is my first – and quite possibly only – collection of short fiction to be published. I say 'only' because it's taken me around 30 years to accumulate what you hold in your hand now … so unless a sudden burst of prolific inspiration hits me, then it could be some time before the next.

Most of my writing career has been spent writing non-fiction. Whether books about the making of that great BBC television show *Doctor Who*, or reviews of horror books for various magazines, or interviews with some of my literary heroes, one way or another I have been lucky to have pre-sold just about everything I have written. But fiction doesn't work like that. More often than not, fiction is written as a speculation, with little chance that it will be published, and in a commercial world, if the choice is between writing something that you have already been paid for, or that you know you will be paid for; or spending the same time writing something that might stand little chance of ever being published … then the food-on-the-table angle usually wins out.

So the fiction herein is a collection of pieces that I have written over the years; some were commissioned, some were speculative submissions for specific anthologies or projects; but all were great fun to write and have been greatly enjoyable to revisit for this book.

I have decided also to include a couple of started but unfinished novels, plus two screenplays (one was made, the other sadly fell by the wayside), as well as two drabbles (writings of exactly 100 words). My fiction writing has been nothing if not diverse. I decided against adding the script and plot of an interactive *Doctor Who* telephone line that I developed with a company that then canned the whole project, as I felt it was perhaps too obscure out of context; and some other fictional exploits involving the good Doctor have also been excluded – though I have included 'Goodbye Rembrandt' as it is a story I am very, very proud of, and the one I feel works the best.

I hope you enjoy this little visit into my mind … a place of darkness and horror sometimes, but often tinged with a little black humour, and of course papered with old horror film posters, and full of *Doctor Who* toys, games and references.

David J Howe
August 2011

Moonlighting

Jakki burst onto the platform as the train edged its way towards London. She was seconds too late. She stood, hands on thighs, panting as she watched the carriages pick up speed and vanish down the line.

'Damn!' she said.

She slumped onto one of British Rail's curiously uncomfortable benches and stretched her denim-clad legs out. Her gaze swept over the filthy platform, littered with cigarette butts and sweet wrappers. A shining example of British Rail's 'Keep your station tidy' campaign. When was the last time this station had seen a broom, let alone a coat of paint?

Her eyes scanned the familiar graffiti on the opposite platform wall. 'Ken Loves Tracey', 'Tes is a fat slag', 'For sex phone me', and now almost obscured by one of those flash American-style graffiti words – all bulging letters and multi-coloured paint – one that always brought a smile to Jakki's face; 'Jak 4 Tel 4 Ever'.

Terry had been her … how many was it? … fifth or sixth boyfriend at least. Anyway, he had been okay for the four weeks they were seeing each other semi-seriously. She smiled and looked up and down the rest of this shit-hole of a platform. Stonevent. What a pit. One train an hour. No toilets. No staff. Just two facing platforms that only ever saw life twice a day. Once when the workers set off for London and once when they came home in the evening.

The outside of the station was as scabrous and depressing as the inside. Peeling paint (somehow, despite BR's Southern Region clean up, Stonevent kept getting put to the back of the list), deserted car park and the strangest array of small shops you would ever expect to see. A travel agent's, a dusty and seemingly deserted watch repair shop and an equally dusty but apparently open for business leather-goods store that always seemed to have a profusion of bulging black dustbin liners piled on the pavement in front of it.

Jakki looked at her watch. An hour to wait for the next train. What to do now? Should she wait here, or catch the bus back home and then set off again almost as soon as she arrived, or should she go for a long aimless walk? Damn British Rail.

She pushed herself to her feet and wandered down the deserted platform, kicking stones over the lip of the platform onto the rails. Weeds poked their heads through cracked asphalt, a tattered newspaper page fluttered feebly as it tried to escape through some tired and battered wire fencing, and small furious balls of dust tumbled and skittered around between the rails, endlessly chasing each other.

The rusting station sign above her head creaked as the wind eased it into hesitant motion, and across the platform from her a door swung free on protesting hinges.

The door caught her attention. It was sturdy and

wooden and set into a brick and pebbledash construction. Twelve foot square, the box-like building extended for one storey above the platform and, for all she knew, one storey below as well. There were no visible windows and the only port of entry other than the door on the platform seemed to be another wooden door, set right at the top of the structure, which had no way of being reached from the outside – a door that would open into thin air.

Normally, the platform door would be securely padlocked and bolted shut, but here the wood of the door-frame had been splintered and the door forced open. Jakki peered across the track. She had always been intrigued as to what this strange building was actually for, and here was an opportunity not to be missed.

She quickly crossed to the other platform via the leaky and graffiti-ridden tunnel. A quick glance around confirmed that, as usual, there was no-one about, so she quickly pulled the door fully open and slipped inside.

She found herself in a plain and unremarkable room. Over to one side some rough boards covered a square arch that led into the main portion of the structure. The boards only came up about four feet and were covered with splashes of paint and more graffiti. Jakki moved across to the boards and peered over into the darkness beyond. This portion of the room extended both up and down. Up was wreathed with black cobwebs and grimy brickwork, while down disappeared into the darkness, although Jakki could make out some vague shapes clustered at the bottom. As her eyes grew accustomed to the gloom, the shapes coalesced into recognisable objects. An abandoned chair, one leg broken. A stepladder leaning drunkenly against one wall, all but two of the treads smashed. On one side Jakki made out what looked like another door, in the side of the structure that faced the platform, but right at the bottom. She craned her head to get a better view, and the boards covering the arch gave way with a loud crack. Arms swinging wildly, Jakki toppled into the cavernous pit.

When the dust had settled, Jakki cautiously opened her eyes. She was lying on top of some ancient cardboard boxes that had cushioned her fall. If she had landed on the chair or on some of the other debris that littered the floor then she would surely have broken something. She sat up and shut her eyes tight again as pain speared through her ankle. She explored the offending region with her hands. No bones seemed to be broken, just a nasty sprain.

Gingerly she got to her feet and hopped to the nearest wall for support. Looking up, she estimated that the ledge from which she had fallen was a good ten feet above her. Had she been uninjured then there was a possibility that she could have constructed some means of reaching it with all the junk that had accumulated down here, but with a bad ankle, forget it.

She looked around. Just by her feet was an old bristle-less broom. She scooped it up and used it as a makeshift crutch to take the weight off her foot.

That was when she heard the noises. At first she thought it might be a train arriving but then she realised that it wasn't getting louder, just a faint irregular thunking noise and a machinery hum. Casting around for the source, she arrived at the wooden door set into the wall at the base of the tower. There was no handle so she pushed against it. It gave slightly so she pushed harder and with a grinding of grit and a squeal of oil-free hinges it opened enough for Jakki to squeeze through.

At first Jakki wasn't sure where she was. The door opened into a long tunnel that disappeared into blackness in either direction. The far wall was plain brick, but at intervals along it, dusty and cobwebbed air-bricks provided welcome but meagre spots of light. Jakki tentatively moved into the tunnel and looked in both directions. Of course, she realised, she was under the platform. Pausing to re-locate the noises she had heard earlier, she moved down the tunnel.

The grit crunched under her feet as she moved towards the source of the machine noises. As she got closer she heard another noise as well, a hesitant scraping sound, as if a sack of something was being dragged carefully across the floor. Jakki stopped but the scraping continued.

She took another couple of steps and came to another door set in the wall of the tunnel. Jakki pulled at it and it creakily swung open. In the dim light she could only make out piles of discarded train seats. Suddenly a light flicked on and flooded the small room with light through another entrance in the far wall. Jakki hobbled across the room and stood in the lighted doorway. She looked in on a partially tiled ante-room. There was a generator humming away in one corner, and in the tiled portion a man in a British Rail uniform was bent over something that Jakki could not see from where she stood. There was a solid thunk and the man jumped back as the thing he had been bending over spasmed and thrashed on the floor. Jakki silently gasped as she saw that it was some sort of animal – perhaps a large dog – and that its body was covered with blood. She mused that perhaps it had been caught on the line and electrocuted as well as run over, but then what was it doing here and what was the BR man doing? The creature shuddered and lay still. The white-tiled floor and walls were splattered with bloody streaks left by the thing's thrashing movements. As she watched, a snaking red river slowly made its way from under the creature and crawled towards a drain set into the floor.

At that moment, the man turned and saw Jakki standing in the doorway. She saw that he was holding a large stubby pistol, from the barrel of which protruded a six inch bolt. The bolt was smeared with blood and gore and Jakki guessed that this was a humane killer, normally used for slaughtering cattle in an abattoir. The man looked directly at Jakki and their eyes met but, almost in the same movement, the man put down the pistol-device and, completely ignoring the watching girl, went to another door, switched off the lights and left the room. Jakki came to her senses as she heard the key flick in the lock.

'Wait!' she cried and hobbled in the darkness to the door. It was locked. She hammered on it a couple of times and listened.

'Hello' she called, 'Anyone there?'

No answer.

She banged on the door a final time with the flat of her hand and then gave up. Glancing at the still-humming generator as she limped past, she made her way back out to the long, gloomy under-platform corridor.

When she got to the doorway she paused, listening. Furtive scrapings could still be heard echoing slightly in the gloom. She stepped out into the tunnel, intending to continue along it until she found a way out.

Suddenly something hit her in the back of the legs and she collapsed forward, mashing her lips onto the gritty floor. She rolled onto her back as a pair of sticky wet arms shot from the gloom to grab her ankles. She pushed backwards with her legs, ignoring the pain throbbing in her damaged ankle as the owner of the arms pulled itself into view. Only the head was recognisable as human; the rest of the body was a bleeding, suppurating mess of raw tissue and exposed veins. Mad wide eyes stared out of a skinless face. Hair hung in bleeding clumps from its skull, and where the nose should have been, a gaping scab-filled cavity remained. But worse was the mouth.

The remnants of lips were pulled tightly together and held there with a criss-crossing black twine. Rivulets of blood and pus seeped from the points where the twine entered the flesh of the lips and ran down the creature's chin.

Jakki screamed as this bloody apparition clawed its way up her legs, shaking its head wildly and rolling its eyes. She kicked out, catching the thing a blow on the head with her boot. The mad eyes rolled and one of its hands slipped. Jakki kicked out again and again until, with a muffled gurgle, the creature let go and scuttled to the far wall where it curled into a shuddering heap.

Jakki lurched to her feet and limped hurriedly away down the tunnel, desperate to get away from the nightmare that shook and moaned on the floor behind her. As she moved, she heard other scuttlings and scrapings, both from in front of and behind her, as if a legion of these beasts were even now creeping up on her.

Suddenly there was another door set into the wall. She grasped the handle and pulled. The door flew open and Jakki crashed through. Regaining her balance she pulled the door shut again and pressed against it, listening to the harsh sound of her own breathing. After a minute or so, a faint scratching and tapping on the bottom of the door could be heard. Jakki noticed a bolt at the base of the door so she hurriedly threw it closed and then allowed herself to relax.

She was in what seemed to be a storage room. There

were dusty boxes and crates piled up against the walls and, by the light she now saw filtering in through a soot blackened skylight, another door. She moved over to it and gingerly tried the handle. It was torn from her grasp as the door was flung open and a man stood framed in the doorway. The same man that she had seen before. Behind him looked like the back room of some sort of shop, shelves filled with boxes, all labelled. Jakki took all this in during the few seconds before the man raised the wooden club he was holding and smacked her hard on the side of the head. The impact flung her crashing into a pile of boxes. Handbags tumbled and poured over her from the rent cardboard. She reflexively pushed them off her and staggered to her feet, groggy, hurting and confused. She fell to her knees as the club connected soundly a second time, and sank into blissful unconsciousness on the third impact.

When she came round, her head throbbed and she could not move. Blurred shapes were moving just past her field of vision and she became aware of a burning pain on her right thigh. She heard a man's voice say 'She's coming round'.

Jakki looked towards the source and saw someone in a white apron holding up to the light a small, square sheet of thin, translucent cloth. He laid the material carefully down and spoke to someone else,

'She'll do. Prepare her.'

The last things Jakki saw before her mind closed down

were the backwards sign on the shop window ('SDOOG REHTAEL'), the square patch of bleeding, skinless flesh on her right thigh, and a hand approaching her face with a large, curved needle threaded with black twine.

'Moonlighting' came about, as far as I can recall, from a challenge given by a girl at work. Jakki Fallon was her name, and she asked me to write her into a story. The other inspirations were my then local British Rail station at Tolworth, which has a strange tower-like structure, just like the one I describe, and a painting by Les Edwards showing a woman's face with the lips stitched together, a single tear trickling from her eye. It was originally a cover painting to a book called *Terror by Night* (a horror anthology edited by R Chetwynd-Hayes) and also appeared in a hardback book called *Echoes of Terror* along with many other brilliant horror paintings.

What happens to poor Jakki in the story, however, is hopefully not true at all, and I have never seen a leather goods shop at Tolworth station ...

The Ultimate Test

The Doctor flexed his fingers and concentrated. All his friends were against him. Nyssa was by the TARDIS doors, knees bent, hands tense, waiting for the Doctor's next move. Adric crouched by the inner door – the Doctor would not pass, not this time. Tegan faced her opponent. In her hand she held the intended instrument of the Doctor's downfall. The Doctor crouched lower, testing the balls of his feet against the floor. He was ready to run. Tegan's arm moved swiftly and a small pile of tin cans behind the Doctor clattered to the ground.

'Owzat!' yelled his companions triumphantly.

The Dream

Over the course of many years the fan had obsessively climbed the BBC's echelons. Often taking hated jobs but ones that would bring him closer to his ultimate goal.

He had started in accounts and moved swiftly, changing jobs until he became an assistant floor manager and finally production assistant, where he lay waiting for the moment.

Then it came. The producer was leaving. Favours were called and then, after several weeks bargaining, he became producer of *Doctor Who*.

The fan sat back in his empty office. He stared at the wall.

He had absolutely no idea what to do.

These two pieces of writing are 'drabbles', a name apparently coined in a *Monty Python* sketch, and they consist of exactly 100 words each. They are therefore quite challenging to write and are often used as an exercise in writing.

These two were written for a book of drabbles that I edited for *Doctor Who*'s thirtieth anniversary in 1993.

The Third Time

Slumped, he looks around him. Grey tiled walls. Grey tiled floor. Grey tiled ceiling. Grey. He tries to remember when there had been colour, but that was another time, another place.

Blue.

He remembers blue. That was the colour of the shirt he was wearing the first time. Had that been only two nights ago? He looks down at his clothes. Grey. Perhaps they had been blue.

Once.

'Go on, just this once.' A voice echoes from the past.

'No. I mustn't. I can't. I shouldn't.' Thoughts from the past.

'Go on. It won't hurt you.'

Cajoling. Persuading. Seducing.

His stomach clenches as it has done often in the last few hours. The bile of need bubbling up inside him, erupting like grey pus on the floor. He pulls together foetally as he has done before and squeezes silent tears out of his blindly shut eyes. The pain subsides. For now.

On the grey floor beside him stands a grey tube. Its open end beckons him to explore further. He knows there is only one small grey capsule left.

One more chance to live.

To die.

Deep in his mind he knows what he has done. He

knows now that all the warnings, the threats, the films, the examples have been for nothing. This is buried deep. Nearer the surface, in the part of him that has come alive, there is music. Deep and throbbing. Pulsing to an inner beat, gaining in intensity as the small, bittersweet voice of tainted reason worms its way through his meagre resistance.

He knows he wants to. He knows he has to. Why does he resist?

He knows why. There is only one grey capsule left for a start, but there is another reason. One that he refuses to let surface for fear that it may crack the thin grey ice of sanity that he is currently skating upon. The other reason: it involves what happened the second time.

He opens his eyes to the greyness and remembers.

The first time had been great. The capsule slipped down his throat. A great blossoming, ballooning sensation of pleasure and magnitude followed. A soaring, expanding knowledge of the how and the why. He remembers the feelings. The tingling nerve ends, the heightened awareness of self. He remembers the bittersweet smells, the sheer radiant beauty of a vibrant daisy seen through new eyes. The tang of rain on his tongue, of salt on his skin. Life flowing and throbbing wherever he looked.

He could actually see life. It encircled all things with a brilliant halo of electric sensation. Life was good and life was everywhere. He felt honoured to be a part of it. His friends had not understood – how could they? They could not see what he could, feel what he felt.

When the sensation was spent he vowed through a pounding headache never again. It had been good. It had actually been bloody brilliant, but frightening. As if he no longer knew himself, as if something else had been in control. Yes. It had been good but once was enough.

Until

Report from the Staffordshire Herald

18th April — Staff Reporter

… Mr Staple's friends admitted that he had acted strangely during and after the party on the 16th. He seemed to be hooked on something that he would only describe to them as 'life'. This behaviour may be in some way connected to his disappearance following the unprovoked attack on him the following afternoon. Police are still trying to trace the woman seen distributing drugs outside the venue …

the second time. He tries hard not to remember the second time. If the first had been his best dream then the second …

His arms encircle his legs and touch the scabs that still mark him under his dirty and tattered grey trousers. His face, marked and bruised. His mind – only just there. Clinging to sanity by a thread. Listening to the inner voices that tell him alternately that he should go for the third time and that he should seek help – somehow.

He really does not understand. He cannot understand.

He shakes his head and buries another part of his soul as the memory leaks back to haunt him.

He remembers.

A summer's day by the river. The sun is shining. The birds are singing. Fairy-tale material. He is lying on his back gazing at the cloud animals as they caper in the heavens. He misses the rush of sensation, the elation of being alive. Real life is fine, but to really appreciate it you need more. He knows what his friends have been saying, that whatever drug is in the little capsule is no good, that he is only hurting himself, but then they didn't experience what he experienced. They don't know.

He comes to a decision and slips the second plastic-coated wonder out of the tube. He downs it in one and waits.

Nothing.

He waits some more and then he feels it. This is not like the first time. This is different. Worse. As he looks around the colours bleed out of the world as if a watercolour painting had been left in a shower of rain. Colours run and mix together into a uniform grey and then, without warning, pain. The throbbing and beating music of blood in his ears. He sees a woman walk by. She glances at him and he watches as she transforms. She takes one glittery-eyed step towards him and hesitates. The human mask slips and her eyes flash gold as she smiles a welcome of needles and razors and sets about enjoying the summer afternoon with him.

Pain

Report from the Staffordshire Herald

18th April — Staff Reporter

… Miss Lucy Bodwin, a local resident, is still being held by police following her unprovoked and vicious attack on Mr Staple. Eyewitnesses say that she set upon Mr Staple as he sat by the river on the afternoon of the 17th. Miss Bodwin denies the charge but cannot explain how Mr Staple's blood and skin came to be under her fingernails and on her dress. Investigations are continuing as to the whereabouts of Mr Staple.

lances through him and now he is here. Sitting in a puddle of dirty grey water in a deserted lavatory in a dead town. The world is grey and populated by shining-eyed, sharp-teethed monsters. He feels another cramp in his belly. His body is screaming to go for the third.

He reaches out with a shaky hand and grasps the tube. The small piece of potential paradise rattles into his other hand. It remains clenched there. The pain and fear well up once more. The bubble bursts and he cries again. Great heaving sobs as grey tears course down his ashen cheeks. Hopelessness and resentment. Loss and wretchedness. Why me? He screams to an internal audience of none.

Half way to his mouth his hand stops. He heard a noise. He looks up to see and then wishes he hadn't. He is no longer alone in his grey, forgotten ceramic world.

The golden eyes pierce the greyness and draw him in. The creature smiles its poisonous welcome, the needle teeth glinting and gleaming. His eyes open wider and he falls into the golden light. Held as a snake holds a mouse, he stays motionless as the creature stalks delicately forward. It gestures that he stands and he does. It stops before him and its gaze flickers up and down his bruised body. Consciousness floods back as soon as it looks from his eyes, and his arm, still half lifted to his mouth, completes its journey with a rush. The pill is in and down his throat before those glorious golden eyes drown him again.

Strings.

The smiling puppet-master pulls his strings and he removes his tattered clothing. A smile grows wider as his scabbed and bruised flesh is revealed.

The mouth smiles wider and thin needles slide from their sockets in anticipation of the fun to come.

As he watches the saliva-coated razors tenderly slice through his flesh, he realises that there is no pain.

Grey tears continue to trickle from his eyes.

From his mouth.

From the myriad holes and slits where the creature has opened him to the world. The golden eyes lock onto his once more and his mouth is jerked upwards in a smile as the man-thing tenderly grasps the sides of his head with scalpel fingers. The mouth moves closer for a lover's kiss and his tongue and lips are devoured. The creature tenderly caresses his eyelids and all goes dark. A moist tearing noise reaches his ears as two eyeballs are pulled from their sockets and sucked like gobstoppers.

His hearing turns grey. The white noise of oblivion.

Then there is nothing but a mind.

Realising

Report from the Staffordshire Herald

19th April — Staff Reporter

A man turned himself into Stafford Police Station yesterday evening reporting that he had killed a man that he had found in the public lavatories in the centre of town. The man, whose identity is being withheld at present, apparently entered the lavatory and found what he described as a tramp slumped in the corner. The next thing he remembers is finding himself standing in the lavatory, covered in the tramp's blood. The man, who has no previous record of violent assault, is helping police with their enquiries.

This is the second case of violent assault by a normally law-abiding citizen within two days. Miss Lucy Bodwin is being held in custody after being charged by police yesterday evening with assault and grievous bodily harm to Mr Paul Staple. Mr Staple is still missing and police welcome any information as to his current whereabouts.

that the third time explains a lot. Why are there murderous lunatics that take pleasure in the mutilation and defilement of flesh? It is not the fault of the perpetrator, it is all in the mind of the victim. They bring it on themselves.

The power of the mind.

I have no idea where 'The Third Time' came from. It's obviously drug-related but I have never taken drugs. It was written one day, after considering an idea about a drug which affected everyone *other* than the taker …

It's also written in the present tense, which is not something I'm used to doing at all. However, it felt appropriate to write this narrative in this way and I feel it adds immediacy to the story – making the reader feel the action is happening there and then.

Record Collector Blues

The door to the house crashed back against the wall as Jerry bounded through. Wrenching his key from the protesting lock he leaped up the stairs three at a time to the room that he shared with his long-time girlfriend Gina.

'Gina!' he gasped, wheezing a little as the exertion of the run from the bus stop started to take its toll. 'Gina! I've found one! I've finally found one!'

As he rushed through the door to his room, it became obvious that Gina was out – her voluminous multi-coloured woollen coat wasn't hanging in its customary place by the door, and her large canvas tote bag was missing from beside the sofa.

'Damn.' Jerry breathed as he went across to the stereo system, gently and almost reverentially laying the paper bag he had been carrying on the top.

Red faced, he went over to the small, cluttered sink and eyed the mugs suspiciously, wondering which was the least offensive. He spotted an old chipped *Snoopy* mug lurking under a pile of foil take-away cartons and wrenched it free, sending cartons clattering onto the floor. He sniffed the rim and inspected the stained interior – good enough!

Placing the mug down on the pile of magazines by the sofa, he set about brewing a cup of coffee. The tap complained as it always did, and finally disgorged a kettle-full of murky water, and the stove took three matches before the gas ignited with a satisfying whumph. Finally, the coffee jar yielded just enough to make a one final cup. Jerry dutifully noted this fact down on the wiper-board fixed to the wall by the refrigerator – More Coffee. Gina would take care of that next time the groceries were bought.

Coffee poured and gently steaming in the mug, Jerry perched on the sofa and eyed the prize that he had placed on the stereo.

Jerry collected records. Not any records, but only those that he deemed to be particularly worthwhile. On the whole these were anarchistic, incomprehensible, power-packed blasters from the heady days of Punk and New Wave. Groups with names like Inflated Lilo, The Scum, Move And You're Dead, Death Sex and Penile Fascination filled his collection. The more obscure the record, and the more controversy it caused when first released, the more it met the criteria for Jerry's selection.

The record in the bag was one for which Jerry had been scouring the country for some time now. It was the second and last single release by a band called Reptile Youth, whom Jerry had first encountered through an article on obscure Punk bands in the *NME* several years back – he still had the article, cracked and yellowing now, pasted into one of his scrapbooks. Reptile Youth had released only one single and one album before vanishing off the face of the Earth as the second single was released

– or so it seemed. The band members, Scud, Rape, Phil and Brute, had arrived direct from art college with little or no practical experience of music – and in Brute's case no knowledge of which end of a guitar to hold, let alone how to play it. They were ideal material for an enterprising A&R man to mould into a controversial money-making enterprise.

Their music was loud, rude, offensive and controversial, with tracks on the album entitled 'Kill the Queen', 'I Fucked My Sister (And My Sister Fucked Me)', 'Heroin Overload' and 'Dead Dog Curry', sure to cause major headaches for numerous parents up and down the country whose rebellious kids were addicted to the anarchistic and violent undertones contained in the music. To Jerry, however, all this controversy was as nothing to the scandal associated with their second single. Released to tie in with the album (although, strangely, the track did not actually appear on the album), it was never to be found on sale anywhere as all the copies, like the group, mysteriously vanished under circumstances claimed by many to be part of a massive hype operation to boost the group into the charts. One day they were there, large as life, having wrecked and vomited all over yet another hotel room, and the next day, another wrecked hotel room, more vomit, but no sign of the group. The fact that they never reappeared seemed to have escaped the enthusiastic propounders of the hype theory.

What really piqued Jerry's interest, however, was

the mention in the *NME* article that the missing single supposedly contained material offensive to the Devil himself, and that rumour had it that the group was currently entertaining in the hot court of Old Nick. This latter comment was appended as a rather tongue in cheek aside by the author.

Now Jerry had finally found a copy of this elusive and much-sought-after (well, by him anyway) single, and it was currently sitting in a paper bag on top of his stereo in his flat.

He shook his head, remembering the pile of records from which this treasure had emerged.

'You can look through that lot,' the shop owner had said. 'But I doubt you'll find anything!'

Jerry had doubted too until he saw the unique and familiar violet and orange label that signified a Reptile Youth product. When he looked closer and saw the title – 'Heart Death' – he couldn't get the record out of the pile quickly enough. He stayed cool enough to casually offer the shop owner a pound for it, which was accepted without a glance, and then he was out into the sunshine with a big grin on his face and a definite spring in his step.

Sipping his coffee, he replaced the cup on the magazines and went over to his prize. He slipped it out of the bag. There was no sleeve, but that was to be expected, and the clashing colours of the label never looked so good.

Balancing the record expertly on one hand, he flicked on the stereo and opened the lid of the reproduction turntable. After inspecting the vinyl for marks and scratches (there were none), he placed the record on the platen, twisted the volume up to something he considered would do it justice, set the play count to three and placed the needle at the start of the track.

A crack, a pop, another pop and then the worst noise that Jerry had ever heard committed to vinyl poured over him. It seemed to be a combination/cross between a baby crying, feedback, a power drill and 300 electric guitars being trashed with a sledge-hammer. The noise erupted out of the speakers for what seemed like an eternity before the familiar beat of a Reptile Youth production broke through the crescendo and nailed a rhythm to the wall. Then came the gargling wail of Scud's vocals, sounding even more tortured and incomprehensible than usual. It was said that Scud gargled with bleach to 'improve the quality of his voice' and, listening to the records, Jerry could well believe it.

Jerry was in seventh heaven. His skin broke out in goose-bumps as the noise echoed around him, driving all other sounds into the background. The beat thudded and throbbed in his ears, and the tearing guitar and power-drill sounds ripped through the fabric of his very existence. Closing his eyes, Jerry could imagine the group performing, leaping about, shedding their clothes, destroying their instruments and finally leaping on the dozen or so female groupies that seemed to flock to all pop-weirdos.

Three minutes later and the noises abruptly ceased, leaving Jerry's ears ringing, his hands trembling and his heart palpitating wildly in his chest.

Jerry slumped to the sofa. Overwhelmed and sated. He blinked the tears from his eyes, and pushed his hair back over his ears. That deserved a second listen, yes indeed. He watched as the machine reset the stylus and then waited for the blast of noise following the crack and two pops. He was not disappointed. The racket flowed over Jerry as he sprawled on the sofa, a happy, imbecilic grin plastered to his features. The grin vanished abruptly when, about half way through the record, he felt a sharp pain in his chest, as though something had violently pricked him through his clothes. This was followed by another pang, and another. Jerry hurriedly pulled open his shirt and was shocked to see a vivid red weal on his chest, just above the nipple on the left hand side.

The record ended, and in the sudden silence, Jerry tentatively examined the mark. It seemed to be in the form of a spiral, concentric circles getting smaller and smaller towards the centre. Jerry tentatively probed the centre of the spiral with his finger and a dagger of pain shot through his chest, radiating from the middle of the mark. Jerry gasped and convulsed as the pain flooded through his body, and his eyes squeezed tight as the record started for the third and final time.

Engulfed in the blast of sound, Jerry watched helplessly as the spiral was gouged deeper into his skin, a throbbing, scarlet spot moving along the curve until it reached the centre. As the mark was etched more deeply into his skin, so the pain increased. Suddenly a spot of blood appeared in the middle of the weal and began to trace the pattern backwards. Bleeding profusely, Jerry tried to stand, clapping his hand over his chest. Blood oozing from between his fingers, the combination of noise and white hot pain caused him to stumble and fall back onto the sofa. His breathing started to spasm and as he lost consciousness he finally made out what Scud was gargling on the record: 'Death is in the heart, Needle's gonna stop, Dart is in the heart, Heart is gonna pop.'

Silence.

Jerry lay on the sofa. His head was buzzing and there was a throbbing pain in his chest.

He cracked open one eye and looked about. It was his flat, nothing odd about that.

Pushing himself into an upright position, he rubbed distractedly at his chest. In a flash of memory, he pulled open his shirt and looked down. There was a faint red mark above his left nipple, but nothing like what he remembered. He launched himself to his feet and went over to the stereo – there was a single on the turntable, but it was one of his old favourites, not the sought-after Reptile Youth one.

'God, what a dream,' he muttered, running his fingers through his dishevelled hair. Remembering the blood, he pulled his hand away and inspected it carefully. No blood. Nothing.

He glanced at his watch to check on the time, but the digital face was blank. He raised it to look more closely and shook his wrist to try to jog it into some semblance of life. The face stayed resolutely blank.

'Shit!'

Jerry stood in the centre of the room for a moment, listening to the silence outside and the ringing in his ears, when he realised that there was another sound. There was a thumping noise coming from the room above. This was not a new experience for Jerry as he was well used to the neighbours banging on the walls and ceiling to try to get him to turn the volume down. Old Mrs Price lived upstairs and she used her walking stick to hammer a beat on her floor whenever Jerry jacked the volume up too high.

'All right, all right,' mumbled Jerry. 'It's off now.'

But Mrs Price seemed intent on hammering her way through the floor as her banging just carried on.

Jerry suddenly had a thought that maybe she had fallen or otherwise hurt herself, and that she was simply trying to attract attention. Sighing to himself, he went out of the door to his flat and ascended the narrow flight of stairs to the next floor. Up here the banging noise was louder, and there were other sounds mixed in with it.

Jerry put his ear against Mrs Price's door and listened to shouting, banging, occasional crashing sounds, and the noise of water running.

'Mrs Price?' he called softly. 'Mrs Price, are you there?'

There was no answer so Jerry tapped on the door with his knuckle. 'Mrs Price? It's me – Jerry – from downstairs.'

Still no answer.

Looking right and left, Jerry placed his hand on the door handle and gently tried the door. To his surprise it opened, and he pushed the door fully open in front of him.

The sight that met his eyes immediately made him think that Mrs Price was entertaining burglars and that he had disturbed them. The short hallway was littered with papers and clothes. The pictures on the walls hung askew and the glass was shattered. Quietly Jerry moved down the hallway to peer into the main room from which all the noise was still coming.

In the centre of the room, a man stood with his back to Jerry. He was holding a coffee table above his head and using it to trash a television set that was lying crumpled and smoking at his feet. Jerry's eyes, however, were not focused on the table or the television. They were drawn to the words picked out in metal studs on the back of the man's leather jacket: Reptile Youth.

Just then, another man bowled out of the small

bathroom beside Jerry. Jerry glanced at the hooded eyes, the smile revealing the shattered teeth, and the earlobes bristling with rings, chains and pins, and knew that he was looking at Phil, the quietest member of that notorious group.

'Aya Jerry!' burbled Phil. 'Ow ya dooin mate?'

Phil wiped the back of his hand over his mouth and stumbled out into the room.

'Brute! Scud! Look oos ere.'

The man holding the table turned, and Jerry saw the bland, piggy face of Brute. Innocent-looking but for the tattoo on his forehead that proclaimed 'Fucker' to any who wished to know. Brute pulled his face into a twisted grin and let the table fall to the ground.

'Jerry!'

The new voice came from the ruined sofa, where Scud lay in several congealing pools of vomit.

'Glad you could make it!' Scud said, his voice guttural and gurgling. 'Rape'll be pleased.'

As if in reply, Rape's shaven head popped up from behind the sofa, a sly grin plastered to his features.

Jerry stood at the end of the hallway as Phil, Brute, Scud and Rape all looked at him, almost expecting him to speak.

'Uhh … Hi guys.' he managed.

'Guess wot,' said Phil, pushing his face into Jerry's. A gust of halitosis and stale vomit wafted over him, and he gagged.

'That's right,' said Phil happily. 'You're our audience!'

At this, Brute reached down with one Neanderthal hand and picked up a chair leg that lay beside his foot. Scud pushed himself up off the sofa and sashayed across to the curtains. Rape popped back down behind the sofa, returning to whatever was occupying him there. With a flourish, Scud pulled open the curtains, revealing, not the vista of houses and gardens that Jerry was expecting, but a swirling white mist.

As Jerry puzzled over this, he noticed that the mist was moving. It was also filled with faces. Crying, screaming, yelling, shouting. Expressions of pain and hopelessness pushed and jostled against the window. Men, women and children all crushed together. Fingers scrabbled at the glass, screeching like fingernails on a blackboard.

'Fans,' grunted Brute, his vocabulary no doubt doubled by this observation.

Jerry looked from the window to the faces of Reptile Youth.

'B-b-but ... I I I ...'

'Don' worry,' said Phil, staggering up to Jerry and draping an arm around his shoulders. 'You only get to go ousside if we don' like you as an audience!'

Phil looked enthusiastically at his fellow band members. 'Ain' that right chaps?'

Jerry found himself cajoled and encouraged across to the sofa, and pushed back onto it and a puddle of vomit. Phil gestured to no-one in particular. 'Cum on, less play a set.'

'Wait!' stammered Jerry. 'Who … I mean, how long … why?'

'You mean you ain't realised?' gargled Scud from the window.

'You'd better tell im!' said Phil seriously.

Rape giggled while Brute tested the stick in his hand against the wall with a crash and a dusting of plaster from above.

'Eternity's wot the man in black sed,' smiled Scud. 'An eternity of gigs, birds and dosh.'

'We ain't seen no birds or dosh yet,' explained Phil earnestly. 'But they'll cum when we got our audience sorted.'

He dropped to a crouch in front of Jerry. 'An' you're our audience!' he repeated.

Jerry started to protest, but Rape popped up behind him like a lunatic jack-in-the-box and grabbed him around the neck, holding him still. Phil smiled his broken-toothed grin. 'The bitch woman wouldn' sit still an' watch,' he explained, glancing at whatever Rape had been working on behind the sofa. 'So we gotta make sure you can't look away while the boys and me perform.'

Jerry's eyes flicked from side to side as he wondered exactly what Phil was talking about. Rape increased the pressure on Jerry's neck and giggled in his ear as Phil reached up to his right earlobe and extracted a large safety pin from it. Jerry's eyes bulged wider as Phil, with all the delicacy of a drunk searching for a keyhole, fumbled for Jerry's eyelid with his free hand.

'Just … gotta … make … sure,' he mumbled, concentrating on the task in hand. With one swift movement, he inserted the pin up under Jerry's eyelid and into the brow. Ignoring Jerry's frantic thrashing, he clipped it home and obtained a further pin from his other ear.

Jerry screeched incoherently as Phil repeated the operation with his other eye, not so effectively this time; the pin struck bone on the first attempt, and Phil had to jiggle it to get it through.

Jerry gazed manically up at Phil with bloody and staring eyes. The pain he had felt was now replaced with a lunatic buzzing as he went into shock. When he tried to close his eyes, he found that he could not. In fact the only way to keep the pain and blood at bay was to keep his eyes wide open.

'Hit it, Brute!' shouted Scud, and the band launched into an impromptu rendition of their debut single 'Smash the Palace' to an accompaniment of screaming, crashing plaster and gurgling water.

Jerry sat on the sofa. His staring and bloody eyes took in the show as the noise washed over him. In his mind he was huddled into a small ball. His internal screaming echoed a counterpoint to the madness that raged outside. He'd got his wish. He'd found his violent and controversial Punk band. For eternity.

'Record Collector Blues' was an idea that gestated after thinking about all those stories of records that allegedly summon the Devil if played backwards and so on. Combine that with some of the trash music of the '70s, when Johnny Rotten and the Pistols were the epitome of rebellion ... and Reptile Youth was born!

Party Girl

I can't sleep now. Just can't. I'm afraid. Afraid that the heating will fail and the house will grow cold around me. And that must not happen. Must not. So I sit here, with the heating on full. With a fire in front of me, another by my side, another plugged in and ready … just in case. My hands are sweaty and sticky and the pen keeps slipping as I write this. My face is burning hot but that is good.

Must keep warm. Must keep the cold away. Must write this down to warn others.

She's still out there. I can't see her – what's left of her – but I can hear her. Frozen fingers scratching oh so softly on the window pane. Her voice like tin foil picking at the edges of my mind. She traces the patterns the ice has created on my walls. But the ice does not melt.

It started weeks ago. Newspapers reporting missing kids. People who, for whatever reason, found themselves out alone and late, and never returned home. If this was America, we'd have seen new faces staring out from milk cartons at breakfast. But this was not America. It was England. And people were going missing.

And then there's what I saw earlier tonight. It was one of those winter nights when the air is crisp, still and silent. The sky was infinitely clear, the stars sharp and gleaming. Underfoot the grass and leaves were brittle and white, echoing the frozen panorama above. The weather had been like this for … well … probably since people started to vanish.

From my window I could see the shadowy park, orange and silver light filtering through the trees, dappling the landscape with sepia hues. The only sounds as I stood gazing out were distant echoes from far away streets and the furtive creaking of frozen trees as an icy breeze caressed them.

On a glinting bench not 50 yards from my window sat an attractive girl of about 19. As if to spite the weather she was dressed only in a black velvet sleeveless party frock and a flimsy silk wrap. Her stockings were twisted and her once-pristine shoes were scuffed. She sat there, and I could see frozen tears, or perhaps glitter, sparkling on her cheeks. She stared out into the cold, dark night and I could sense her cold, dark thoughts.

I imagined her predicament ... She had been dumped. Christmas Eve and she had been dumped. Her boyfriend – correction: ex-boyfriend – had invited her to a party and then gone off with someone else.

As I watched, she shuddered and hugged herself. Moments later I too felt the same chill breeze as it investigated the open window at which I stood. My breath steamed as I copied her actions.

My unknown companion in the park stood and wandered slowly towards my window and the park exit below. I could hear the crisp cracking of grass crunching under her feet. A quick flurry of movement behind her caught my eye and she also turned. Frozen leaves rustled in a whirlpool of air, but otherwise there was nothing to see but the cold and ice.

An inner chill pulled at me and I sensed rather than saw the presence. The feeling was undeniable and the girl obviously felt it too as she turned and began to walk more briskly for the exit.

Ahead of her, and from out of a clump of bushes, an amorphous mist rolled over the path and a sighing whisper carried through the air. I peered closer, as the effect was of someone hidden in the bushes exhaling mightily. The sense of presence magnified, and the girl stopped as she (and I) caught a fleeting glimpse of something pale, pink and glittering moving arrow-swift towards her through the sibilant swirling mist. Her mouth opened in a gasp as wintry tendrils reached for her, and seconds later I heard her intake of breath. She quickly glanced about. Nothing. Just the cold, desolate, darkness of the park …

And the mist …

And the strong, frosted hand that emerged from the cloud to grip her upper arm.

She inhaled to scream, but the mist flowed in with her breath, blazing a crystalline trail down her throat. A second pale arm emerged and grasped her ankle. I could see its fingers bury themselves in her stocking. A third set of fingers crept sinuously around her other ankle and she found herself held motionless as the rolling, icy mist tenderly caressed her.

I watched as her struggles slowly lessened as her

body became covered with glinting ice crystals. Her hair, whipping as her head tossed from side to side, slowed and then shattered into pieces. Her arms and legs slowly stiffened as the heat was removed, and then, to my horror, the hands holding her flexed, and her limbs were pulled from her torso with a series of sharp retorts that echoed through the desolate night. Her glittering torso fell to the hard ground, and the once-soft dress shattered around her with a gentle tinkling sound. The mist rolled over to cover her and that is when, in unthinking panic, I slammed my window shut.

I tried to run. I really tried. As I opened my door, the shimmering, whispering mist scooted across the road towards me, an indistinct shape, the colour of putty, writhing in its centre. I slammed the door and bolted it. The wood frosted and protested as cold fingers scratched against it. I watched as ice crystals formed around the edges, and then turned and ran back to my upper room.

She's calling me now, the party girl. Whispering in my mind that she is so cold and would I just open the door to allow her some warmth. Promising me untold pleasures if I will just let her in. Her voice reminds me of someone I think I know, reassuring and calm.

Perhaps I will open the door. Just a crack.

Her voice croons to me. Alluring and calm. I can see the steam from her breath dance through the gap under the door. It makes shapes in my mind. Sensual, writhing shapes. Promising so much.

Is that what the party girl felt just before ... before ... So hard to think. It's so hot in here.

I can feel her touch, her pale blue hand pressing to my fevered forehead. Blessed coolness after all this heat.

Opening the door just a bit can't hurt. It can't matter.

A cool hand on my forehead would be so nice. Soothing.

The door is opening ... My hands have undone the bolt and turned the key ...

She's singing to me now ... so cool ... so cold ...

'Party Girl' was written as something of an experiment to see how far I could describe a scene, to really try and get the sense of the cold, the freezing conditions. Once I had completed it, I quite liked the result as it turned into a somewhat sinister tale.

Goodbye Rembrandt

ONE

Eight-year-old Danny Walker was pushed back against the muddy wall. He could feel his fists and arms sinking into the yielding grey ooze and yet it was impossible to run. Before him the walls of the underground tunnel curved round out of sight and a familiar quirky tune started up, which could mean only one thing … the Mud People were coming.

Before Danny's frightened eyes the walls of the tunnel seemed to shift as featureless grey mud gave way to humanoid forms. These forms started to struggle and push themselves away from the walls of the passage, dripping blobs of wet dirt and clay. They reached out with lumpy, fingerless hands, and as Danny stared in paralysed horror they turned their misshapen faces towards him. As the music continued, Danny watched as they lurched away down the tunnel in search of Danny's hero, one Flash Gordon, who was on Mars to try and foil the schemes of the dastardly Ming the Merciless.

Danny risked a sideways glance but the seat next to him was empty. His elder brother had no doubt slipped away to enjoy some time with his new girlfriend Tanya. Bob was eight years older than Danny and had just discovered the wonders of girls: Danny however could not understand why *anyone* would want to spend time with

47

them. They couldn't throw ball properly, were hopeless at football, and, unless properly prepared by forward-thinking mothers, couldn't even go climbing trees and exploring the riverbanks nearby for fear of getting their dresses spoiled.

Danny sighed and looked back at the large cinema screen in front of him. The mud men had been replaced by Gordon's rocket ship, shooting through space and emitting an impressively large number of sparks from its rear end. Danny had seen *Star Wars* and knew that rocket ships did not throw out sparks. Real rockets made a kind of howling noise as they powered through space, lasers blazing away at the enemy. Danny briefly entertained the thought that in a battle between Flash Gordon and Darth Vader, then Vader was almost certain to win … but if Lord Vader then decided to go up against Ming, the outcome was perhaps less certain.

As Gordon's ship hurtled towards the surface of Mars, a familiar caption appeared telling people that the adventure would continue next time. As the music swelled and the credits appeared, Danny pushed himself up out of his seat. He noted that the scuffed fabric *was* very like mud and experimentally pushed it with his finger. The resultant dent stayed when he removed his finger. Danny pushed at another point with the same result.

A sharp pang in his bladder told him that he had not been to the loo since the start of the presentation and that, if he didn't want to miss the next feature – an episode featuring Captain Buck Rogers – he had better do something about it.

Danny crab-walked his way down the row of seats to the aisle and, stepping over someone who had apparently gone to sleep on the stairs, made his way up towards the back of the cinema towards the toilets. All around him children were laughing, screaming, shouting and calling to each other. Paper missiles flew about, and every so often a lump of indefinable toffee-like substance was thrown. The management had long since abandoned any hope of controlling the 50 or so kids who had made the Saturday morning pictures such a success during the school holidays. It was easier to simply spend an hour or so after they had all gone cleaning up, than suffer the constant abuse and harassment that ensued should any of them appear in the cinema during the two-hour session.

Danny reached the back of the cinema and turned to survey the seats leading to the screen. The cinema was an old, turn-of-the-century construction, and the screen was massive, dwarfing all before it. The seating was all on the cinema's balcony, and at the very front there was a massive pit falling away to where the stalls would have originally been. They had long been removed, however, and the whole 'downstairs' area had been converted into two other cinemas, allowing the management to show three films at the same time and so treble their income.

Access to this dark front area was blocked off by gratings across the spiral staircases at each side of the auditorium, and a wall prevented any children from risking life and limb by falling over the edge. This was the only thing that was forbidden, as far as Danny could tell. The management were blissfully absent at all times, except for when someone decided to clamber up on the wall. Then, torches blazing, the manager and two female ushers (one, Mavis, was usually to be found behind the cash desk dispensing tickets, while the other, Susie, was in charge of the ice cream fridge and the coke and popcorn machines) would appear as if from nowhere and escort said child off to await his or her parents.

It wasn't worth the hassle, so most of the kids stayed on their side of the wall.

Danny carefully scanned the rows of seats but he couldn't see Bob and Tanya anywhere. They normally nipped to the back row, but today that row was empty. Danny shrugged. Maybe they had gone to the loo themselves. He pushed aside the heavy red velvet curtain that blocked the rear exit and wandered along the corridor to the loos. All along the walls were hung frames containing faded posters for old films. Danny had seen the posters hundreds of times, but had yet to see any of the films. One, for something called *Them!*, was a particular favourite, and Danny liked to stop and study the images, imagining what marvels the film must contain. Today, however, he hurried on past, mindful of his need to use the loo, and slightly concerned as to where his brother had gone.

He pushed open the door to the gents and hurried to the porcelain urinal. When he had finished, he dutifully washed his hands. Then he realised that Bob was not in there. In fact, the toilet was completely empty. Danny stood still for a moment and listened. All he could hear was the dripping of the cistern.

He returned to the door and entered the corridor once more, not seeing the shadows that skittered across the floor of the toilets behind him.

Odd. The silence continued. Normally you could hear the screams and shouts from the auditorium back here, as the old velvet curtain was not that good at blocking them out, but as Danny listened he could hear nothing at all.

He wandered back along the corridor, past the posters, and paused at the curtain. He still could hear nothing. Behind him, the darkness seemed to intensify, and the posters along the walls shimmered slightly, the images faintly moving as though seen through a haze of heat. He grasped the curtain and pushed it to one side, slipping past it into the cinema once more.

As the curtain dropped back, Danny looked around. The light reflected from the screen lit up the rows of chairs at the front. He blinked. It has to be some kind of joke. There was no-one there. No-one at all. The cinema was deserted.

TWO

Tanya saw Danny make his way up the aisle towards the back of the cinema. She and Bob were shrouded in darkness about three rows from the back, below the wall lamp that Bob had disabled some weeks back by removing the bulb and then jamming a wad of chewing gum into the hole before squashing the bulb back into place. This resulted in an impressive area of gloom to which she and Bob made their way once the films had started.

Tanya closed her eyes in pleasure as Bob started kissing and running his sharp teeth along her neck. Goosebumps rose on her bare arms as he ran his hand around the back of her neck and tickled the fine hairs there. She shifted in her seat and sighed.

Bob's other hand braced against the seatback as he started to suck at her earlobe, at the same time blowing gently into her ear. The sensation of air blowing against the dampness of her ear sent shivers running right down her legs and she curled her feet in pleasure.

Through her closed eyelids she suddenly caught a flash of light and opened her eyes to see what was going on. The flickering grew faster and she struggled to push Bob off her.

'Bob ... stop ... look.'

Bob raised his head lazily from her neck and smiled. 'D'you really want me to stop?'

As his hand started a slow stroke up her side towards

her breasts, she gasped. 'Yes … No … Just stop!'

Bob opened his eyes and looked at her. Tanya was looking right past him at whatever was causing the light to strobe across her face. He twisted in his seat and looked towards the front of the auditorium.

All the noise had stopped and everyone in the cinema was looking towards the source of the light.

The giant screen was flickering and strobing, coloured lights flashing out and playing over the faces of the people gathered before it. Within the light Bob could see something curling and moving. A sinuous shape that coiled and writhed in the light. He sat up and peered closer. It was like one of those magic-eye pictures that came to life before your eyes when you least expected it. But there was something oily and wrong with this picture.

As Bob watched, a sudden tendril of mauve light flicked from the screen and silently engulfed a group of children near the front. There was a burst of light as though someone were taking flash-photographs in the cinema, and then the children were gone. Just vanished.

Bob grabbed Tanya by the hand and tried to drag her from her seat.

'There's something not right here, Tanya. Come on. We've got to …'

She seemed strangely reluctant to leave the seat and sat there, wide eyed, staring at the lights that flashed and flickered across her face.

Bob grabbed her arm and lifted her from the seat. 'Come on!' he shouted and started dragging her along the row of seats. She followed him meekly, still entranced by the light-show taking place at the front of the cinema. Reaching the aisle, Bob started to make his way up the steps towards the exit. He looked back to see another tendril flick out and caress his girlfriend's face briefly.

Tanya stiffened and shuddered, before the sight of her was blotted from Bob's eyes by another brilliant flash. He lifted his hands to his face and blinked until he was able to see again. Tanya had gone. In fact, practically everyone in the cinema had vanished, leaving an eerie stillness lit by jumping shadows and pulsing lights. Bob turned and bounded up the stairs towards the velvet curtain that led to the exit.

Just as he reached the curtain, he felt a tingling in his leg. He looked down to see purple light flickering around him, and then, with an agonising jolt, everything went black.

THREE

The Doctor was worried. Normally this would not have bothered Romana much, but his worry made him grumpy and uncommunicative. Ever since they had attached the randomiser to the TARDIS controls, he seemed to have grown more moody. She would have thought that he would have relished the prospect of unplanned and unannounced adventures through space and time once more (apparently he had enjoyed a good few of those in the years before she met him) but instead he seemed more concerned with whether their random trips were, indeed, random at all.

First they had arrived on the planet Skaro. Nothing too unusual about that, but their arrival had coincided with a plot by the robot Movellans to excavate the body of Davros, the creator of the Daleks, in order to use his knowledge as a lever in their war against his creations. From there they had tried to have a holiday in France – Paris to be precise – but somehow the TARDIS again arrived right on top of a time distortion caused by an alien experimenting in the vicinity.

After that, he had made some adjustments to the randomiser, and the TARDIS had homed in on yet another source of time distortion. Again on Earth, and again she and the Doctor had gone out to investigate.

Now, here they were again. Once more on Earth (What was it with this planet?, she wondered. Why was it the focus for so much alien attention?) and once more checking out some anomalous ripples in time.

Romana had to admit, however, that this time the ripples had flared across the TARDIS's navigation systems like a lighted strip of magnesium. There was no denying it, and no ignoring it either, as the Doctor adjusted the controls minutely and brought the TARDIS down to Earth.

Standing by the doors to an enormous cinema in 20th Century England, the Doctor was an imposing sight, and yet at the same time friendly and calming. A pair of wide, twinkling blue eyes peered from under a shock of curly brown hair. His full lips were parted in an almost permanent gentle smile, and atop the head a battered felt hat rested at a jaunty angle.

'Localised disturbance of the time lines,' he muttered to himself. 'Whatever is going on is still going on, so to speak.' As he spoke he waved an object in his hand at the doors before checking a small dial set into its face.

As usual, Romana had dressed for the occasion, and was wearing a tight pair of black corduroy trousers and a short scarlet blazer over a white, collared shirt. Unlike the Doctor, she liked to look her best when investigating unexplained time disturbances.

She looked around her. The Rembrandt cinema was perched on a hill alongside a railway line, and below it a stream of traffic passed in both directions on a busy South London road. She turned to see that the Doctor had opened the doors to the cinema and was striding across the red-carpeted foyer towards a flight of stairs that led to the upper level.

'It's stronger here, see?' The Doctor called out to Romana. She hurried across and looked at the time sensor he was carrying. A handy device, and one that he had knocked up in the TARDIS labs once he had decided that he was going to seek out these anomalies. Romana idly wondered if the Guardians' intent in setting up the search for the Key to Time had not been a ruse to draw the Doctor into enjoying the thrill of the hunt, and that this was the result ...

'Oh, Doctor,' she exclaimed in mock exasperation. 'There's nothing here! It's just a cinema. England, London, late 20th Century ... *again*', she added under her breath. 'If there were some distortion then it would be showing itself.'

As she spoke she took a step backwards up the steps leading to the upper level and felt a cold chill down her back. Before her, the foyer seemed to ripple and twist.

She jumped forward abruptly and looked back up the stairs. 'What was that?'

'What was what?' asked her companion, innocently munching at the contents of a carton of popcorn he had found on the sales counter.

Romana reached out her hand up the stairs, and saw her fingers ripple before her. 'The time distortion. It's here,' she whispered.

The Doctor strode over and reached out with his hand too. 'Mmmm,' he murmured around a mouthful of popcorn. 'Hold this.' He thrust the box of corn into Romana's hands and held forward the time sensor. The small needle started to shudder back and forth. 'About 25 ... give or take. And fading.' He stepped up the stairs, still holding the device in front of him. 'Fading ... fading

… gone.' He looked back at Romana. 'Whatever it was, it's retreated upstairs.' The Doctor looked up into the darkness. 'Shall we follow it?'

Without another word he started stalking up the staircase, leaving Romana standing down in the foyer.

'You wait there …' the Doctor's voice came echoing down the staircase.

Romana gulped. 'It'll be all right. The Doctor knows what he's doing,' she muttered to herself. With the fingers of her left hand crossed behind her back, she added: 'I hope.'

FOUR

The Doctor could feel that something was very wrong in this cinema. The portable time sensor was registering wildly and, as a Time Lord, he didn't need his electronics to tell him that time was being manipulated here.

As he ascended the dark staircase, he thought he could hear snatches of music and voices, as though he was tuning a radio through various stations. He stopped just before the top of the stairs and listened hard. As though from a great distance he could hear the distinctive twanging music that heralded the start of Orson Welles' film *The Third Man*. He took another step forward and the music dissolved into an out-of-tune rendition of John Williams' *Star Wars* theme. One more step and he was at the top of the stairs. From nowhere he heard Jack Nicholson announce his arrival: 'Here's Johnny!'

The Doctor slowly walked forward. With each step he caught more snatches of music and dialogue: 'What's up Doc?'; music from *Twin Peaks*; Woody Woodpecker making his distinctive call; 'Frankly, my dear, I don't give a damn!'; the whistling theme from *The Good, The Bad And The Ugly* … all mixed and merged together to form a whispering accompaniment to his steps.

He approached the velvet curtain that led to the seating area and paused for a moment with his hand on the rich, red cloth. Mixed in with the whispering and snatches of music he could now hear crying and screaming. Children reacting in pain and confusion. From around the curtain could be seen a flickering, multi-coloured light that pulsed in time with the fading of the sounds.

He swept the curtain aside and revealed the blackness of the auditorium. All the sounds stopped and the lights were extinguished. Breathing heavily, the Doctor took a step into the room beyond.

He peered into the darkness and fumbled in one of his voluminous pockets for a torch. He located what he was after and switched it on. The narrow beam cut through the darkness and illuminated the ghostly shape of the vast cinema screen before him. Swinging the light up the rows of seats, the Doctor thought he could hear sobbing once more. He made his way slowly across in front of the screen and up the central aisle, his feet crunching on discarded popcorn.

A furtive movement at the back of the auditorium caught his eye and he swung his torch up. He carefully made his way up the wide steps. Right at the top, huddled behind the seats, he found a small boy curled into a ball. The boy was crying, and when the Doctor reached out his hand to gently shake his shoulder, he squealed and tried to scurry away along the row of seats.

'Hello there,' smiled the Doctor, gently. The boy stopped and looked back at the Doctor, terror glinting in his eyes.

The Doctor gently removed his hat and smiled at the boy again. 'Hello. I don't think we've been introduced. I'm the Doctor. I'm a friend ...'

The boy made another muffled cry and launched himself at the Doctor. Burying his face in the folds of his voluminous scarf, he started sobbing more loudly. The Doctor hugged the child to him and patted his heaving shoulders. 'It's all right ...' he muttered, looking around the gloom warily. 'It's all right.'

FIVE

Romana was starting to wonder what was taking so long. There seemed to be nothing out of place. Nothing unusual whatsoever. Her gaze took in the doors they had just come from – now closed. The popcorn machine, the ticket booth, the red carpet … everything *seemed* normal.

She sighed and lithely jumped up onto the counter beside the coke machine, her legs swinging in front of her.

… trouble … go now …

She shook her head. She could have sworn she had heard something. Like a background buzz in her mind.

… help … now … urgent …

There it was again.

'Doctor?' She called out quietly. 'Doctor, is that you?' Silence.

She pushed herself off the counter and loped across to the flight of stairs. Peering up she could see nothing.

She took a tentative step up and her attention was suddenly grasped by a framed poster on the wall opposite her. It was for a film called *The Texas Chainsaw Massacre* and showed the leading character, an unsavoury character called 'Leatherface', wielding a large chainsaw against a blood-red sky.

Romana blinked. The poster had seemed to shift and move, and suddenly the crashing roar of a chainsaw being revved up echoed around. With a sickening twisting and wrenching feeling, Romana felt the world tip sideways, and suddenly, rather than standing on a flight of stairs in an English cinema, she was lying on a hot tarmac road. The sun was setting behind her, casting a blood-red glow over everything and, in front of her, revving his chainsaw, stood Leatherface.

She blinked rapidly and clutched at the gritty tarmac. It was real …

Romana's eyes widened in horror as the man with a mask of human skin took a step towards her.

SIX

The Doctor had managed to calm the boy down, and as his sobs had died away, he sat him down in one of the seats.

The Doctor crouched down beside him. 'I know it's hard,' he began, 'but you've got to tell me what happened here.' The boy looked at the Doctor and shook his head stubbornly.

The Doctor looked thoughtful. 'If you do, you can have a jelly baby …' In the Doctor's hand had miraculously appeared a crumpled white bag. He dug into it with his other hand and emerged triumphantly with a green baby-shaped sweet. 'There!'

He thrust the bag at the boy. 'Go on … before I eat them all.'

The boy looked uncertain, but the Doctor rustled the bag at him again. 'Go on,' he whispered.

The boy delved into the bag himself and came out with a black sweet, which he popped into his mouth.

The Doctor smiled. 'There you go. Now. How about

we start from the beginning.' He cleared his throat and held out his hand. 'I'm the Doctor, and I'm pleased to meet you ...?'

'Danny,' whispered the boy around the half-chewed jelly baby. 'Danny Walker.'

'Well I'm pleased to meet you Danny Walker,' said the Doctor, grasping the boy's hand and squeezing it. 'Now ... can you tell me what you saw?' The boy pulled his hand from the Doctor's and shook his head.

'Now ... come on Danny. I haven't got enough sweets to keep this up all day, you know. Nothing's going to hurt you ... I just need to know what you saw. Hmm?

'Were you here on your own?'

Danny shook his head. 'My brother ... and Tanya ...'

The Doctor looked around. 'Do you know where they are now?'

'Gone.'

'Gone? Gone where?'

'Just gone.'

The Doctor sighed and stood up. He flicked on his torch once more and shone it around the room. 'Gone.' He muttered to himself.

'Come on Danny.' The Doctor held out his hand to the boy. 'Let's get you back downstairs, eh? And then we'll see if we can't find out where your brother went to.'

Danny looked up at the Doctor and managed a smile. 'Okay.'

'That's the spirit!'

They made their way back down the centre aisle and across to the staircase leading back down to the foyer. As they made their way down the steps, the Doctor noticed that something wasn't right. Where was Romana? He bounded down the last few steps.

'Romana? Romana? Where are you?' The Doctor stood in the middle of the foyer and listened. Faintly, he could hear the sound of someone trimming a hedge in the distance. And screaming.

The Doctor shut his eyes and slowly pirouetted on the spot. He came to a halt facing the staircase once more, on which Danny was still standing with a scared expression on his face. The Doctor opened his eyes, and walked back towards the boy.

'Oh dear.'

The Doctor's eyes alighted on the poster of *The Texas Chainsaw Massacre*, where the maniac with the chainsaw was bending over a female figure on the ground before him. The figure had long blonde hair and was wearing black jeans and a red jacket. 'Romana!' hissed the Doctor.

SEVEN

Romana!

Romana heard the Doctor hiss her name. Even above the overpowering roar of the chainsaw, she heard it as though it were in her head.

'Doctor?' she spluttered. 'Help me!'

Romana. It's not real. You're not really there. Concentrate.

The Doctor's words seemed to make no sense. She could feel the hard tarmac under her hands, hear the roar of the ripping chainsaw, smell the belch of petrol fumes each time the lunatic revved it up. Of course she was here …

Keep thinking … It's not real … You're not really there.

Romana glanced around her. How could she do that? The maniac stepped closer and swung the spinning blade in a lazy arc towards her. She tried to scurry away but the lunatic could walk faster than she could crawl. She fought back the impulse to scream again.

Romana. Listen to me.

It was the Doctor again. She struggled to concentrate through her fear. She dragged herself a little further away from the man across the gritty road surface.

Shut your eyes. It's not real!

'Shut your eyes!' she muttered. 'It's all right for you. *You* don't have a bloody great chainsaw being waved in your face!'

She clenched her hands into fists and with a momentous effort of willpower closed her eyes. The chainsaw roared once more and she felt a breeze as, presumably, the man made another swinging pass before her face.

Say it. It's not real.

65

'It's not real,' agreed Romana. 'It's not real.'

Again.

'It's not real … it's not real … it's not real.'

Suddenly the sound cut off, and Romana felt herself twisting again. The hard, gritty road surface softened, and she unclenched her fists to feel the velvet pile of a carpet under her. She opened her eyes a crack to see the Doctor's face looking concerned.

'Oh, Doctor,' Romana gingerly got to her feet and dusted herself down. She could still smell the acrid tang of burnt petrol in her throat. 'What was that all about?'

'I was about to ask you the same question. Where were you … correction … where did you *think* you were?'

Romana glanced at the film poster on the wall. 'In there … with that … that maniac. He was going to kill me.'

The Doctor looked at Romana and then at the poster. 'Really? Kill you? Are you sure?'

Romana nodded. 'It all seemed so real.'

'I expect it was meant to.'

'What do you mean?'

'I mean,' said the Doctor grimly, 'that whatever, or whoever has taken control of this cinema intended it to seem real. There's something very evil here. Something that has been here for a long time. Something that has just managed to break through and, if left unchecked, may destabilise the very fabric of time.'

'You don't mean …'

The Doctor suddenly brightened. 'No I don't mean …
and neither do you.'

He looked at Danny who was still standing on the
stairs beside him looking bemused. 'Danny, this is my
friend Romana. Say hello to Danny, Romana.'

Romana smiled at the boy. 'Hello Danny.'

Danny looked back at this lady and thought she had
the most beautiful smile he had ever seen. He could not
help but smile back.

The Doctor stepped towards Romana. 'Danny's had a
bit of a shock. Maybe if you talk to him, you can find out
what happened.'

Romana nodded and held out her hand to Danny.
'Come on Danny, I think there's still some coke in the
machine. Shall we?' Danny nodded, still entranced
by Romana's smile. He took her hand and the two of
them walked down the stairs towards the confectionery
counter.

EIGHT

Down in the pit in front of the cinema screen, something
stirred. Gently at first but then with more vigour. A
gentle, pale violet glow coalesced into a shifting form,
and air stirred as dust motes gathered together to create
a shape. The light flickered in intensity and the shape of
a skeletal arm formed from the dust. Slowly, the arm was

coated with veins and muscle, before a layer of skin crept across it. The arm tentatively flexed.

Around the cinema auditorium, the numerous posters from times past glowed with an inner light. In each of them could be found figures that had not been there previously. In one, the bestial form of a Morlock was throwing its shadow over the forms of the peaceful Eloi, but among their number could be seen several children dressed, not in the cloth and flowers of those future inhabitants of the Earth as seen in George Pal's *The Time Machine*, but in jeans, sneakers and T-shirts of the late 20th Century. These children were screaming and screaming as the Morlocks approached ever closer.

In another, the image of Michael Caine standing proudly as his British troops rallied against the ruthless Zulu warriors was at odds with the group of strangely dressed teenagers who were being threatened by three spear-wielding aggressors. As the terrifying Zulus advanced, one of the teenagers, a girl, started crying uncontrollably, while the two boys stood their ground, terrified beyond belief as to what was happening to them.

In yet another, a space-suited alien being from Planet X stood over an attractive brunette, while in the background another woman looked on as a further group of children were being bundled into an alien spacecraft. Once more, all were confused, crying and terrified out of their wits.

In a poster for *The Brides of Fu-Manchu*, the collage of scenes behind the green-hued image of Christopher Lee as the dastardly Chinese villain now included Tanya and Bob, huddled together in a cell, waiting for whatever fate lay in store for them. Tanya was crying and Bob had his arm around her, unsure of what had happened or what to do or say.

All this pain and emotion fed the entity that writhed and rolled below the screen. Sucking up all the projected emotion that this building had known throughout the years, and intensified first through the capture of the children, and then through Romana's own terror at finding herself trapped, the entity now had enough latent energy to form itself a real body, something that would serve until it could gain sufficient suffering to expand once more.

The muted cries and screams from the posters fed it, making it grow and giving it life.

NINE

Down in the foyer, the Doctor and Romana had left Danny eating popcorn on the counter, and were standing over by the doors.

The Doctor pushed against the door once more. 'Definitely locked.'

'But how can it be locked?' asked Romana. 'We got in

here and it was unlocked then.'

'Well, you can try yourself, but it's locked now.' The Doctor sighed. 'It's not as if we really know what's going on or where all those children have vanished to.' He pulled his time sensor out of his pocket and checked the readings once more. 'Whatever it is,' he said, 'it's growing in strength.' He showed the sensor to Romana, who was looking over his shoulder at the stairs. She gently shook her head and patted the Doctor's arm.

'I … I don't think we have to go looking for what's causing this, Doctor.' She swallowed. 'I think it's found us instead.'

The Doctor muttered 'What?' and slowly spun round on the spot.

At the top of the staircase, swathed in shadow, was an abomination.

It took a step down towards them. On top of a misshapen torso was a lumpy and malformed head. Wisps of hair dotted the skull, and the features kept shifting and moving, flowing like mercury into new formations. Now it looked like Humphrey Bogart, but those features shifted into Madonna, and from there into Mel Gibson, Meryl Streep, Peter Cushing and Roddy McDowell. No face remained for more than a few seconds before it shifted. A constant moving panoply of movie stars through the ages.

The torso was red and unfinished. One stumpy arm emerged from the left side, while on the other grew a strong and muscular limb. A second set of limbs could be seen waving ineffectually below these. The legs were functional and ended with two stumps as though the creature wasn't sure what happened below the knee. Romana realised in horror that the majority of films mostly cut the actors off below the knees – it was rare to see feet on screen. This creature, whatever it was, had a million faces to choose from, but very little idea about the rest of the human body. Or else, pondered Romana cynically, it just couldn't be bothered.

As it stepped down closer to them, Romana left the Doctor's side and hurried across the foyer to where Danny had not as yet noticed their visitor. She grabbed his hand and pulled him off the counter and away to the far end of the foyer, where they crouched down behind the ticket booth.

'What is it?' asked Danny, again happy to have this beautiful lady all to himself. 'Nothing. It's nothing,' said Romana. She looked at Danny sternly. 'Now I want you to stay here. All right? Just stay here and everything will be fine. Nothing will hurt you. We'll make sure of it.'

Danny looked up at her with trusting eyes. If his new friend said that if he stayed here, then he'd be fine, then he believed her. 'Okay,' he said, 'but you'll come back?'

Romana nodded. 'Yes. Promise.'

Danny settled back to munch at his popcorn, and Romana stood up and made her way back around the ticket booth to where she could see the Doctor standing at the bottom of the stairs, looking up at the hulking creature that was now about half way down. As Romana watched, she could see strands of violet light attaching the creature to the posters along the staircase wall. It seemed to be drawing energy from the images.

Romana hurried across the foyer and arrived at the Doctor's side. 'You've noticed the light?' she hissed.

'Yes,' replied the Doctor, not taking his eyes off the thing in front of him. 'It seems to be drawing energy from them. You can see that as it gets close to a poster, the light flares brightly, and then fades off as it moves away.'

'What do you think it's doing? What's it taking from the posters?'

'Energy … emotion …' the Doctor's voice was bleak. 'A creature bringing itself into life using the emotions of people who come to watch films at the cinema. Interesting analogy. Film makers constantly try to outdo each other in creating ever more real spectacles on the screen, and to engage the viewers' emotions while doing so. Now those emotions have taken on a life of their own, so to speak.'

'But what about the children?'

The Doctor gestured to the posters. 'They're in there. Trapped. At least for the moment. Trapped in a world of make-believe. I think that our new friend here,' the Doctor gestured to the creature on the stairs, 'has put them all somewhere to generate the maximum amount of terror to feed it. And you know what that's like, don't you?'

Romana nodded. 'Horrible,' she whispered.

'So,' said the Doctor. 'Let's see what we can do about it.'

He took a step towards the hulking shape. The head twisted from side to side, like a snake seeking its prey. The ever-changing faces became quizzical, and then the thing's mouth opened in a smile.

'Of all the bars ...' the voice of a thousand people hissed around the foyer.

'Oh, give it a rest!' exclaimed the Doctor. 'You've got all the films ever made, and all the actors. I'm sure you can come up with something more original than that!'

'Where are you going, little girl?'

Romana elbowed the Doctor. '*The Wizard of Oz*?'

The Doctor nodded. 'Our friend here may look like every child's nightmare, but it's not very original.' He looked at the creature. 'That's your problem, you see. You've access to time displacement, you can tap into all the things that exist on the silver screen, but you can't be original.'

The creature took another step towards them, and the head whipped round to fix the Doctor with a steely gaze. Through a myriad different voices, it tried again.

'You ... mock ... us ... We ... *can* ... talk ... through ... the ... voices ... of ... many.'

'Clever.' The Doctor nodded sagely. 'It's breaking the speech up into individual words and then playing them back to us one word at a time to give it a voice.'

'What do you want?' The Doctor flinched backwards as the questing head flicked back in his direction once more.

'We … want … experience … Recorded … histories … not … enough.'

The creature swayed from side to side. As it breathed, so more violet flashes of light came from the posters, and the faint, echoing sound of screaming increased in volume slightly, before fading away once more.

It reached out its good arm towards the Doctor.

'You … who … are … you … you … are … not … like … the … others … more … like … one … we … tasted … fear … from … earlier.'

The Doctor shrugged modestly. 'Oh, we're just travellers, you know. Been there, done that, seen the other.' He smiled at the creature on the steps. 'You can't win, you know. We won't let you.'

Laughter echoed round the foyer. It was the laughter of a million people in a million cinemas at a million films. 'You … threaten … us?' the creature asked. 'We … can … draw … on … the … power … of … film … any … time … we … like.'

'But that's just it. It's only film. You can't experience true life. You can't enjoy what it means to grow up, to love, to hate, to bleed, to cry…'

'All … these … things … we … know.'

'Ah,' the Doctor shook his tousled head sagely. 'But you don't. You only know what the films have shown.

A Hollywood-glossed version of what some group of faceless studio executives *think* it means to do those things. You're just a third-rate copy of some fourth-rate film ideas. There's not a spark of originality in you.'

The creature surged forward another step, and the Doctor and Romana stepped back.

Romana caught at the Doctor's sleeve. 'Careful, Doctor,' she said. 'Maybe it only has second-hand sensitivity as well.'

The Doctor looked at Romana. 'I've an idea,' he said. 'But you're not going to like it.'

'What idea?' Romana looked concerned.

'You're really not going to like it.'

'Well how can I tell, if you don't explain it to me.' Romana was getting used to the Doctor's word games, but this was hardly the time or the place.

The Doctor looked back at the creature on the stairs. 'Well … what our friend there wants is to experience a real life rather than a fiction.'

Romana nodded. 'I'm with you so far …'

'So what we could perhaps do is give it what it wants.'

Romana frowned. 'What …?' She followed the Doctor's gaze to the ticket booth where Danny was still hiding.

Romana's eyes flashed. 'No. How could you even think …? But the boy … he's just a child.'

The Doctor looked sad. 'I know. But what's done is

done. You and I know, Romana, that we can't change the course of events. And sometimes we must live with the consequences.'

The Doctor turned back to the multi-faced creature. 'How much power do you have? How long can you last?'

'We … have … a … million … audiences … to … draw … from …nothing … can … stop … us.'

'Yes, yes, yes. I know all that. But what would you say if I could offer you what you want. What you need. To experience a life.'

The creature paused. 'You … have … the … power … to … make … this … offer …?'

The Doctor smiled. 'Well, it's not really a power, so much as the ability, and anyway, I think you need to move on. You need to find out the truth,' he grinned. 'It *is* out there, you know.'

'Explain.'

The Doctor took a breath and, out of the corner of his eye, saw that Romana had edged back to the ticket booth. 'It's simple,' he said. 'You release all these people you have trapped and I will let you have a single life. One that has a lifetime of potential ahead of it. This act will subvert the laws of time itself, and will allow you to live forever.' The Doctor cocked his head. 'After a fashion,' he added under his breath.

The creature paused as though thinking. The legion of faces flickering across its head also seemed more thoughtful. Eventually, it spoke again. 'If … you … can

… do … this … we … agree …'

The Doctor nodded. 'So, you return to where you came from and release the other people.'

'It … is … agreed.'

The creature clumsily turned and stomped back up the steps into the darkness.

TEN

'Romana! I think we've done it … Romana …?'

'Go away!'

'Romana … we've got to talk. It was the only way.'

She rounded on him. 'The only way! *The only way*! You want to send an innocent child to … to … that monstrosity, and you expect me to understand.' Romana's eyes blazed with anger. 'What gives you the right, eh? Who put you in charge? You play with people's lives as though … as though they were pieces on a chess board.' She strode across the foyer towards him. 'Sacrifice a pawn here, a bishop there … it's all a game to you, isn't it? We could have found another way! We *should* have found another way! But, oh no, you have to start playing with people's lives. You have to make deals that cost so much!'

The Doctor nodded. 'There's always a cost, Romana. Always something to pay. We can't always negotiate the best deal, but we try … We *always* try.'

'So, go on then. What's your excuse this time? What

great master-plan-in-progress is this move a part of?'

The Doctor's face broke into a broad grin. 'I had to make it think I was being serious. Your reactions just established that I was.'

Romana looked confused. 'What?'

The Doctor stepped towards her. 'You don't really believe that for one moment … for one moment … I would let Danny there walk into the lion's den unprotected?'

'Well … I …'

'Oh, Romana …'

'Well what did you expect?' Romana sniffed. 'So you're not going to sacrifice Danny.'

The Doctor shook his head.

'You never were going to do that?'

The Doctor shook his head again.

'So,' Romana walked to the foot of the stairs and stood looking up. 'What do we do then? Mr Movies is up there waiting …'

The Doctor ignored her and wandered over to the ticket booth. 'Danny?'

Danny's head popped up and the boy smiled.

The Doctor gestured to the boy. 'You can come out now, Danny.'

'Is it safe?'

The Doctor nodded. 'For the moment.'

Danny emerged and the Doctor hunkered down on his haunches to talk to him. 'We're going to have to be very brave now, Danny. We've got to go and find your brother

78

and his friend, and try to stop them being frightened too. We've got to find as many of the people who were here as possible, and, if we can make them not be frightened, then we can all get out of here.'

Danny nodded. 'It's all just films, isn't it? Like on the screen. Nothing can hurt you if you just close your eyes.' Danny leaned closer to the Doctor, and whispered conspiratorially, 'My dad ... my dad says that when he was young, he used to hide behind the sofa when things got too scary on the television.'

The Doctor smiled and nodded sagely. 'I've seen shows like that,' he said. 'They can be very scary.'

'But they can't hurt you,' said Danny with finality.

'Right.' The Doctor looked over at Romana, who was watching this exchange with a smile on her lips. He turned back to Danny. 'My friend there ... Romana ... she gets a little bit frightened at times. But it's all right. Do you think you can help her not to be afraid?'

Danny looked at the beautiful woman and smiled. He nodded and walked across to where Romana was standing. 'The Doctor says I'm to look after you,' he said.

Romana took his hand. 'Well, that's very kind. Thank you.'

'Right,' said the Doctor, picking his battered hat off his head and then jamming it back on his curls so that it rested at a jaunty angle. 'Ready?'

Romana and Danny looked at each other and then at the Doctor. 'Ready,' they both said together.

ELEVEN

In the main auditorium, all was quiet. The Doctor, Romana and Danny edged their way past the velvet curtain and along the front row of seats. The screen was glowing slightly, and down in the pit shadows stirred and roiled.

'I was looking at the posters,' hissed Romana.

The Doctor nodded. 'Not all of them have been used,' he whispered back. 'Obviously our friend has only used those that will elicit the most emotion.'

The Doctor clicked on his flashlight and swung it round the empty seats. 'Where … I wonder where?'

'Where what?' Danny was getting over his initial apprehension and, with his new-found role as Romana's protector, he felt that maybe he ought to contribute something.

'Where are the posters?'

Danny pointed up to the back of the cinema. 'All the really good ones are in the corridor back there.'

The Doctor nodded and started to make his way up the flight of stairs towards the darkness. Romana and Danny fell into step behind him. As they reached the top, the Doctor snapped on his torch again, and found the velvet curtain that led to the fire exit, the toilet and the hallway of posters.

'Um, you can stay here if you like …'

Romana and Danny looked at each other. 'Gulp,' said

Romana. 'What a choice. Go with you into the hallway of horrors there, or stay here with whatever decides to come and investigate what's taking you so long to deliver on your agreement.'

'It's all right, Romana,' said Danny. 'There's nothing to be scared of.' He squeezed her hand reassuringly, and Romana smiled weakly.

'That's easy for you to say,' she muttered.

The Doctor stepped forward and pulled the heavy velvet aside, shining the light down the corridor. Nothing moved.

'Come on then.'

They moved into the corridor, and Danny let the curtain fall back into place behind him.

The Doctor stopped by the first poster, and clicked off the torch. The image was glowing slightly, a faint purple light shimmering round the frame. At the top of the image, stark white letters spelt out the subject of the film: 'A horror horde of crawl-and-crush giants clawing out of the Earth from mile-deep catacombs!' The film's title followed: '*Them!*'

TWELVE

The army were in charge and, as usual, they were taking a thrashing at the hands of the invading enemy. Tanks, jeeps and land-rovers lay scattered about like a child's toys. The air was full of dust and smoke. Several bodies were strewn on the ground; their heads turned away, faces hidden from sight. Water ran down the gutters. Shop windows were smashed. Alarms blared. In the distance the sound of sporadic gunfire echoed, along with the crashing of breaking glass.

The Doctor, Romana and Danny stepped into the street. The smell of burning rubber hit them, and the Doctor waved his scarf around to try and clear the air. Danny coughed and stumbled on a broken brick underfoot, and Romana inspected the glass-strewn ground with distaste.

'Not as unpleasant as it could be ...' said the Doctor through his scarf.

Romana huffed. 'So where do you think the kids are?'

'Somewhere frightening ... Now where might be frightening?'

'You're enjoying this, aren't you?'

The Doctor flashed one of his winning smiles in her direction. 'Whatever gives you that idea? This way.'

With that he strode off towards where the shooting and crashing noises seemed to be originating. Romana and Danny hurried to catch him up. Danny was looking around in amazement. He'd never seen anything quite like this before. It was like television or the pictures, but all around him. He decided that he quite liked it, really, and mentally reminded himself that it wasn't real.

The Doctor turned a corner and abruptly stopped. Romana and Danny cannoned into his back and then stood and looked in amazement at the scene in front of them.

Three enormous black ants were being bombarded with gunfire from a group of soldiers stationed in a gutted shop. The ants were screeching and waving their legs and antennae around as the bullets and grenades hit them, but, aside from this, the weapons seemed to be having little effect on the creatures. Over to one side was the shattered wood and glass front window of a general store, and inside people were screaming.

The Doctor, Romana and Danny edged their way round some overturned vehicles, and made their way carefully towards the store. The soldiers were totally preoccupied with letting everything they had fly at the ants, and didn't notice the three figures as they slipped through the broken window and into the darkness beyond.

Inside the shop, the screaming was louder, and it was joined with sobbing and crying. Making their way through the shattered debris of several shelves of food to the back of the shop, the Doctor found the source of the noise: a large group of boys and girls, all dressed in '90s clothing, and all terrified out of their wits.

His eyes roving over the group, the Doctor turned to Romana. 'We've got to calm them down, stop them being afraid. Then we can get them back to the cinema.'

Romana nodded and, still clutching Danny's hand, moved to the nearest group. With gentle words, and calming gestures, she managed to quiet the first couple of girls enough to stop them crying. With Danny's help, she moved on to the next group, and the next.

The Doctor, meanwhile, was nervously scanning the front of the shop. The gunfire had died down a little, but he was certain he had seen something moving in the shadows. A low chittering emerged from a pool of darkness at the left, and the Doctor swallowed. Time to set up a distraction.

Glancing back to where Romana and Danny were talking to the other children, the Doctor turned and carefully made his way down one of the aisles. His feet crunched on the contents of several bags of sugar that had burst as they hit the floor.

Reaching the junction of a cross-aisle, the Doctor poked his head around. Nothing. He listened intently for a moment and thought he heard a furtive scuffling noise. He ducked around the aisle and, on hands and knees, crawled to the next junction. He risked a quick look.

About 20 feet away, a giant ant was standing, antennae tasting the air and mandibles scissoring together with a faint clicking noise. It was not quite as large as those outside – this one was around six feet long as opposed to the 12 feet of the monsters attacking the soldiers. – but it still presented a formidable adversary. As the Doctor watched, the ant took a couple of steps towards him and then stopped again, its gleaming black head slightly cocked as though it were listening for something.

Gently, the Doctor pushed himself backwards. He stopped for a moment and thought. How to dispose of one giant ant without sending all the children at the back of the shop back into shock? He looked around and his gaze alighted on a rack of garden produce. He rose to his feet and slowly moved closer. Plant fertiliser, garden forks, sturdy gloves, DDT dust … DDT!

The Doctor picked up one of the plastic tubes of DDT. 'Dichlorodphenyltrichloroethane,' he muttered under his breath. Looking at the instructions, he checked that it was guaranteed to kill all garden pests. Humans … thought the Doctor. Only humans could develop a synthetic chemical to kill insects that would also eventually poison themselves.

He quickly picked up five of the tubes and quietly tiptoed back to the aisle with the spilled sugar. He grabbed hold of some unbroken bags, and put them on the floor. Then he opened the first DDT canister and started pouring the white powder onto the sugar.

THIRTEEN

Senses working overtime, the ant sniffed the air once more. It could smell humans, but this was mixed with other tastes. Fruit and sweetness. Just the sort of thing to make an ant want to go tell its friends and then come back for the gorging.

Suddenly, the ant's head snapped up. In front of it was one of the two-legged creatures. The creature made a sharp, fluting whistling noise and vanished off to one side. The ant scuttled further along the aisle, its legs easily manoeuvring past the fallen produce, and came to the junction. Its multi-faceted eyes just caught a flash of movement as a long, knitted object was dragged out of view a little further on.

The ant scurried forward again and twitched its antennae as it picked up the smell of sweet sugar syrup. On the floor in the middle of the aisle was a slowly spreading puddle of golden syrup, sugar, and vanilla ice cream. The ant tentatively moved towards it, chittering gently to itself. It lowered its mandibles into the sticky goo and tasted. Then, it moved closer and started to suck up the sweet concoction.

Above it, resting precariously on top of the rack of shelves, the Doctor gently lifted his arm and started to sprinkle the ant with DDT dust from the tube. The fine white grains fell like snow and coated the coarse hairs on the black carapace of the creature.

Just as the Doctor emptied the tube and was about to start on the next, the ant stiffened and backed away from the puddle. It started to twitch, and then fell down on its own legs before struggling back up again. Its movements became more violent as the DDT started to take effect, and it stumbled into the pool of syrup. Unable to control its movements, it slumped into the sticky goo and drummed its legs on the ground for a time, before the movements subsided and it dropped its head into the puddle.

The Doctor dropped down from the shelves and stepped closer to the barely-twitching form. The ant was not going anywhere else in a hurry.

The Doctor tutted to himself and shook his head. Even the taking of hostile insect life was against his deeper principles, and yet sometimes even a Time Lord had to do what a Time Lord had to do. He turned and swiftly made his way back to Romana and the children.

Romana had managed to calm the group down, and as the Doctor approached she was just finishing telling them that everything would be all right. The Doctor cast his gaze over the children and beamed one of his smiles at them.

'Now … Who wants to go home?'

Immediately hands shot up and voices were raised in agreement. The Doctor hushed his hands at them and put his finger to his lips.

'Shhhh.'

When all was quiet again, the Doctor spoke. 'Now, to get home, we're all going to have to close our eyes.'

Some of the children looked worried, but Romana smiled encouragingly at them.

'It's like a dream in reverse,' piped up Danny. 'Only

you have to close your eyes to get out of it, rather than opening them.'

'That's right,' beamed the Doctor. 'So, can you all close your eyes, and repeat after me …'

He looked as all the children screwed up their eyes.

'This is not real …'

A chorus of voices repeated the line.

'We're not really here …'

'We want to go home …'

'We're not afraid …'

As the voices chimed in again, the Doctor could see that the surrounding walls were starting to fade, to be replaced by the dimly-lit corridor of the cinema.

'We're not afraid …' he said again, and smiled as the cinema replaced the shattered shop before his eyes.

'Stay calm, everyone,' he said, 'and open your eyes.'

Twenty pairs of eyes opened and then opened wider in astonishment and pleasure as they saw that they were back in the cinema.

'Now, stay very quiet and gather round.'

In the confines of the corridor, this was hard, but somehow the Doctor managed to cluster the children to him.

'We're going to go down to the foyer now and wait. So, everyone follow Romana there …' Romana smiled and gave a little wave before moving off towards the curtain.

The children all followed her; all, that was, except Danny, who stayed by the Doctor and watched as they silently trooped out.

The Doctor looked down at him. 'You don't have to stay, you know, you can go with them.'

Danny nodded. 'I know that … but … well …' he leaned in to the Doctor as though about to confide a great secret. 'Romana was a bit scared in there …'

The Doctor frowned in a serious way and nodded thoughtfully.

'… and I think she might need me to stop her being too scared.'

The Doctor marvelled at the capacity of human children to put themselves before others.

'Okay, Danny,' said the Doctor, 'but next time might be even more scary.'

'That's fine,' said Danny lightly. 'I know it's only make-believe anyway. Those things can't really hurt us, not as long as we know they don't really exist.'

The Doctor smiled and looked up as Romana re-entered the corridor.

'They're all down in the foyer and everything is *very* quiet. On the way we picked up some more children. It looks as though others are escaping as the power weakens. I've left a couple of the older children in charge and warned them to stay together and not to go close to any of the posters.' She held up her hand in which was a screwed up ball of paper. 'And just to be on the safe side I took the liberty of removing that chainsaw poster … just in case.'

The Doctor nodded sagely. 'Very wise.'

'I suspect,' Romana continued, 'that our removing the children from this poster has acted to alleviate the flow of power into the conglomerate mass, thus depriving it of much of its latent power.'

Danny looked confused.

'We've weakened it,' said the Doctor in a stage whisper, and Danny nodded.

'So,' said the Doctor in a normal voice. 'Where next?'

He moved along the corridor and saw that of the three remaining posters, only one was glowing faintly.

'Are we ready to do it again?' he said.

FOURTEEN

International super-criminal Fu Manchu was having a bad day. First, his secret underground base had been infiltrated by an impostor: one Franz Bulmer, pretending to be the scientist Otto Lentz. Bulmer had escaped, but Fu Manchu had no intention of letting this get in the way of his plans. He intended to destroy a world arms conference with his powerful sonic weapon, and to discredit the dastardly Commissioner Nayland Smith into the bargain. More worrying was the sudden appearance in his Tibetan lair of a group of English children. His guards had them all under lock and key, but Fu Manchu was certain that this might be the start of a convoluted plot to stop him.

The tall Chinaman stood up and walked to one side, gazing off into the distance thoughtfully. He still had all the girls – his 'brides' – under lock and key. Even the latest acquisition to his ranks, Marie, the so-up-tight daughter of Otto Lentz, was now under control. Perhaps he could deal with all his problems in one swoop.

'Feng …'

Fu Manchu barked for his current number two. His previous number two had been a loyal servant … until the incident with the snakes. He sighed. Sometimes you needed to make sacrifices if only to impress upon the others how important it was to be diligent at all times, especially when the safety of Fu Manchu was at stake.

Feng appeared by his side, head bowed.

'Fetch me the new English girl.'

The black-clad servant nodded and then hurried away. He well knew the penalty for keeping his master waiting.

Fu Manchu glided with a cat-like grace across the control room and entered his main hall. Sawdust covered the floor, and there was a series of stone pillars along the edges. Each pillar was fitted with iron rings where his guests could be tethered as he performed his dastardly rituals. To one side was a regal-looking chair. It was from here that he made his announcements to the world. Settling himself down, he waited for Feng.

Another servant entered from the communications room. 'Master,' he said humbly.

Fu Manchu glanced at him. 'Speak.'

'Master, we have heard voices in the passages. More people have arrived.'

'From where?'

'We don't know. A man and a woman at least.'

Fu Manchu narrowed his eyes. Maybe this was the real attack. No matter. He would have the situation under control before long. He dismissed the servant with an imperious wave of his hand. Feng shouldn't be too much longer, not if he valued his life.

Shortly, Feng entered, dragging a dishevelled and crying girl behind him. He pushed her forward and then all but threw her at the foot of the steps leading up to Fu Manchu's chair and the covered snake-pit beyond. She landed in a heap, and lay there crying, not understanding anything that was happening.

Fu Manchu gazed at her. A strange specimen, and so oddly dressed. He took in the tight blue trousers and white top, cut to reveal all but her upper arms and torso. The neckline dipped alarmingly, and Fu Manchu considered that he could almost see the top of the girl's breastbone. This in itself was not unusual by Fu Manchu's standards. He liked his brides to wear as little as possible. Peasant blouses seemed to be the staple wardrobe for young girls these days, but this one was somehow ... different.

He waved his hand at Feng, who retired to stand at the back of the room by the door, his head bowed in deference.

'Child?' The Chinaman's voice was not entirely unfriendly.

Tanya looked up and took in the sight before her: Christopher Lee dressed in emerald green oriental robes, sitting on a throne looking down at her. None of this made any sense.

'Child?' said Fu Manchu again. 'What is your name?'

Tanya swallowed a sob. 'T – Tanya, sir.'

'Tanya …' Christopher Lee rolled the name around his lips like a fine wine. Tanya felt like smiling, but was still somewhat bewildered as to how she and Bob came to find themselves locked in a smelly cell by a bunch of Chinamen when the last thing she could remember was snogging with her boyfriend in the cinema.

Fu Manchu rose from his seat and descended the steps towards Tanya. He held out his hand. 'Stand.'

It was not a request, and Tanya struggled to her feet, grasping onto his proffered hand for support as she did so.

'What are these clothes you wear?'

Tanya looked puzzled. Her fear was starting to ebb away now. 'What?'

The man lifted his hand and fingered the arm of her T-shirt. 'What is this material?'

'It's a T-shirt … and jeans. Excuse me, but who are you?'

The man smiled and stepped closer to her. 'You'll find out soon enough,' he whispered before gently reaching

93

out and placing his hands on either side of her head.

Tanya drew in a breath and her eyes opened wide as the man gazed levelly into her eyes. The pressure from his hands intensified slightly, and his eyes bore into hers. She found that she could not blink. There was something … something attractive about his eyes. She stared into them and listened as the man spoke.

'You have no will, no mind of your own. You will do only what I command you to do … even until death.'

As the words registered in her brain, so she found herself getting dizzy. The man's eyes bored into her. He was right. She was not thinking for herself. As the edges of her vision started to grey, she heard, as if from a great distance, a soft, smooth voice talking to her.

'You have no desires but to please your master … This is what you will do …'

FIFTEEN

Corridors, thought the Doctor. Why do we always end up in corridors?

They had found themselves standing in a stone passageway lined with locked doors. Each door contained a small window, and, after checking one or two, the Doctor decided that the rooms beyond must be cells. The first had a ragged-looking man crouching in, while the second seemed empty at first, before the Doctor noticed a grubby foot protruding from underneath a pile of straw.

The corridor was lit with a flaming torch set into a holder in the wall. The Doctor lifted it down and used it to light their way.

He led Romana and Danny along the passage, and found another passage, almost identical to the first. They were part-way down it when the Doctor heard the sound of someone approaching, and hurriedly pushed the others back the way they had come. From the relative safety of the corner, the Doctor watched as a black-clad Chinese man, wearing a black cap and red belt, dragged a crying girl along the corridor and through one of the doors. The girl was dressed in a T-shirt and jeans and the Doctor felt sure that this must be Tanya.

When the footsteps and crying had died away, the Doctor and his party made their way back down the corridor. The Doctor checked the doorway that the Chinese and Tanya had taken and found that it led onto a flight of steps leading up. Romana, meanwhile, wandered further along the corridor.

Her whisper sounded loud in the enclosed space: 'Doctor! Here.'

The Doctor hurried to where she was looking through the grille on another cell door. Inside was a youth of about 16, sitting on the floor and looking despondent.

'Psst!' The Doctor attracted his attention.

The boy got up and jumped to the door. 'Who are you? How did you get here? Have you come to get me out of this?'

The Doctor smiled. 'Yes, a form of magic, and yes. Stand back.'

The Doctor rummaged in his pockets and came out with a penknife. He opened one of the implements and started poking it in the lock. 'Atraxian penknife,' he muttered. 'Never leave … the swamp … without … one. Ah!'

There was a loud click and the door swung open. The Doctor beamed like a child and even Romana looked impressed. 'Not the sonic screwdriver, then.'

'No,' the Doctor smiled some more. 'But that would have been my *second* choice.'

'Bob!'

As the boy left the cell, so Danny saw him and rushed to him. Bob grasped Danny by the waist and swung him up, giving him a swift hug. 'It's all right now, Danny-boy. We're gonna get out of this mess.'

While they were talking, the Doctor was moving down the row of cells, checking them and opening any that contained 20th Century children. Soon there were about ten kids standing in the corridor, all talking together and looking a little confused. Some of the younger ones were still crying to themselves, but the older kids had done their best to try and quieten things down.

The Doctor looked round at the assembled crowd and pondered the significance of his performing like the pied piper. 'Right,' he announced to no-one in particular.

'Time to get you all back home.'

'What about Tanya?' Bob looked round at everyone. 'She's not here. They came and took her away.'

The Doctor nodded. 'Don't worry about her. We'll go and get her.'

'But, Doctor,' said Romana, 'if we've weakened the entity already, won't Tanya be freed when we return all these?' She gestured at the assembled kids.

'Maybe …' muttered the Doctor darkly. 'Or maybe she'll be so terrorised that it supplies sufficient energy for our friend to start trapping people again.' He gestured for Danny to come over, and the small boy complied. 'Do you think you can stay here and look after this group until we get back with Tanya?'

Danny nodded. 'I'll tell them what's been happening.'

The Doctor walked back to the stairway, as Romana ushered all the children back into one cell. Although the door would not lock, it would be far less conspicuous than a crowd of children thronging the corridor should anyone wander past.

She then hurried back along the passage to the Doctor, and the two of them started up the stairs.

SIXTEEN

As the Doctor and Romana reached the top of the stairs, they heard crying. A girl. Romana listened intently and then led the way through dark corridors until they came to an impressive wooden doorway that opened onto a room with pillars all round the edge. To one side of the room, in an alcove, they could see Tanya lying on a pile of straw, crying to herself.

The Doctor and Romana edged into the room, wary of traps, but there was nothing to be seen. After four steps with no phalanx of guards emerging to cut them to pieces, the Doctor hurried to where Tanya lay.

As he approached, she looked up and her crying stopped. She stared up at the Doctor, tears sparkling in her eyes.

'Oh, please … please don't hurt me.'

'I'm not going to hurt you,' said the Doctor. 'Now stay calm.'

As he reached the girl she wrapped her arms around him and started crying with relief. The Doctor saw that she had a heavy iron collar manacled around her neck, and attached to a ring in the wall by a chain. He felt in his pockets again and came out with a handful of assorted money. He shoved it back in and rummaged again. This time, he came out with a paper-clip. He unfolded the wire and then, asking Tanya to hold still, gently probed the lock on the ring around her neck.

After a few moments, he frowned. Nothing happened. He tried again, but still nothing happened. He sat back and looked at the paper-clip and the key-hole.

Romana, watching what he was doing with a wry

smile on her face, gently took the paper-clip from him and, with an endearing smile at Tanya and a withering one at the Doctor, inserted it into the lock. With a sharp twist of her wrist, the lock clicked and the manacle sprang open.

'Beginner's luck,' muttered the Doctor as she pressed the paper-clip back into his hand.

Romana helped Tanya to her feet and she stood there gingerly rubbing her neck. 'Time we got out of here,' said Romana, and she started to walk back through the room the way they had come.

'Not that way,' said Tanya. 'They'll be waiting now.'

The Doctor stopped and looked at her. 'Who'll be waiting?'

'Oh. Those … Chinese people,' said Tanya vaguely. 'I think it's this way.'

With that she turned and walked off between two of the pillars and through a doorway that had been concealed there. The Doctor looked at Romana. 'This is all getting a little serious …'

Romana nodded. 'I know … We mustn't get too involved, as it's not real. Fun though, isn't it?' With a grin she strode off after Tanya. The Doctor took up the rear, nervously looking about him for the trap that he was sure should have been sprung by now.

Tanya led the Doctor and Romana through a veritable maze of corridors. Some brick-lined, some stone. Along the way, flaming torches lit the way and the smoke caught in their throats. Eventually she led them out of a flickering tunnel into an antechamber where she stopped.

'About time,' said the Doctor. 'Now where are we …? We have to get back to your friends, Tanya.'

As the Doctor and Romana looked about them, Tanya moved to stand to one side of the room. Romana looked across at her and saw that she was staring fixedly into space.

'Tanya?' Crossing to the girl, Romana waved her hand across Tanya's eyes. No reaction. Not even a blink. 'Doctor … I think we have a problem.'

The Doctor looked across and saw Romana standing with the mesmerised Tanya.

'She does not even hear you.'

The voice was rich and cultured, tinged with the Chinese accent that had terrorised the politicians of the world for so long.

The Doctor and Romana turned as the regal form of Fu Manchu stepped forward out of the darkness at the other end of the room. On the left of him was the figure of Feng, head bowed as always, and on the right was another figure, a young Chinese girl. Like Fu Manchu she was dressed in oriental robes – black with a pink motif embroidered on the front – but unlike Feng, she carried her head high and, the Doctor noted, there was an arrogance in her stance that marked her out as being someone of importance … or, he corrected himself, someone who *thought* they were someone of importance.

'Thank you, my dear,' continued Fu Manchu. 'You have done well.'

Tanya gave no sign that she had heard, but continued to stand immobile, eyes staring at her master.

'Now,' the elegant Manchu glided forward until he was standing in front of the Doctor. 'Who exactly are you, and why are you here? Did Nayland Smith send you?'

'Well,' the Doctor began with a chuckle, 'if I told you that, I don't think you'd believe me, and anyway, I don't think we've been properly introduced … I'm the Doctor. How do you do?' The Doctor grasped Fu Manchu's manicured hand and pumped it up and down enthusiastically.

Fu Manchu looked aghast and withdrew his hand as Feng leaped forward and placed himself between his master and the stranger. Fu Manchu looked down at his hand as though it had been defaced in some way.

'No-one,' he hissed. '… no-one touches my person without permission and lives.'

'Father.' The Chinese girl, who had been watching the proceedings with amusement, stepped forward. 'Your methods can be somewhat … damaging?' She flashed her eyes over the Doctor and then walked towards Romana. 'Let me have this one. I'll try not to hurt it … for the moment … and I guarantee the information you need.'

Fu Manchu smiled. 'So be it, Lin Tang. But this one …' he pointed with his little finger at the Doctor, '… will suffer.'

With that he swept around and stalked away down the corridor, head held high.

'Oh good, he's gone,' smiled the Doctor. 'Perhaps we can have a sensible conversation now. Any chance of a cup of … oh. You're still here then.'

Feng had moved around behind the Doctor and was holding a viciously sharp-looking knife up to the Doctor's throat. The Doctor risked a look down and winced. 'I hope you're careful with that. You could hurt someone.'

'Silence.' Lin Tang spoke without looking at the Doctor. Her gaze was fixed on Romana, who was looking back with cool detachment.

The Chinese girl stepped forward and placed her hands gently on Romana's head, drawing her gaze towards her eyes. She stroked the sides of Romana's face with her thumbs and then carefully pulled them down over Romana's eyes, closing them. With a slight pressure against Romana's eyeballs, she whispered: 'You have no will, no desires but to please your masters.'

When she removed her thumbs, Romana's eyes stayed closed.

The girl looked across at the Doctor, and smiled. It was not a nice smile. She then returned her gaze to Romana.

'You may open your eyes.'

Romana's eyes flicked open and looked into the slitted brown eyes of the Chinese girl. 'Everything I command ,you will carry out,' said Lin Tang.

'Everything I command, you will carry out,' repeated Romana, her eyes locked in place.

'You will obey me,' whispered the girl.

'You will obey me ...' repeated Romana.

For a full minute, Lin Tang and Romana remained in place, both gazing into each other's eyes. Then, Romana raised her hand, and palmed the Chinese girl's eyes closed.

'I think,' said Romana, 'that this may be our way out of here.'

She looked at the Doctor and smiled. Feng was watching the exchange and growing increasingly agitated. The knife was starting to wobble, and the Doctor was becoming uneasy as well.

'Umm, Romana, I don't want to sound impatient, but can you deal with our friend here?'

Romana nodded and turned to the girl. 'Lin Tang, can you get our friend with the knife to maybe go off to sleep, eh?'

Lin Tang opened her eyes and turned to Feng. 'Feng!' she snapped. 'Feng, sleep now.'

In an instant, Feng's eyes clouded over and he slumped to the ground at the Doctor's feet. Leaving him snoring gently, the Doctor walked across to where Lin Tang was standing. He waved his hand in front of her eyes and saw that she didn't flinch.

'Impressive ...'

'Practical,' said Romana. 'That's the trouble with these

evil oriental dictator-types, they don't know when to call it a day. I was top of my hypnosis class at the Academy.'

'I didn't think they graded them,' said the Doctor quizzically.

Romana smiled. 'They didn't, but by the time I'd finished, the tutor was convinced that they did.'

The Doctor smiled. 'I'm sure he was.'

Romana stood in front of Lin Tang. 'Why don't you see what you can do with Tanya there,' she said to the Doctor, 'while I give this young lady some instructions that might make life slightly trickier for her father.'

Before long, Tanya was looking around herself in a somewhat bewildered state, while Lin Tang hurried off after her father. She would soon discover that Romana had made it difficult for her to exert quite as much power over her victims as before.

The Doctor, Romana and Tanya made their way back through the passages and down into the lower levels. Just before they arrived at the cells, they heard a commotion break out above them. Running feet and shouting. Romana smiled. 'Sounds like the cavalry have arrived.'

In the cell, Danny had explained to the rest of the children what was going on, and they were sitting in a circle, trying hard to be calm. When the Doctor, Romana and Tanya walked in, Danny jumped up in pleasure. Bob was also overjoyed, and he and Tanya hugged each other tight as the Doctor returned Danny to the circle.

'Okay everyone,' he said. 'Now just close your eyes

and repeat after me …'

SEVENTEEN

Back in the foyer of the cinema, the Doctor and Romana counted the children. There were well over 50, with more wandering down from the upper level every moment. There were also three adults present: the cinema manager, Mr Stevenson, and the two members of staff, Mavis and Susie. All had become trapped in posters, and had found themselves freed as the entity loosened its grip. Like many of the kids, they were still somewhat shocked by their experience.

'Doors are still locked,' said Romana, giving them an experimental shake.

'I expect our friend upstairs is channelling whatever available energy it has into keeping them that way.' The Doctor looked around. 'What we need is a distraction …'

'You don't mean …'

The Doctor looked at Romana. 'Yes I do, and why do you always state the obvious?'

'Sorry.'

'Accepted. What we need are some games …'

'Games?'

'Yes. Games. To distract it from keeping the doors locked. Romana, I want you and Danny to start up some games, while I go and see how things are upstairs.'

Romana looked up the flight of steps into the darkness that lurked at the top. 'Okay,' she said, without much enthusiasm. 'We'll see what we can do.'

The Doctor turned and re-adjusted his hat on his head before taking off up the stairs four at a time. Behind him he could hear the sound of Romana and Danny organising a series of games for the kids. Choosing sides for an impromptu round of coke-can football by the sounds of it. As he turned the corner at the top, the Doctor was engulfed in darkness once more. The sounds faded to be replaced by a sighing, dripping noise, which grew in intensity as the Doctor neared the auditorium.

Pushing through the curtain, the Doctor tentatively approached the front of the cinema. Before him, the giant white screen stretched up and across, and all around shadows skittered and skimmed. He leaned over the balcony as far as he could and saw a faint purple glow roiling in the pit.

'So … not out of power yet …,' the Doctor murmured as he made his way to one of the gratings leading to a spiral flight of steps leading down into the pit. He vaulted over the gate and paused at the top of the steps, listening intently. From the foyer he could hear happy cries and screams as the kids indulged in whatever game Romana had concocted for them.

Warily, the Doctor made his way down the steps.

EIGHTEEN

In the darkness by the front of the screen, something roiled and pulsed with a faint violet light. The Doctor stopped at the bottom of the spiralling stairs and peered into the gloom, trying to allow his eyes to grow accustomed to the darkness.

He stepped off the stairs and his feet sunk into a soft and mushy layer of dust, accumulated crisp packets, coke cans, popcorn and other debris that had fallen – or had been thrown – from the balcony above. He warily took another step, the rubbish crunching gently under his feet.

There was a sighing whisper, and the rolling purple-hued darkness moved in front of him. The Doctor pushed his hat down on his head, and, shoving his hands deep into his trouser pockets, affected a look of seriousness.

'You can't win, you know …?'

The sighing whispering paused for a moment, and then the Doctor heard words, weakly at first, but growing in strength.

'What … have … you … done?'

The cadences were the same as before. A million voices speaking the words, one overlaid on top of the other. Extracts from film soundtracks, broken down and replayed at the wrong speeds.

'Well,' the Doctor pushed at the rubbish with his foot in a nonchalant sort of way, 'I've taken away your energy supply. The children you trapped, and from whom you were draining the emotional power, are no longer trapped. You had no intention of freeing them anyway …'

'We … sensed … interference,' the voices confirmed. 'But … we … can … survive … You … can … not … stop … us …'

'Bold words from a thing that doesn't even have a body,' taunted the Doctor. 'Come on. Show yourself if you're not beaten. Face me.'

There was a stirring in the darkness, and the Doctor watched as, slowly, a form emerged. It was a smaller version of the monstrosity that had appeared on the stairs earlier. Stumpy white legs, and a torso topped with a face on a long neck. The face kept changing as before, although the rate of change, noted the Doctor with some satisfaction, was far slower.

The creature stumped towards the Doctor and stopped a few feet away. The Doctor shook his head. 'Is that the best you can do? It's pathetic. Pathetic. You hide yourself away down here like a … a … mole, and only pop out to say hello when it suits you.' The Doctor turned his back on the creature, and made as if to return up the stairs. 'There's no point,' he said. 'I've faced Daleks, Cybermen, Sontarans, Drashigs and the Master and all were uglier than you. I'm wasting my time.'

With a roar of rage, the creature surged forward and caught the Doctor's arm with a flailing misshapen hand, spinning him round.

'You … dare … mock … us!'

The Doctor looked the morphing face in the eye. 'Yes, I dare.'

With another bellow, the creature flung the Doctor across the pit. He skidded through the muck on the floor and landed in a heap, cans and crisp packets flying and clattering around him. Checking to make sure he was all right, the Doctor jumped back to his feet. 'I dare …' he shouted, '… because you are nothing. You came from nothing, and you'll go back there. Go on, attack me again, if you can!'

The creature surged across the floor, but the Doctor could see that his plan was working. The energy now being expended was not being replenished, and the creature was weakening. Purple tendrils of light were breaking through the creature's joints, and it slowed as it came nearer.

The head on its sinuous neck whipped from side to side. 'What … is … happening?'

'It's the end,' replied the Doctor. 'So sorry you couldn't stay.'

'No … no … no … *No!*'

The creature roared out its rage, expending more energy in the process. The head whipped down and saw that the purple light was spilling from its leg, and the leg was unravelling beneath it. With a thump, the creature fell over and tried to push itself back up again with its arms, but they too were spinning away into vapour.

The Doctor watched as the physical form of the entity grew smaller and smaller, and its thrashing became weaker.

'You … tricked … us …' it shouted faintly. 'We … cannot … die … We … are … imm–'

With a flash of light, the creature unspun its physical presence of rubbish back onto the floor, leaving ropes of purple light, which coiled and writhed. The roiling darkness from which the being had emerged also started to contract until the Doctor was standing in front of a globe of streaked darkness, which was contracting in on itself.

'Roll credits …' muttered the Doctor.

The ball grew smaller and smaller until it vanished from sight with a faint popping sound.

'The End.'

The Doctor shook his head. Defeated by its own ambition. What a way to go. With a final look around the basement pit, the Doctor started to climb up the spiral staircase once more.

NINETEEN

Back in the foyer, the Doctor found that the main doors were open, and all the children, with the exception of Danny, Bob and Tanya, had gone.

Romana looked up as the Doctor descended the

stairs.

'The doors flew open a few moments ago, and the kids decided that they'd had enough and went.'

'Except me,' said Danny. 'I wanted to make sure that you were all right, but Romana wouldn't let me go upstairs.' Danny grasped the Doctor's hand and pulled him down to crouch at his level. 'I think she's still a bit scared,' he whispered.

The Doctor grinned. 'And so she should be,' he boomed. He gripped Danny's hand firmly and shook it. 'Thank you, Danny,' he said.

Danny smiled and shook the Doctor's hand back. 'Are you going now?' he asked.

The Doctor nodded. 'Our work here is finished, for the moment.' He looked over at Romana, who smiled back.

The Doctor stood up and looked around the foyer. 'Somehow I don't think there'll be many more films shown here.'

'1998, isn't it?' said Romana. The Doctor nodded. 'That's when the Rembrandt was demolished,' she confirmed. 'Against public opinion, of course. Turned into another housing estate.'

Danny smiled again at the Doctor and returned to Bob and Tanya, who were standing by the doors, ready to go.

'I'm not sure what happened,' began Bob, 'but … thanks. Both of you.'

Romana smiled and bent to give Danny a kiss. 'Thanks for looking after me,' she whispered.

Danny blushed beetroot red, and grasped Bob's hand firmly. With a final look back, the three of them walked out through the doors and into the sunlight.

'That stuff about the cinema being demolished,' said the Doctor. 'How did you know that?'

Romana looked guilty. 'Well a girl's got to have a hobby.'

Together they stepped out of the cinema and looked up at the impressive art deco façade.

'A shame, really,' said Romana. 'It's a great looking building.'

'Mmmm,' mumbled the Doctor. His eyes flashed and he grabbed Romana by the hand. 'Come on, Romana,' he smiled. 'Places to go … people to see … worlds to save … games to play …'

Romana sighed. The Doctor, she supposed, had to have a hobby too.

'Goodbye Rembrandt' is a story with a lot of influences, and I think they probably all show. The title actually comes from words that were put up on the front billboard area of our local cinema when it closed down in the early '90s. The place had been sold for housing development, and I started wondering if the people who lived in the houses built on the site of a cinema might see ghosts of the films that were played there. This then developed into the idea that a cinema might trap all the emotions of the viewers over the years – a sort of riff on Nigel Kneale's *The Stone Tape*, with elements of Clive Barker's 'Son of Celluloid' thrown in.

In the '90s there were a number of charity *Doctor Who* anthologies being published, and I was asked if I had something for one of them … so I decided to write a story inspired by some of my biggest childhood loves: *Doctor Who* of course, but also a show called *Sapphire and Steel*. 'Goodbye Rembrandt' reads as a *Sapphire and Steel* story, but with the Doctor and Romana cast as the eponymous heroes of that show. Then there is my love of horror films. I decided to use *Them!* and *The Brides of Fu-Manchu* as the main two featured in the story, though there were a lot to choose from … The opening scenes of the young lad watching *Flash Gordon's Trip to Mars* are a flashback to my own childhood when I used to go to Saturday morning pictures at the self same cinema and watch the black and white exploits of Flash and Buck Rogers each week.

The end result is a story that I'm very fond of, and which I hope others might enjoy.

My Garden

There is something at the bottom of my garden.

Now I know all the stories and I know all the myths. They're meant to be fairies, but if they are, they're not out of any children's bedtime story.

So what happened, you ask. Why am I talking about fairies? Well it's partly to explain. That's if anyone actually believes me. If anyone cares enough to listen.

And why should they? I still consider myself a reasonably attractive woman of 25 years. I can just see the thoughts rushing across your face as you look at me. You don't know whether I'm a raving nutter, or a publicity-seeker, or something else entirely.

Let me try and explain. Amazing as it may sound, it started only yesterday. It was Saturday, if today is Sunday, and I think it is, so it must have been Saturday. I was out in my garden as usual for the weekend, checking the pond, seeing if the frogs and toads were still thrashing about in the water, doing what frogs and toads do in the spring. My fish idly swam about, pretending to ignore the frogs, and the black water-boatmen skittered across the surface looking for food. I picked a few good daffodils that had bowed their heads to the grass overnight, intending to put them in a vase once indoors. My meandering in the garden took me to the bottom, where a large and ancient oak tree stands twisted and knurled. When I was a kid, I used to play in its branches, and my dad once built a swing up on one of the higher boughs. I can still remember him pushing me higher and higher as the sunshine dappled my face and dress with patterns of light filtered through the leaves.

At the base of the tree is a bole; a knotty, lumpy area that makes the old tree look as though it is wearing a legwarmer, or so I always thought. I did notice, as I was growing up, that no grass ever grew around the tree. We tried one year to plant some. Raking the earth to smooth and break it up, scattering grass seeds, and then watering the area every day. Nothing. Perhaps I should have thought that this was strange, but I didn't. I didn't even think it was odd that the grass stopped in a neat circle around the tree, about three feet from the trunk. I suspect that I thought it was just some nature thing – maybe the tree roots sucked all the moisture from around the soil making it impossible for other plants to grow there.

Yesterday, however, I noticed that the bole had a split in it.

I love that tree, and so I investigated further. There was a break in the bark about an inch across at its widest. It was seeping some whitish liquid, and within the split I could see something glinting. I crouched down and looked closer. To my amazement, there then clambered from the hole a tiny person.

No. Honestly. Swear on my life. It was a small person with wings.

The creature made its way out of the slit in the bole, and sat preening its delicate wings, which twinkled and sparkled in the shifting patterns of sunlight. I crouched there silently, not quite believing what I was seeing. I remember blinking several times, but every time I opened my eyes, this little green-tinted person was still there, gently rubbing its wings with its hands, rather like a cat cleaning its fur.

Then another head emerged from the bole, and a second little figure joined the first. This one had a reddish tone, and it too sat and started unfurling gossamer wings from its back.

They wore no clothes, these creatures, and their tiny bodies were shifting and changing hue as the sun hit them – a little like a cuttlefish can change its colours as it swims along lightening-swift, pulsing and shifting the whole time.

As I watched, the first creature finished tending to its wings and looked up suddenly, as if seeing me watching for the first time. With a flicker, it was airborne, and, like a humming bird or a hoverfly, was hanging in front of my face. I think I must have smiled with delight as it flitted to and fro, glinting wings a blur on its back, while its body flushed purple and green. It hovered closer to the ground, and by instinct I raised my left hand – the one not clutching a posy of daffodils. As I held my hand out flat, the fairy hovered closer, peering at my large and ungainly fingers. Then, it settled gently on my palm, its feet soft and light. So light, in fact, that I could barely feel it there at all.

My Garden

I couldn't believe it. There was I, sitting on my haunches in a sunny garden, under an aged tree, with a real live fairy standing on the palm of my hand. Just then the second creature appeared in the air by my head. It too flitted down to my hand and joined the other standing there. I watched them in a daze.

The first fairy held out its hand to the second and they clasped their own tiny fingers together. Then, in unison, they bent down and bit me.

I think I screamed and frantically shook my hand in the air to try and dislodge them. They had both sunk their tiny, needle-sharp teeth into the fleshy area at the base of my thumb, and were hanging on for dear life. I shook my hand even harder and watched with satisfaction as one of the creatures lost its grip and flew off to hit the tree-trunk with an audible slap. The other let go on its own and hovered momentarily, looking at me with its head cocked to one side, before flying to its partner, which was caught in the bark on the tree.

I stood up and examined my hand. It was throbbing painfully. At the base of my thumb were two sets of circular marks. Both in perfect rings about half a centimetre across, and both consisting of seven red pinprick points. The tiny rings almost matched the ring around the oak tree, except on a much smaller scale.

I looked back at the tree to discover that my two attackers were now nowhere to be seen, then I hurried back up the garden to the kitchen.

I doused a cotton wool pad with TCP and pressed it against the painful punctures. Further investigation showed that gently squeezing the bitten area produced a milky white fluid from the pin pricks and shooting pains up my arm, which made my head spin. I felt sick and dizzy. There was this bizarre feeling of unreality swimming behind my blurring eyes.

I headed for the telephone, intending at that point to phone my doctor to explain that I had been bitten … but then hesitated. How could I possibly tell him what had caused the marks? Fairies? He'd never believe that for one moment.

I looked again at my left hand, which was now cradled in my right. The marks had become puffy and raised from the surface, and my whole arm was throbbing. I went to pick up the telephone, but found that my hand was aching so much that the muscles were too weak to grip the receiver. My head started to spin so much that I couldn't concentrate on anything, let alone find the number and dial the doctor.

So I went back out into the garden and sat down on the steps leading to the lawn.

My hand was not a pretty sight. After about ten minutes the skin started to stretch and change colour. The reds and oranges were vibrant, but as I watched, I could see other colours blossoming and blooming under my skin: purple and vermilion and green. It stopped hurting, but then other things started to happen.

Take my stomach for example. I used to be a size eight, but my waist started to stretch to fill my jeans. And there was movement too. Ripples under the skin, small lumps sliding backwards and forwards. I tried pressing them, but they just slid out of the way.

I can see you're shaking your head. Perhaps you don't believe me. Perhaps you think you've come to the wrong house.

As I stood in my beautiful garden, with my once beautiful figure bulging, I found that I could see colours, light and movement that I never noticed before. Everything seemed so alive. Everything, that is, except me. When I looked down at my swollen and distended arm all I could now see was black, and as my jeans started to tear with the pressure, I could see my once-shapely legs – the ones I could halt a line of traffic with just by stopping in the street to adjust my skirt – swelling and bloating along with the rest of my body.

But it didn't hurt much. I was just dizzy and giddy, and everything ached. Like growing pains you get sometimes when you're a child. Or when you've spent a long day out walking in intense heat.

I remember blinking, and in the instant my eyes were closed, the light changed. It was moving like treacle, slowing down somehow. I could see shapes and colours in the grass, and with a jolt I realised that the two small fairy creatures were coming back. I tried to head back to the house, but found that my feet would not move. I was too tired, bloated, swollen and aching to be able to stagger anywhere.

The two creatures came closer, and they were moving a lot more slowly than they had been before. They were almost graceful and stately as they fluttered their bright wings and flew up towards my head. They landed on my shoulders, and I found that I could not move my head to see where they had gone. Then, the aching subsided, and I felt two gentle pin-pricks on my neck, one on either side. I felt my eyes closing as a sense of great lethargy overtook me, and I slowly, oh so slowly, moved my arms up to try and brush the creatures away.

When I opened my eyes again, I saw you there. I know you think that there's something wrong, as you looked concerned as you slowly stooped to pick up the remains of my jeans. Now you're looking at me. Studying me. But you haven't answered me yet, or made any comment regarding my story.

What is it? Why are you gently rubbing my arm with your hand. Does the roughness of my skin worry you? You look worried. I can see you frown as you turn and slowly walk to the house. No. Don't go. It's me. Can't you hear me? Can't you see me?

Why won't my arms move? It's as though they're locked in place above my head. I can just glimpse them out of the corner of my eye. But they're brown. It's not skin at all. It's bark. Why are my arms covered with bark?

I close my eyes again, and feel a tear gently run down

my trunk. I cannot move, but the sun is pleasant enough. The ground beneath me is grassy, but soon a bare ring of earth will start to surround me. The sun will dapple the ground around me as I stand here, the light filtering through my leaves.

I'm not hungry. Not thirsty. I don't ache any more. I can watch my beautiful garden grow up around me. I can watch the fairies as they flit about. See the frogs and toads in the pond.

My garden is my life, and I feel that soon I'll be bringing more life into it. A feeling of love and satisfaction creeps up my roots as I feel the tingling spread of a bole gathering around my trunk.

There is something at the bottom of my garden. Now I know all the stories and I know all the myths … and I think that just maybe I now know where fairies come from.

'My Garden' is another story of which I'm unsure of the origin. I wanted to write a fantasy rather than a horror … but it ended up being a horror anyway. This story explores the innocent approach children have towards fairies, Santa Claus and the Tooth Fairy, even though the main character is an adult. How would we feel if we found that mystical fairy ring and dancing, miniature, winged people in our garden? How harmless would these creatures be? Would our childhood innocence let us fall into some hideous trap?

Blackfriars

From: 'Sue' <rich-bitch@hotmail.com>
To: 'Keith' <kbarber@lineone.net>
Subject: Lunch
Sent: Fri, 31 May 2002 19:19:25 +0100

Hi Keithy

Love to do lunch tomorrow. You know I miss you loads
when I'm not with you. Last week was just fab … you
know what I'm talking about.

    See you at 12. Usual place.

Sue

xxx

From: 'Sue' <rich-bitch@hotmail.com>
To: 'Mike' <antiquekid@yahoo.com>
Subject: You *are* dumped
Sent: Fri, 31 May 2002 19:23:45 +0100

Mike

I don't know how many times I'm going to have to tell you,
but I really don't want to see or hear from you again.

    Please stop calling my mobile, and stop hanging

round my flat.

Seriously. If you bother me again I'll be contacting the police.

Sue

Mobile Phone Transcript:

Call Made: Sat, 1 Jun 2002 11:50:43

Sue: Hi honey
Tony: Hi there. Where are you?
Sue: Just out shopping. Listen. I'm going to be a little late back this afternoon. Got to pick up some stuff.
Tony: Okay.
Sue: Just didn't want you to worry, babe.
Tony: See you later then.
Sue: Okay. Byee. Kiss kiss.
Tony: Love you. Bye.

CALL ENDS

The restaurant was, as usual, packed. Waiters circulated attentively with bottles of wine and water, the swing door to the kitchen was overworked, as a constant stream of mouth-watering dishes emerged while plates piled with detritus and cutlery returned.

At her usual corner table, Sue surveyed the organised

chaos around her. It was a wonder that all these people managed to get through their lives intact. She picked up the slim stem of her champagne flute and sipped at the ice cold liquid. Her plate of *moules meurnieres* sat finished in front of her, while opposite, Keith sat holding her free hand gently, and gazing into her eyes intently.

She gently placed the wine glass back on the table. Keith was older than her – all the men in her life were – but only by about ten years. He was handsome in a rugged kind of way, but had the most beautiful hands. He was also pretty good in bed, which, quite frankly, was a great bonus. So many of her men were just too old, portly, and past it to manage anything more than a quick fumble before dropping off to sleep. But with Keith … Well, he had some staying power, and was handy with his tongue as well.

Her attention switched back to Keith as he raised his eyebrows at her in anticipation of her response. She smiled. Not just any smile, but her special, patented, make-any-man-in-the-room-look-at-me smile.

'So that's a yes then?' asked Keith, his own face breaking into a grin.

Sue nodded. 'Just as soon as you have the paperwork ready, then I'll be happy to sign.'

'That's brilliant,' said Keith, raising her hand to his lips to kiss it gently. 'And as we agreed, you'd be starting with me as a partner, with, of course, the salary you wanted. I had to pull quite a few strings to get this through with

Harry, but he can see the sense in having a younger head joining us.'

'I'm sure it will all go swimmingly,' said Sue with another grin. She picked up her champagne once more. 'To us.'

'To us,' echoed Keith, clinking his glass against hers.

'There is just one thing,' said Keith. He leaned closer to her. 'It is okay for us to be seen together now, is it? It's just that, with Tony running a rival firm and all that …'

Sue laughed and, shifting in her seat, gently ran her foot up the side of Keith's leg. 'It's fine,' she insisted. 'In any case, I'm about to dump the loser.' Putting down her glass, she picked up Keith's hand and gently sucked on his thumb. 'You are so much more my type than he is,' she muttered, raising her eyes to look directly into Keith's.

Keith smiled dreamily. 'I'll see you later on, then …?'

'You bet, lover.'

A waiter swooped on their table and spirited away the plates. Their glasses were refilled, and, at a gesture from Keith, the bill was presented.

At that moment, Sue's mobile phone rang. She let go of Keith and dived for her bag to get it. Removing the phone, she checked the caller, put it to her ear and started out of the restaurant, looking back at Keith with a 'see you outside' glance.

Keith nodded and watched her go, as did most of the male clientele of the restaurant.

Sue was gorgeous. She was radiant. Today her fine blonde

hair was brushed, conditioned, and shining down to the middle of her back. She was wearing a smart pair of pinstripe trousers, with a low cut white T-shirt and stylish jacket. Her face was elfin and perfectly proportioned. Plucked eyebrows, alabaster skin, and just a touch of lipstick and powder completed a look that turned most men into babbling idiots the moment they saw her.

Keith really could not understand why she was still with Tony, partner in a rival antiques firm and some 30 years her senior, when Tony's company seemed to be in such a shambles. No wonder that when Sue had first met him at a trade fair some three months back, she had joined him for dinner, and then for sex – both on the same day. Keith shrugged. Tony's loss …

He picked up the bill and grimaced at the cost – over two thirds was the bottle of champagne that Sue had chosen to celebrate her new job. Shaking his head, he added his MasterCard to the bill and gestured for a waiter. At least he would get his just rewards later in the week, when Sue was due to visit for their now-regular sessions of sex and debauchery. He smiled. There was nothing that fazed that girl. Endlessly imaginative, energetic and sensual … what a catch.

Mobile Phone Transcript:

Call Made: Sat, 1 Jun 2002 13:26:32
Sue: Hi Tony!

Tony: Just wanted to see how late you were going to be?
Did you get what you wanted?

Sue: Oh yes. Not too late.

Tony: You know I love you.

Sue: I know. I love you too.

Tony: Did you eat yet?

Sue: I picked up a quick sandwich on my way. I'm fine.

Tony: Well tonight I've something special planned for us.
Some good news.

Sue: That's excellent. Listen, I'm going to have to dash. I'll
see you about four. Okay?

Tony: Okay. Don't be late. See you then. Love you.

Sue: Love you too. Bye.

CALL ENDS

Keith walked out of the restaurant to see Sue just putting
her mobile into the Gucci bag she carried. Stepping up
behind her, he held her round the waist. She turned and
looked into his grey eyes.

'All done?' she asked.

'Paid and ready to go.'

Sue slid her hand up around the back of Keith's head
and pulled his face towards her. Her tongue snaked
out and tickled around his lips before moving closer.
Keith's hands cupped her perfect buttocks as she kissed
him passionately. When he came up for air, she stepped
backwards, smiling that million watt smile once more.

'So … see you tomorrow, then,' she said.

Keith looked confused. 'Tomorrow?'

'To discuss the paperwork. Needs a lot of discussion does paperwork …'

Keith smiled. 'I see. What time should I expect you at the shop?'

Sue looked at him. 'Who said anything about the shop? The paperwork I want to discuss is in your bedroom. I'll be at your flat at 11.30 for a pre-lunch discussion.'

'11.30 …' Keith remembered that he was supposed to be meeting Henry for lunch the next day. However, Sue was at that moment adjusting her bra strap, giving him a glimpse of more of the perfect pair of breasts struggling to break free from her T-shirt. 'That's fine. See you then.'

Sue suddenly looked worried. 'Oh, sorry, Keith, could you lend me 20 … I'm a little short at the moment.'

'Sure, no problem.' Keith extracted a note from his wallet and passed it over.

Sue took it and grinned. 'You know … when this deal has gone through and I'm partner in your company … I promise you the night of your life.'

With a leery wink and a final peck on Keith's lips, Sue turned and walked off down the street, Keith's eyes watching her long legs and perfect shape as she retreated from him. He suddenly realised he was standing there on a busy street with his wallet and mouth open. He shut both, and returned the wallet to his jacket pocket.

Sue Cavendish. What a babe!

An hour or so later, as Sue turned the corner into the street where Tony's flat was, she became aware of a figure hovering behind her. She stopped and turned, hand instinctively going for the small attack spray she always carried with her.

'Oh – it's you.'

The figure was that of Mike, ex-boyfriend, ex-antiques dealer, ex-member of the human race.

'Sue ... I ... I ...'

'Didn't you get my e-mail?' Sue looked him up and down. Mike was unshaven, and looked as if this had been the case for at least a week. His shirt was stained and rumpled, two buttons were missing, and the shirt-tails were pulled from his grubby jeans at one side. His eyes were red and slightly unfocused, and he swayed a little.

'No ... no ... I don't suppose you did.' She muttered to herself. 'What do you want? I told you it was over.'

Mike started crying. 'Sue ...' he blurted. 'Sue ... I'm ruined. The money ... the business ... all gone. Stolen.'

Sue looked worried for a moment. 'But that's all your fault, Mike,' she stated. 'No-one asked you to make those investments. No-one told you how to spend your money.'

'But I thought ... I thought you loved me. I loved you – I love you, Sue – Come back to me, and we can sort it all out.'

Sue shook her head. 'Whatever did I see in you, Mike? – except for your money, of course. Thanks for the car, the holidays – oh, and the bag, of course.' She lifted the £1,000 Gucci object before him. 'The rest I just took. Silly of you to leave passbooks lying around, of course – such a temptation for a girl.'

Mike's eyes widened. 'But Sue …'

She turned on her heel and started walking away from him. Mike had to shuffle along beside her to keep up.

'*But Sue … But Sue …* Is that all you can say? You really were useless. Useless in business and useless in bed. But I got what I wanted. Thought I was just a pretty face, eh? Thought I'd be just some arm candy for those important meetings. Well I got what I wanted. I got your money. I got your business. I got your life.'

Sue stopped walking and turned to Mike. 'You see, Mike, you never realised that I was using you all along. You were so blinded by the fucking, that you never saw the rest of me coming. Oh, and you *never* made me come, either, just in case you thought you did.'

Sue smiled as she saw the impact of her words hit home. 'So, Mikey, *darling*, there's nothing you can do. If you lay one finger on me, then I'll have you in court on a harassment charge. If you try and tell anyone about this discussion, then I'll deny it – who would believe a hopeless, washed up, drunken old lech anyway. That's even if you had the money to afford the legal bills, because … oh yes … in case you forgot – you're bankrupt. You're a jealous fool, Mike. Maybe next time – if there is a next time – you won't let your pathetic cock make your decisions for you.'

Sue turned and stalked off down the street, leaving Mike crying in the gutter. He fell to his knees and wept. Not just for his business, his ex-wife whom he left and divorced for Sue or his bankruptcy when he finally discovered that all the money had mysteriously vanished, leaving bills unpaid and angry creditors at his door. He cried because Sue was right, and he knew she was right. He had fallen for the worst bitch in the world, and she had taken everything.

Sue meanwhile was quietly smiling to herself. Things a girl has to do to get on these days …

She strutted on down the street, and as she approached Tony's flat, she suddenly had the sense that someone was watching her. She spun round. There was no-one to be seen. Even that miserable prick Mike had gone. She walked on down the street, slower now, and as she reached the entrance to the flat, she looked around again. Standing opposite her on the other side of the road was a figure wearing a black monk's habit. She looked at the figure, but could not see his face, as it was in darkness inside the cowl. A car passed by, and, in the blink of an eye, the figure was gone. Sue looked up and down the street, but there was no sign of the figure. She narrowed her eyes. Maybe another ex-boyfriend out to cause her trouble – well, just let him try. She smiled to herself and let herself into Tony's flat.

The first thing she saw was a massive bunch of flowers

on the dining table. The spray was of red and white carnations, her favourites, and she smiled when she saw the note attached to them: 'To Sue. Missing you. Tony.'

'Surprise?'

Sue span round to see Tony standing in the doorway to the kitchen. She squealed with pleasure and leaped at him, almost knocking him over. Planting little kisses all over his balding pate, she hugged him tight.

'Oh, Tony, they're wonderful. Thanks so much. I'm just popping upstairs to freshen up. Could you put them in water for me? Thanks hon.'

She hurried out of the room and up to the bathroom, leaving Tony smiling happily to himself. He could not really believe his luck. That a 54 year old ex-bank manager, running his own antiques company, could have landed one of the hottest girls he had ever laid eyes on, was amazing. He rubbed his hand over his head, smoothing down the grey hair at the back. He picked up the bunch of flowers and headed for the kitchen. As he prepared the bouquet, he heard the shower go on, and smiled again at the thought of Sue under the water. She liked to make love in the most unusual places, and the shower was one of her favourites. Even though he sometimes slipped – being on the wrong side of 50 certainly slowed down your reactions – she never seemed too disappointed.

By the time Sue reappeared about 45 minutes later, the flowers were proudly displayed on the table. Tony looked appreciatively at Sue, who had changed into a figure-hugging pair of velvet tracksuit bottoms and a crop top, her damp blonde hair held back in a ponytail. He poured her a glass of wine, and she idly flicked through a newspaper as he fussed in the kitchen, creating a meal of crusty bread and fresh pâté, baked salmon and lemon with asparagus and rice, and a rich chocolate mousse for dessert. His ex-wife may have hated his passion for food (to which his expanding waistline bore testament) but Sue seemed not to mind, and she also loved being looked after. From the moment he had first set eyes on her, two years ago in the local auction rooms, Tony had known she was all he wanted. She had flirted with him outrageously, and it wasn't long before she had been taking him to her bed on a weekly, then daily basis. He had left his wife, sold the house and moved in with Sue, whose knowledge of antiques promised to reap dividends for his company. Before long, she had been all but running the business with him, taking care of all the paperwork – a task for which Tony had never had much aptitude. His two partners in the company seemed uncertain, but Tony had faith in Sue, and was good at arguing his case.

After the courses had been dished up, and Tony been vaguely disappointed that Sue had only picked at her food, he decided to share his big news.

'We've agreed a bonus for the work so far,' he explained. 'I had to talk them round, but I think you'll be well pleased with the amount. Five thousand.'

'Five thousand!' Sue looked aghast at Tony. She had been

expecting ten thousand at least, although, as she hastily checked herself, with the money she had been quietly extracting from Tony's business, maybe they couldn't afford more. 'That's brilliant,' she concluded after a pause.

Tony looked apologetic. 'It would have been more,' he explained hastily, 'but cash flow is a problem – we're really looking to you to start to turn things around.'

Sue nodded. She was turning things around all right. Right around into her bank account. One of the things about looking good, she reflected, was that people seemed to trust you. And also they underestimated what you knew. Sue knew her antiques. She had read and studied hard until she could tell the difference between the real thing and a fake at ten paces. She knew what to buy and when, and also where to go for the best bargains, and the best profits. However, for the most part she let this knowledge out a little at a time. Gaining the trust of others, and a reputation for being a good money-maker. And this was certainly true. At only 24 years old, she currently had a personal wealth of far more than the firms who paid her. This was mainly because, for every item she sold for her various bosses, strangely, another two would not appear on inventories, only to surface some weeks later in certain private sales, netting an impressive amount of money from the right buyers.

Now, thanks to her liaison with Tony, she knew that his company was very nearly bankrupt. Bad investments and poor sales would be nominally to blame, and no-one would ever think to look to Tony's mistress and lover as the root cause of the problem. She had made sure that she was entirely blameless in all dealings, and the money she ended up with directly from the company was mainly through payments for her work and, of course, gifts from Tony.

She realised that Tony was still speaking to her, and tuned in to catch the tail end of his sentence: '… belonged to an old lady. Should be some nice stuff there, and we've got in first this time.'

'Sorry, where's that?'

'Tomorrow … I just explained …' Tony smiled his long-suffering smile. 'We're going to clear a house tomorrow, up Blackfriars way. An ancient pile by all accounts. Belonged to an old lady who died a month or so back. Untouched since.' He grinned and laid his hands over his ample belly. 'We might strike lucky.'

Sue smiled back, deep in her own thoughts. 'We might indeed. We might indeed.'

From: 'Sue' <rich-bitch@hotmail.com>
To: 'Keith' <kbarber@lineone.net>
Subject: Our meeting today
Sent: Sun, 2 June 2002 08:18:54 +0100

Hi Keithy

Sorry babe. Something's come up. Have to miss our chat at lunch. I'll make it up to you next time.

Love

Sue

xxx

To say that the house was untouched was an understatement. Tony blew gently at the mantelpiece and a cloud of dust and dead insects took flight. He flapped his hand and shook his head.

Sue rubbed a finger experimentally across a table, leaving a deep groove in the dust. She rubbed her fingers together in a vain attempt to clean them.

'This place is a pit,' she said with a sniff. 'How could anyone live in these conditions?'

Tony nodded. 'Incredible,' he agreed. 'But just look at some of this stuff.' He removed a mounted plate from the wall, muttering to himself, Shame about the clips, they've chipped the edges a little. Still – not often you see one of those.' He made a note on the clipboard he was carrying and moved off around the room.

Sue checked that Tony was occupied and gently eased open a drawer on the cabinet she was standing by. Inside was a drift of papers: bills, receipts, letters, demands – the detritus of a life. She idly plucked one out. It bore a 1965 date – had this old lady never thrown anything away? She closed the drawer and opened the next one along. Her eyes widened imperceptibly as a velvet case was revealed. She gently extracted the case from the drawer and opened it. Diamonds sparkled. Sue smiled to herself and, with a glance to see that Tony was occupied with a selection of canes and walking sticks in an elephant's foot by the door, slipped the velvet case into her bag to join the other items hidden there.

She checked that there was nothing else in the drawer.

'Just off to check another room,' she called. Tony mumbled something, absorbed in trying to date a silver cane top.

Sue ducked out of the room and headed to the stairs. Her passing raised eddies of dust along the edges of the floor carpet, which was filthy and matted, and in places slightly tacky. Sue climbed the stairs without touching the banister rail, which looked like it had been coated with some sort of jam.

Upstairs, she pushed gently at the first door, and entered the dark room beyond. It was a bedroom, the curtains pulled tight shut. She moved to the window and tentatively grasped one of the curtains. Giving it a quick shake, she pulled it open in a cloud of dust. A large, grey cobweb held the curtains closed, but Sue tugged harder and the cobweb finally tore free and the cloth parted, revealing a grimy window matted with more cobwebs, dust and dead insects. A few small spiders scurried for safety, and a colony of woodlice tumbled progressively from a hole in the rotten wood of the window frame.

Sue dusted her hands off and turned to survey the room now that there was some light. Her eye was caught by an ancient tallboy in the corner, stacked with trinkets, crockery and figurines. She moved closer and her expert eyes scanned the contents. A small Victorian pill box and a set of Lalique glasswork figurines found their way into her bag before her eye was caught by something right at the back of the tallboy.

Masked by a swathe of cobweb was a chalice. Not a normal drinking cup, but a dull metal chalice inset with coppery swirls and the glint of gemstones. Sue moved some of the other worthless junk to one side and brushed away the cobweb so she could see the thing better. Certainly something unique. She grasped its stem and drew it from the back of the shelf. It was filthy dirty and encrusted with muck, as though it had been found in a riverbed and never cleaned. She rubbed her thumb across the rim to reveal several green and red gems. They certainly looked like genuine emeralds and rubies, and the object had a good heft, suggesting it was made from pewter or bronze. Sue pondered as she looked at the object, turning it in her hand.

'Sue? You up there?'

Tony's call snapped her back to reality, and she hastily added the chalice to the other objects in her bag, moving back the trinkets on the shelf to obscure the fact that something was missing from the tallboy.

'Yup!' she called.

'Anything?' Tony asked, coming into the room.

'A few bits and pieces. She gestured to the tallboy, and

Tony moved across with his clipboard and pen poised to record anything that might be of value. Sue wandered out of the room and back downstairs. Outside the front door, she took a deep breath to clear her lungs of the dust and grime from within the house. She patted her bag and smiled. Not a bad day's work.

From: 'Sue Cavendish' <antiquelady@hotmail.com>
To: 'Jacob' <jweigler@warwick.ac.uk>
Subject: Chalice identification
Sent: Sun, 2 June 2002 13:43:23 +0100

Hi Jacob

I wonder if you might be able to help with some identification.

Attached is a pic of an object I came across today. I've been checking on various internet sites for information on this chalice but so far have come up blank. The usual sources are also vague on the subject.

As this is one of your favourite subjects, I wonder if you have any other clues as to its origin, history and so on.

Sorry I've not been in touch of late. Work's keeping me in London. I promise I'll get up to Warwick soon for one of our special sessions. You know I can't keep away for too long.

Meantime I look forward to hearing what you can dig up about this object.

Love

Sue

xxx

From: 'Jacob' <jweigler@warwick.ac.uk>
To: 'Sue Cavendish' <antiquelady@hotmail.com>
Subject: re: Chalice identification
Sent: Sun, 2 June 2002 14:05:43 +0100

Hi there antiquelady,

You're a naughty girl! I don't hear from you for months and then you want my help … However on the promise of seeing you again … :->

The reason you probably can't find any information about your chalice is that it isn't a chalice at all. It's a goblet (and I could go into all the differences, but I'm sure at this stage you're not that bothered).

Check out the papers held at the Institute site at www.c-tec.gov.org (I didn't tell you any of this by the way – kind of classified information as this is a government site). The entry code changes each day, and so today click on the words 'unauthorised' and 'special' in turn. They're in the historical artifacts section, and you'll need a login id and password to access them. Use 'Warwick' as the ID, and JacoBA34526 as the password (it's case dependent as well). I think the one you're looking for is in case file L57935/C – but there are several there, and maybe you can figure out which one you have.

If this is what you're after, then look after the object. It seems to be quite rare and maybe if you clean it up a little, it might be more obvious what you have.

You owe me big time for this (as usual :->) so try and get up to Warwick as soon as you can to pay your debts.

Yours

Jacob Weigler
Art History Department
Warwick University Campus

Sue read Jacob's note with growing pleasure. Looking at the filthy chalice – correction, goblet – it was hard to imagine that it could have any real worth. But then Jacob was rarely wrong on these things, and was a useful person to know. She made a mental note to try and get to Warwick soon, if only to ensure that Jacob remained faithful to her as a source of knowledge. She smiled – amazing what you can get with the occasional blow job and flash of your boobs.

She opened up an internet browser and entered in the web address that Jacob had given her. Almost immediately a 'Cannot find server' page appeared. Sue looked at it blankly and followed Jacob's instructions as to which words to click. Suddenly the page changed and she was presented with a sign in/password screen. She shook her head. Strange. Entering the details Jacob had supplied, she found herself faced with an impressive library search function.

Everything seemed to be here. What an incredible resource, and trust Jacob to know all about it. Before long, she had located the catalogue and was comparing images of goblets with the one on the table in front of her. The one Jacob had suggested was pretty close, but on comparison, Sue decided that it wasn't the one. Shame, as Jacob's choice was a one-of-a-kind piece from the 13th Century, missing for more than 500 years and worth pretty much whatever the buyer wanted to charge. Several world-renowned institutes, including the Getty in America and the British Museum in England, were offering substantial prices for information as to its whereabouts.

Several pages later on in the online catalogue of lost treasures, Sue came across an ink sketch of something that looked far more promising. She looked at the simple sketch, and then across at the goblet sitting on her desk. The gemstones seemed to be in the same places. The patterns of the copper etching were very similar indeed, and overall the shape of the fluting on the stem, the base and the rim seemed to match her find.

'The Goblet of the Black Friars,' she read, 'was lost around the early 1700s during a publicly-suppressed spate of witch hunts in central London. It was rumoured to be at the centre of rites carried out by the Black Friars, based on the banks of the Thames close to the site of what is now Blackfriars Station. The Goblet is still worshipped by several underground cults as being the basis of power, and many of their rites revolve around the quest to locate the object. The vessel is rumoured to grant the heart's desire to the owner, although quite how the rite to achieve this is performed has been lost. This sketch was found amongst the possessions of an ex-cultist when he died in the late 1800s, and its accuracy cannot be verified.'

Sue sat back in her chair and read the text through a couple of times. She thoughtfully picked up the goblet and studied it closely.

'Heart's desire, eh – didn't do much for the old lady though, did you.' Looking closer at the side of the cup, Sue thought she could make out some additional inscriptions under the muck. She rubbed at it with her thumb, and revealed what looked like the rough shape of the Thames. She rubbed harder, revealing more finely etched lines surrounding the line of the river. As she ran her thumb over the cleared space, she suddenly felt a sharp pain. A bead of blood emerged and smeared over the surface of the goblet. The blood seemed to darken as it touched the metal, and a cloud moved over the sun outside, plunging the room into a gloomy darkness.

Sue looked up. 'Shit. All I want is more money than I know what to do with, and a fucking cut thumb and tetanus isn't going to help with that.'

The cloud moved on and the room was lightened once more. Blood continued to run from Sue's thumb and started to drip onto her desk.

'Bugger.' Sue leaped up and carried the goblet into the kitchen area, where she ran her thumb under the cold tap for a moment before studying the damage. A thin slit in the flesh gaped as she squeezed it, and more blood beaded up within. She reached for the antiseptic and liberally doused her thumb, wincing as the stinging started and then faded off. A plaster completed the exercise before she returned to the goblet and, after a moment's hesitation, held it under the tap. One of the key concerns when restoring old and tarnished objects was to take time and to do the research before anything else. Otherwise one always ran the risk of irreparably damaging the item. As the water washed over the goblet, so the muck and grime started to clear and Sue could see that it was etched with sigils and designs. The map section she had revealed resolved into an impressively detailed, if tiny, map of London, showing the bends in the Thames, and a pointer line leading to a location close to Blackfriars Station.

Sue rubbed her sore thumb thoughtfully with her fingers, and gently set the goblet onto the draining board. Returning to Tony's office, she printed out the information on the goblet, and then grabbed the London A-Z book from the reference shelf. Opening it to the overall map of London, she returned to the goblet and started to compare the maps.

Maybe, just maybe, after all this time the marked location might still be there.

Mobile Phone Transcript:

Call Made: Sun, 2 Jun 2002 15:07:35

Tony: Hi.

Geoff: Hi Tony, Geoff here.

Tony: Hi Geoff. Everything okay?

Geoff: Well … no, not really.

Tony: What's up?

Geoff: Well, I'm here with Francine looking through the accounts, and … well … we're in a bad shape.

Tony: What? What do you mean?

Geoff: Basically, unless things turn around very soon, we're looking at having to close or sell the business.

Tony: Wha –

Geoff: I know it's a shock. I couldn't believe it either, but Francine has checked and double checked and basically whatever money we had here has gone. All seems legitimate expenses, but the bottom line is that there's nothing left.

Tony: But I –

Geoff: So the first thing we have to do is to try and cut back. Did you tell Sue about the appointment yet?

Tony: Well … yes.

Geoff: That's a shame. We can't do it, Tony. We can't afford to pay her anything. You'll have to explain –

Tony: What do you mean?

Geoff: It's as I say, we don't have any funds. Sue will have to be dropped, and whatever we owe her will have to be paid later – if at all – in instalments.

Tony: But I don't –

Geoff: Sorry, mate, but that's the situation. We need to get together tomorrow to talk about this, so I'm contacting Alan. I wanted to check the situation with Sue so you can let her know that we won't be needing her. Sorry you've already told her. There's also some problem with the savings accounts – but we can go over that tomorrow as well.

Tony: Okay.

Geoff: Sorry to be the bearer of sad news, Tony. Hopefully we can sort something out, but it really doesn't look good.

Tony: Tomorrow then.

Geoff: Sure. Sorry.

CALL ENDS

Sue left Blackfriars Station and headed to the Bridge, as she felt that this was perhaps the best place to get her bearings. The Blackfriars area of London, just to the north of the Thames by Blackfriars Bridge, is a maze of small alleys and passages, intersected by the newer main thoroughfares of the bridge crossing and the main arterial routes of Embankment and Upper Thames Street alongside the river. From Blackfriars Bridge, Sue looked up and down the Thames, seeing the frontage of the various buildings ranged along the raised river bank. She pulled her A-Z from her bag and opened it to the page marked with a sheet of paper. On the paper was a crayon rubbing of the map from the side of the goblet, and she double checked that against the A-Z before looking up and setting off towards the end of the bridge.

The newer roads were of course not shown on the goblet map, but these had to some extent taken the paths of earlier roads, and Sue followed a series of turnings until she arrived at a small alley leading off Carter Court, which in turn led to an unmarked passageway between two sets of ancient buildings. There was a strong stench of river sewage here, and Sue edged her way down the passage gingerly, her flat shoes crunching over broken glass. She stuffed the A-Z back into her bag and surveyed the passage carefully. This was as close as she could get to the location marked on the goblet. The finely intricate etchings and lines created an impressively accurate view of the location. As she moved further down the passage, Sue's feet scuffed at the ground, and she kicked a small stone along. It span and danced, and then fell with a glassy chink to one side. Intrigued by the sound, Sue crouched down and saw that, half hidden at the base of the wall, was a small window into the building. The pathway had obviously been laid after the building had been completed, as there was a small lip of about a foot between the path and the level of the window's lower sill.

Sue glanced up and down the passage, but all was silent. No-one ever came this way – there was no normal London rubbish cluttering the passage: none of the old newspapers, coke cans, bottles, or even the more modern refuse found in such places: used needles and spent condoms. She returned her attention to the window and pushed against the glass. It creaked gently and gave a little.

Sue stood and looked around the passage. A little way up, she found what she was looking for: an old house brick, caked with bird droppings and half buried in the path. She wrenched it up, being careful not to damage her nails, and carried it to the half-buried window. Then she placed it on the ground before her, and with a final check to ensure that no-one was around, kicked the brick through the window. The glass didn't so much shatter as crumble, and with a few more well-aimed kicks with the flat of her foot, Sue had cleared the window frame of glass fragments.

A musty, dead smell greeted her as she peered into the blackness. From her bag she fetched a small penlight torch, and shone it into the darkness. There was nothing to see except some vague shapes shifting in the gloom and dust. She sniffed, and, looking around her once again, sat down on the floor and fed her legs through the window. Like a child going down stairs she shifted her bottom from the path and down to the sill so her legs were dangling into the building. Then, ducking her head, she braced herself on her arms and let herself drop into the gloom.

It was only about three or four feet to the floor, and she landed with a gentle crunch of broken glass. She shone the torch around her. It seemed to be an empty room. The dust disturbed by her arrival swirled around her, and the torchlight caught constant glimpses of movement as she walked through the room. Her feet were obscured by the murk that swirled around her legs.

To one side she found a black opening with steps leading down, while further along was a hatchway in the wall, securely closed and, it seemed, boarded shut. The only other exit was the shape of a doorway, but instead of a door, it boasted a bricked-up façade, the mortar crumbling with age and spilling out from the uppermost levels, showing that the door had been bricked up from the other side and the masons had been unable to keep the mortar neat towards the top.

She returned to the steps leading down, and, swinging the torch from side to side, started to descend. More than once she had to brush trailing cobwebs from her face, as the steps curled down. The walls to either side were ancient and covered with moss and mildew. The air became damp, and the steps a little slippery underfoot.

Sue's breathing became a little laboured and, she

noticed, her breath started to steam a little in the chill air. After a few moments, she reached the bottom of the steps and was faced with a closed metal door, rusted at the bottom. She shrugged and pushed at it, not really expecting much, but the ancient hinges abruptly snapped with a clang, and the door fell backwards away from her, crashing to the ground with an echoing bang, which reverberated around her in the confined stairwell. She shone her torch through the opening, and, as the dust slowly settled, she found herself faced with another door, but this time of wood. Ancient timbers tied together with cross braces, and enormous hinges made from some sort of metal – not iron this time, it seemed, as there was no rust or corrosion visible. The door also featured an inset carving. Sue smiled to see that the carving was of her goblet. Unmistakable.

She moved closer to the door, and in the dusty silence examined the handle. There did not seem to be a lock, but the handle was bonded to the door with a clay or pottery seal. There were markings there similar to some of those on the goblet, as well as several lines of cuneiform script.

'Abandon hope all ye who enter here,' muttered Sue under her breath, somewhat sarcastically. Holding the torch in her teeth, she examined the seal with her hands. It seemed brittle. She removed one of her shoes, and with a smart tap, broke the seal in two. Replacing her shoe, she pulled the two halves of the seal away from the door with her hands, and placed them to one side. Then, with a deep breath, she twisted the handle on the door and pushed.

Nothing. The door did not budge an inch. Somewhat cross, she put her shoulder to it and pushed hard. Not a thing. She released the handle and stood back, shining the torch around the edges of the door and then again at the handle. Then, with realisation, she grasped the handle once more and pulled. With an echoing wooden creak, it swung towards her, releasing a wave of dust and cobwebs from behind it. The stench was like nothing she had smelt before. Dust and damp and rotting food and ordure. She coughed and held her breath, blinking her eyes to clear them of the dust.

Holding the torch before her, she stepped through the doorway and into the room beyond. She was surprised to find that the floor was dry, and seemed to be of loose earth. Her feet sank into it a little as she stepped in, leaving clear footprints in her wake. The room was fully enclosed, with only the large wooden door she had opened as a means of entry and exit. It was perhaps ten feet across, and circular, the bricked walls soaring up until they were lost in darkness above. So what was the point of this?, she thought.

Sue leaned against the wall at one side and idly swung her flashlight around. A sealed room. No other entrance. So a storeroom, perhaps. But why was there nothing in it? It had been cleared out. But why then go to all the bother of sealing the outer door in such an elaborate fashion? It didn't make sense. She scuffed her foot against the ground.

And why was the floor of loose earth? Perhaps because something was buried here …

Sue crouched down and started to move the earth with her hand. The soil was icy cold and clammy. Suddenly her torch caught a glint of gold, and Sue dug a little deeper to reveal a gold coin. Brushing it off, she looked at it closely. It seemed to be a perfect example of a Roman coin, the sort of thing she would not hesitate to add to her bag should she come across it in her work. She dug a little more and found five more similar coins. It seemed that untold wealth was hers. She pocketed the coins and stood, brushing down her jeans.

Sue smiled to herself. A little excavation work, and who knew what riches she would find? With a spring in her step, she left the room and clattered up the ancient staircase beyond.

The lower storeroom descended into pitch darkness for a moment as the echoes of Sue's departure faded, and then a faint glimmer of greenish light sprung into existence, apparently coming from the fabric of the walls themselves. The damp brickwork was outlined in green, and the light spilled across the rough dirt floor in waves. The earth started to heave. Gently at first in one place, and then in several others. Small white objects burst from the ground and waved gently in the stale air, before pushing up and out of the earth. Skeletal, almost mummified hands attached to decaying arm bones, still with shreds of muscle, skin and fibre attached, waved from the floor as three figures started to clamber out of the ground. Their heads were in shadow, and their bodies clad in rotting and mildewed black robes, tattered and fraying around their emaciated feet. The robes were held together with rope belts, and from the belts hung several rusting and greenly glinting objects. Knives and spikes, stained with ancient blood and dirt.

For a moment the three figures stood silently in the chamber, unmoving. Then there came the hiss of a voice, as unfamiliar air was forced across taut vocal chords, and frayed lips and tongue struggled to form words. 'We are summoned. We must now wait and fulfil the curse.'

With a single movement, the Black Friars stepped back towards the greenly-glowing walls, which faded to darkness, leaving only faint rustling sounds, and the echoes of Sue clambering back out of the upper room onto the pathway.

Having finished her shower, Sue returned downstairs to find Tony there looking extremely sheepish.

'Hi,' he mumbled. 'Sue ... we've got to talk.'

Sue breezed past him. 'About what?'

Tony followed her into the living room and stood by the door as she poured herself a glass of gin, adding a splash of soda from the siphon.

'Well … you know I said yesterday about the bonus and the job …?'

Sue looked at him and nodded, a faint smile playing around her lips. She was enjoying watching Tony squirm.

'Well,' Tony started to wring his hands. Sue could not believe that anyone would actually do that. 'Well,' he started again. 'I was wrong.'

Sue looked at him in the ensuing silence. 'You were wrong.' She repeated flatly.

Tony nodded. 'Wrong about that, and wrong about lots of other things, it seems.'

'So my bonus …'

'… is not going to happen,' finished Tony. 'I had a call – Geoff – he says there simply isn't the money to justify it. I tried to talk him out of it – I tried – but he wouldn't listen. There's a meeting tomorrow and –'

'No bonus,' said Sue in a voice like ice. 'After all the work I've put in …' She took a deep breath.

'Don't worry,' mumbled Tony. 'It'll all work itself out. It'll all be fine. We've still got each other. I …'

Sue laughed at this. Out loud. It was time. She loved these times. When the men she used floundered on the end of her hook, flapping and gasping for one final kind word, for a last fuck, for sympathy.

'Why are you laughing?' asked Tony. 'I can't see what's so funny.'

Sue shook her head. 'That's it, Tony. It's the end. After

all I've done. I can't stay with you now.'

'Can't stay? But why? I love you!'

Sue gestured at him, her velvet dressing gown gaping to reveal her slim and shapely legs. 'Look at you! Just look! You've no money. No looks. And very soon no job. What on earth would I want to stay for?'

Tony frowned. 'What do you mean, "no job"? Who have you been talking to?'

'No-one, my darling Tony. It's obvious. Despite my best efforts on your behalf, the money's just not been coming in, has it? This is why you're trying to fob me off now, isn't it? Well I've had enough. I saw this coming.'

'What?' Tony's mouth gaped open. 'What do you mean?'

'This time next week,' said Sue sweetly, 'I'll be co-partner in Keith Barber's company – remember Keith? Your rival? Well we're the best of friends. More than friends, really. I can see a hostile take-over coming up for your failure of an antiques company.'

Tony staggered in the doorway as the impact of her words hit him. He stumbled to the table and sat down on one of the chairs, his face red and his breath heaving. 'You … you …'

'What's that Tony?' Sue asked sweetly, brushing past him again to the door.

'But I love you – you love me – you said!'

'Oh, I say lots of things, darling. Doesn't mean I mean them.' Sue turned to leave the room. 'And I never loved you,' she fired back. 'Off to pack now. Don't try and stop me.'

And with that she swept from the room, leaving Tony sitting at the table staring into space. His hands trembled as he re-ran the last few minutes through his mind again and again. A tear emerged from his right eye and tumbled down his cheek, where it rested.

From: 'Sue' <rich-bitch@hotmail.com>
To: 'Keith' <kbarber@lineone.net>
Subject: Tomorrow
Sent: Sun, 2 June 2002 18:30:12 +0100

Keith

Hi darling. Just to say that I'm free tomorrow to chat about the deal. See you usual time and place. And bring a bottle – I feel like celebrating.

Love

Sue

xxx

Having hurriedly dumped most of her things in her bags – whatever remained she could collect later on – Sue dropped them off at her own flat before getting changed once more for her evening's entertainment. She slipped into a pair of black jeans and an old black T-shirt, pulling back her hair and tucking it under a black cap. A camouflage jacket completed the ensemble. She hauled an old canvas bag from storage, and included with it a hurricane lamp, trowel and a small folding shovel – relics from when she had had a brief flirtation with archaeology at university before deciding that much better pickings could be had from places where you didn't have to dig them up yourself.

The sun was just setting as she arrived at Blackfriars Station and retraced her steps back to the alleyway and down into the eerily silent and deserted building. The hurricane lamp threw everything into stark relief as she made her way down the damp curving stairs and into the icy lower room, her breath fogging in front of her face from the chill.

She quickly unpacked her tools and returned to where she had found the coins.

'Nothing ventured …' she muttered to herself as she started to dig and sift the earth with the trowel. As a gold coin came into view, she smiled to herself.

Tony had sought solace from the day's events in the only way he knew. His friend the bottle. Aside from Sue, from whom it was impossible to keep secrets, no-one knew that Tony liked his tipple a little too much. That the visits to the supermarkets became more frequent as the stress increased. That the number of trips to the bottle bank likewise increased.

Staring into his glass, Tony reflected again on what could possibly have gone wrong here. He knew Sue loved him. She had told him so enough times. And the sex – the sex was amazing. Well, when he wasn't too drunk to perform it was amazing. What on earth could she be worried about there? And all that stuff about him losing his money and job – well that had to be a bluff, didn't it? Had to be.

He pushed himself to his feet and staggered over to the drinks cabinet to refresh his glass for the umpteenth time since Sue had walked out. As he did so, his eye caught an unusual shape on the drainer in the kitchen area. He frowned and wandered out to have a closer look. It was a goblet or a chalice or something. Obviously Sue had been cleaning it and had left it to dry. But where had it come from?

Tony grasped it by the stem and carried it back into the living area. Slumping back down in his chair, whiskey in one hand and the goblet in the other, he studied the piece. Fairly good looking really, gemstones, some metal filigree inlaid into it, and meticulously etched.

As he studied the goblet, Tony did not notice that the lights in the room seemed to dim, and in their place a faint green glow appeared, seeping from the very fabric of the building.

Without warning, Tony's whiskey glass shattered in his hand.

'Fuck and damn!' he exclaimed, swapping the goblet from his good hand to his cut one as he rummaged in his pocket for the handkerchief that he knew was there. The blood from his hand spread over the surface of the goblet, and seemed to sink into it. Giving up the search for the hankie, Tony started to cry. First his job, then Sue, now this. He'd never wanted any of this. All he'd ever wanted was to be with Sue forever and ever …

The temperature in the room abruptly dropped several degrees, and Tony looked up through tear-blurred eyes as the darkness pressed in all around. There was a faint whispering sound, as though material was being brushed against material. Seated in his chair, Tony realised that he was not alone. From out of the darkness on either side of him, two silent figures in black robes materialised. He was certain they appeared from nowhere, but how could that be possible?

In front of him, backlit by a faint green glow, a third figure seemed to congeal from the motes of dust floating in the air. It took a step towards him, metal instruments clinking gently at its waist. Tony sat staring at the figure. His heart was beating nineteen to the dozen, and, despite the chill air, sweat broke out on his pate and started to run down his temples.

'You have the goblet.'

The voice was like rusty knives gently sliding against each other. A susurrant, whispering, sexless cadence that set Tony's nerves jumping. He looked at his bleeding hand, which was clenched tight around the goblet.

'You have a heart's desire. You have the goblet. Choose. Destroy the goblet and set us free.'

The whispering voice was without threat. The words were clear.

Tony, looking at the goblet, hitched in his breath. 'Will … will I be with Sue if I do?' he asked, saying the first thing that came to mind at that time.

The spectral Friar standing in the gloom before him said nothing. The cowl covering its face slid back to reveal a face of bone, sinew and desiccated flesh. The blank eye sockets gave nothing away, but with a gentle clicking of bone on bone, the creature shook its head.

Tony stared wide-eyed at the Friar. No. The creature said he would not keep Sue if he destroyed the goblet. This fact echoed in his mind for a moment. Then, with an effort of will, Tony lifted the bloody goblet and placed it on the table. 'Then I will not destroy the goblet. Sue is more important.'

The Friar did not respond, but its grinning face turned towards the goblet on the table. 'So be it,' the rasping voice whispered. 'Your choice. Now you will get your heart's desire – but there is a price …'

After about an hour's digging, Sue was filthy dirty, but had a growing hoard in her canvas sack. After the coins, she had found some jewellery. Some work with the spade had revealed a couple of small chests, rusted shut but reassuringly heavy. More coins had followed.

She worked her way around the small chamber, trying to excavate methodically, and trying not to miss an inch. She leaned back on her haunches and wiped her face. Was it getting even colder in here? Her breath suddenly steamed in front of her, and when the fog cleared, she was looking at the legs of someone dressed in a long black cloak or robe.

With a squeal, she pushed backwards, straight into the legs of a second figure standing behind her. She slowly rose to her feet, brushing her hands together.

'Um – look – I can explain … Is this your stuff?'

The figures silently regarded her, and Sue noticed that their clothes were frayed and mouldy. The hurricane lamp cast their faces in deep shadow, their hoods covering whatever features they might have.

She stepped back, and checked where the entrance to the chamber was positioned.

'Well, if it's all the same to you, I'd better be on my way.' She turned to leave, only to find the doorway now blocked by a third figure, one that had not been there a second earlier. Her blood turned to ice, and she looked around frantically. What had she stumbled into here? Who were these people?

'Look,' she began in her best conciliatory voice. 'Can we just talk about this for a moment?'

'You have the goblet.'

The rusty voice echoed around the confined space,

and Sue realised that the creature in the doorway had spoken. 'Goblet – yes – I have the goblet. But it's not here. I'd have to get it for you. Valuable, is it?'

'Immeasurably. You have a heart's desire. You have the goblet. Choose. Destroy the goblet and set us free.'

'Destroy …' Sue was suddenly alert for the money. 'But you said it was immeasurably valuable. How valuable is that, then?'

There was silence. All Sue could hear was the thudding of her heart and the sound of her own breathing.

'So why should I destroy it, then? If it's so valuable. I think perhaps you'd better let me go, and I can bring you the goblet later on? Yes?'

'So be it,' hissed the Friar, and stepped to one side.

Sue took her chance and bolted for the door. Without looking back, she raced up the steps in pitch darkness, and all but threw herself through the window opening and out into the comparatively fresh night air of London.

Sue's hand trembled as she tried to get the key to Tony's flat in the lock. Finally she managed it, and tumbled exhausted through the door. She slammed it behind her and fixed the safety lock. Taking two big gulps of air, she headed off to the kitchen, where she had left the goblet after washing and drying it. When she got to the drainer, however, the goblet was gone. She span round and recoiled in horror as Tony lurched from out of the darkness in the living area and stood in the doorway before her. His face and hair were covered with blood, and blood had also saturated his clothes, which hung loosely on his frame. He swayed a little, forward and backward, until his eyes, wide and shockingly white against the red blood, fixed on her face.

His mouth opened and a thin stream of blood trickled out. 'Sue – I did it ...' he whispered. 'I got what I wanted. But the price ... the price ...' He breathed in, a hollow rattling sound, and Sue skittered away around the kitchen area, searching for an exit that wasn't there. She noticed a pool of blood slowly spreading across the tiled floor towards her.

Tony blinked at her, and his mouth spread in an insane rictus grin. 'See how much I love you, Sue. See how much!' Tony's body swayed once more, and then he fell face-first to the floor. Sue crammed her fists to her mouth in an attempt to stop herself from screaming.

Tony's body had been cleanly eviscerated from behind. His back had been neatly cut open and most of his organs removed. The same procedure had been carried out to the back of his head, his arms and legs. His clothing had been hanging to the front of his body while the whole of his rear had been expertly flayed and dissected while Tony still lived. Blood leaked from exposed veins and muscle, and Sue could see the remains of his heart pumping still in the otherwise empty cavity of his chest. He should have been dead, but was miraculously still alive. His head turned to grin at her.

Sue became aware of a movement in the room behind

him, and looked up to see the three Friars standing there, one holding Tony's guts, another cradling part of his brain in its hands, while the third held the flayed strips of Tony's skin casually by its side. At this she screamed. Long and hard. And after the first scream came sobbing cries of disbelief, as she slowly sank down against the kitchen cupboards, her feet resting in the still-spreading pool of Tony's blood.

One of the Friars stepped forward – it may have been the same one as before, but to Sue all three looked alike. 'Why?' she blurted between hitching gasps for breath. 'Why have you done this?'

'Greed.' The whispering voice cut through Sue's tears.

'Simple greed. We were cursed by our greed to deliver the heart's desire of those who summon us, with an unthinkable price to be paid. We want peace. If you destroy the goblet, we will be free, but you will get nothing.'

Nothing. She would get nothing. The concept horrified her more than the Friars, and she shook her head. 'I … I can't.'

'Your choice,' whispered the Friar with a note of sadness. 'Now you will get your heart's desire – but there is a price …'

Anyone walking through the back streets of Blackfriars might wonder, as they pass a certain alley at a certain time, why they can hear faint crying. Few would investigate further – such sounds can be commonplace in London, and anyway, it's always someone else's problem.

Down the alley and through the shattered window, now boarded over from inside. Into the pitch blackness. Down the chill steps and past the now closed and bolted iron door to the sealed and warded wooden door. And beyond the door, in the circular chamber …

Sue raises her eyes to the flickering green light that plays around the ceiling of the chamber. Her tears are bright. Around her are riches of all kinds: gold and silver ingots; coins from every realm on earth; banknotes and fine jewellery; caskets overflowing with baubles and riches beyond belief. She sniffs and reaches out tentatively to touch her wealth, to handle her riches, but her arms end in ragged stumps, crudely sewn up with black thread, and weeping blood and pus. Seeing her arms, Sue starts crying. She is hopeless with grief.

There is a sound behind her, and she turns her head, eyes wide as she sees a humanoid shape in the room behind her. It is Tony. His skin is sallow and peeling from his bones. What remains of his clothes is hanging in tatters. His back glistens wetly in the emerald light. He cannot walk well, and so collapses to the earthy floor behind Sue and takes her gently in his bloody half-arms.

'Shh,' he consoles her. 'Shh. I got my heart's desire too. Now we'll never, ever, be parted.'

Sue's scream can barely be heard in the street above.

From: 'Keith' <kbarber@lineone.net>
To: 'Sue' <rich-bitch@hotmail.com>
Subject: Where were you
Sent: Mon, 3 June 2002 13:34:09 +0100

Sue

Just hoping you're OK. I waited for an hour but you didn't show. No answer from the mobile as well. Hope all's well. Call me when you can.

Love

Keith
Date: Mon, 3 Jun 2002 13:40:21 +0100
From: 'Postmaster' <postmaster@lineone.net>
Sender: <postmaster@lineone.net>
To: < kbarber@lineone.net >
Subject: Undeliverable Mail

Unknown user: rich-bitch@hotmail.com

'Blackfriars' started life as a treatment for the Channel 5 horror television show *Urban Gothic*. After the first series of the show, I loved it so much that I got in touch with the producers and got the okay to create and publish an anthology based on the stories. This was great fun to do, and I found that I got on well with Steve Matthews, the exec producer on the show. When series two was commissioned, it started out as being a 13 week run, like series one, but Tom deVille, the writer who had provided all the stories for the first series, didn't want to write all of series two, so a number of slots were being commissioned in from other writers.

I discussed some ideas with Steve, and went away and wrote a treatment. It went through a few further discussions and rewrites, and I was about to meet with Steve for a final script editing meeting before I was due to write the actual script. However at that point, Channel 5 decided to cut the series to just nine episodes. Steve and Tom naturally wanted to keep all of Tom's episodes in there – mainly because they formed an ongoing narrative that led to the series climax – and so some of the other planned episodes had to be dropped ... mine among them.

As I had what I thought was a pretty good outline, I decided to novelise it instead, and the story here is the result.

For casting I had in mind Colin Baker for Tony, and someone like Kim Thomson (who had been in a series called *Virtual Murder*) for Sue ... I still think it would make a pretty good short film!

Recursions

Timmy grinned as he put the finishing touches to his latest toy. Using a pair of the finest tweezers he placed his new creation down into the toy box he used to store everything he made. His new toy was called Peter, and Timmy considered the placing before moving him to another part of the toy box.

Timmy had been building things for a year or so now, ever since he had received the latest software upgrades and was now running with an increased CPU and storage facility, courtesy of his parents. Timmy returned to the workbench where he assembled his toys. There were his tools, the microscopes and tweezers, the fine etching lasers and the wetware tanks where he grew the microscopic components he used to build things.

Timmy loved to build things. He always had done, and his workbench was covered with plastic boxes containing what looked like varying amounts of coloured sand, but were in fact all the components he used in his efforts.

He checked his terminal and saw that Peter had auto-registered and was now visible as a tiny caricature on the screen. He tapped in a few commands, and Peter moved towards a different area in the toy box. Good. Everything seemed to be working fine.

At that moment a bell chimed, and Timmy dragged his attention away from the screen. It was time for his daily charge. Without this, Timmy's power packs would drain and eventually he would become sluggish and slow before losing power completely. A daily top-up ensured that this didn't happen.

Timmy hefted himself off his chair and scooted out of the room, pausing only to slap his hand on the light sensor by the door. The lights dimmed, leaving the monitor still showing an image of a tiny animated figure approaching a house.

'Peter!'

Peter heard the voice as he approached Jasmine's house. He liked Jasmine and was glad he was headed over to see her. It seemed like ages since they had last spent time together.

Peter ascended the steps to her door, and before he could knock, it was flung open and Jasmine was there – a bundle of energy about the same age as him – 6 years old.

She screeched and grabbed Peter by the arm, dragging him into the house.

'Wait until you see what I've done!' she proclaimed proudly.

Jasmine was always doing something. She always had a plan formulating somewhere. When they were with other friends, it was always Jasmine who had all the neat ideas, who found the most exciting places to go. It was Jasmine who masterminded the break-in at the abandoned hospital where they had spent several hours scaring each other silly down abandoned and paint-peeling corridors.

Jasmine dragged Peter up the stairs to her room, and Peter hesitated only momentarily before following her in. There was something about going into her room that filled him with awe. He tried to remember the last time he had been there, but he couldn't. He thought this a little strange as he knew he had been there, but the memory seemed to elude him.

'Look!'

Jasmine pointed at a large, glass-fronted case that took up most of one wall of her room. Inside it was mostly black, but in the blackness floated several ball-like objects. Peter approached warily. It would be just like Jasmine to have some practical joke up her sleeve.

'What is it'?'

Jasmine smiled triumphantly and puffed her chest out. 'Good innit!'

Peter nodded. He had never seen anything like this before.

'Hang on … need a charge.' Jasmine pulled a charging cable from the wall of her room and plugged the end into the socket in her hip. She grinned at Peter. 'What's the matter? Never seen anyone charge up before?'

Peter blushed. Of course he had, just never so blatantly. Most folks he knew charged overnight, or used one of the private charging booths that dotted the streets. But this was Jasmine, he reminded himself. Nothing could be taken for granted.

A movement caught his eye in the tank and he looked more closely at one of the little suspended balls. Swirls of colour drifted across its surface like oil on water.

'Cool, eh?' said Jasmine. 'I managed to get the eco-climates working this morning.'

'Eco-climates?' Peter was not sure what these were.

'Yeah. You know, where we can make it rain or snow or whatever, but only in a selected area.'

Peter nodded, vaguely recalling this. He felt tired all of a sudden and wondered when he had last been charged. He looked at Jasmine. Dare he ask if he could use hers?

'I managed to get it all balanced,' Jasmine was saying. 'Everything feeds off everything else, see. The balls circle slowly, the darkness surrounds them, and the friction of the balls on the darkness provides the power to make the light sources work. It's so *cool*!'

Peter nodded again. He remembered his own experiments with making things – or at least he felt he should remember these things. He definitely *needed* a charge. He considered that working at the micro level was fun, but he couldn't really see the point. He'd rather race through abandoned hospitals. But when he tried to recall where the hospital was, he couldn't place it.

'Do you think …' he started, gesturing at Jasmine's hip.

Jasmine giggled. 'Oh, yes, sorry, rude of me.' She leaped to the other side of the room, the cable in her side flapping wildly, and dug a second cable out from under a pile of clothes.

'My room has two,' she said with a grin. 'We can do it together.'

Peter, with a degree of embarrassment, slipped the connector under his shirt and into the connecting hole there. He felt the charge start to flow and smiled happily. That was better.

Jasmine wandered over to her creation. 'I used the smallest and the tiniest components I could make,' she said. 'And I tried to make as many different things as I could.'

'How can I see?' asked Peter, peering again at the ball with the oil patterns flowing over its surface.

Jasmine handed him a tube-like device. 'Look through that,' she instructed.

Peter looked and frowned.

'You focus it by turning that ring there.'

Peter twisted the ring and an image focused before his eyes. Shapes. Something like a triangle, one shaped like a boot. 'What are they?'

Jasmine smiled. 'That's where I put the other things I make.'

'You put them on these balls?' Peter was astonished.

'Yup. And some of the balls are full up now, and some I've only just started to use. It's hard 'coz you have to match the wetware to the balls. They're all different temperatures you see, and the light is different, and the gravity, so you have to build according to the ball.

Peter was amazed. He had no idea that Jasmine could create such things. He wondered if one day he might be able to construct such tiny objects, but felt that maybe this was beyond him.

Jasmine was fiddling with something on her workbench now. Peter wandered over, but to his unaided eye he could see nothing at all. Jasmine was working with fine wire grips and a microscope to manipulate something unseen.

'If I can just …' Jasmine's tongue poked between her lips in concentration as she moved the grips minutely.

'Ah, there it is,' she smiled. 'I just had to get the wetware inserted into the head cavity, but it's there now. That's usually the hardest bit, as too much and you can damage the container. I slipped a bit there, but I think it's okay.'

She picked up the grips, and carefully carried them over to the glass case. She used her free hand to open a panel at the side, and slid the grips and burden into the cabinet.

'There. That's another one.'

'Another what?' asked Peter.

'Another of my little constructs,' explained Jasmine patiently. 'I called this one Abraxas. Honestly Peter. Don't they teach you anything in your classes?'

Peter shook his head. 'My head is spinning,' he admitted. 'I can half remember things, but then they go again and I can't seem to grasp them.'

Jasmine looked at him. 'I think you need to charge up more often.'

Peter looked again at the balls in the cabinet. 'What about the things you put in there? Don't they need charging?'

'Ah, that's the clever bit,' said Jasmine smugly. 'They do, but they do it themselves. They use the heat and the light and the other stuff I shoved in there, and they are self-sustaining. Neat eh?'

Peter nodded. 'Yeah, neat.'

Jasmine saw Peter's attention start to flag. 'You had enough of that charge?'

Peter nodded.

'How about a spot of underground exploration – I found a way down into the sewer system the other day. Fancy an explore?'

'Try stopping me,' said Peter, unplugging himself.

'Race you to the door,' shouted Jasmine, and scooted out of the room.

Peter looked again at the floating balls, and at the one on which Jasmine had put her latest construct. 'What do you call it anyway?' he shouted after her. 'The ball I mean.'

Peter hurried for the door as Jasmine's footfalls clattered down the stairs. Her voice came back to him.

'I call it Earth! Come on slowcoach.'

Peter crashed down the stairs after her and followed her outside. Another day of exploration beckoned.

On Earth, the night sky scudded overhead like furrows of oil on a pool of water. Spots of rain flecked the pavements and a chill wind moaned through the trees.

Abraxas crouched where he found himself. Part human, part something else, he was hungry, so he sat on his haunches in the shadows and listened and waited. Prey would come soon, he knew, and then he could feed.

Abraxas had no memory of what he was, just that he existed, and that the pain would go when he fed. For he was damaged. Nothing apparent, but something was *wrong* in his brain.

So he waited.

Patiently.

I don't often write science fiction, and so this little piece was quite a surprise to me when it dropped out of my mind. The basic idea is one of worlds within worlds within worlds … and I quite like the idea that worlds are being created by 'kids' in other worlds …

The reference to Abraxas was a nod to the *Time Hunter* series of novellas I was editing for Telos Publishing at the time. In those, Abraxas is a half-human, half-cyborg creature created by denizens of the future to act as a sort of controlled thug. I thought it might be nice to write another 'creation' story for him … After all, if Terry Nation can have three (at least) different stories of the creation of the Daleks, then why couldn't I have two for Abraxas?

It Started with a Rose

Sarah was exhausted as she slumped her way across the office to her desk. *Too many late nights. Sheesh. Come the weekend and I'm shattered,* she thought. *Then a weekend of housework and cooking followed by Monday morning and it's back to the grindstone. 7.45 am is not an earthly time to be at work.*

I wish ... I wish, she thought, *with all my heart, that someone might remember my birthday and get me some flowers ...*

As she approached her desk, Sarah saw that there was something sitting on it. Something red. And small. She realised it was a single red rose. Sarah picked it up.

How sweet. Wonder who it is from?

There was no way her boyfriend would ever do something like this ... unless he was feeling guilty ... She frowned momentarily. Carl had no secrets from her. So someone else then ...

Her work colleagues started to drift in, stopping for coffee, chatting quietly. Normal Monday morning office life. Then at 8.00 am, Sarah's phone rang.

It was reception.

'Delivery for Miss Howard,' said the receptionist.

Sarah went down to reception to find two more roses waiting for her. She smiled and carried them back to her desk.

Then, at 9.00 am, and 10.00 am, and 11.00 am more

calls … more deliveries. Sarah hurried down each time, wondering what was going on … more and more roses. Four, then eight, then a beautiful bouquet of 16. Her desk area was now sweetly scented, and she couldn't help smiling as her office colleagues looked curiously at her flowers as they passed by.

At midday, Sarah was waiting downstairs when a man from the local florist's arrived carrying two large bouquets of roses … 16 flowers in each. She accepted them and smiled sweetly at the doorman and asked if she might leave them in reception as there wasn't really room at her desk.

Leaning forward conspiratorially, the receptionist said, 'Birthday is it, love?' Sarah nodded sheepishly. 'Someone obviously thinks a lot of you, love,' he said before returning to his paper.

Another four bouquets arrived at 1.00 pm. 64 roses in total. As 2.00 pm approached, Sarah was standing looking out of the window as a large florist's lorry rolled up.

She pulled out her mobile from her bag and rapidly dialled.

'Carl? Yes, it's me. Yes, I'm fine. Listen. The flowers. Thank you so much for sending them, but enough's enough, don't you think? I have a pile here and I … What do you mean, "What flowers?"? The flowers you're sending! As I say, they're very nice but … You haven't sent any flowers. Really? So who … what …? Look, don't worry. I'll call you back.'

At 3.00 pm Sarah was lurking in reception, pretending to read the notice board. Another 16 bouquets of 16 roses each were added to the 14 already there. The place was starting to stink.

Two men were delivering the flowers, and as they turned, having placed the last of the new bouquets, Sarah hurried over.

'Excuse me,' she said, smiling. 'Do you know who is sending all these flowers?'

One of the men, a stocky chap wearing a baseball cap, pushed the cap back and scratched his balding head. 'They for you, miss?' he asked.

'No, no ...' said Sarah. 'I'm just interested ...'

The man sniffed. 'Far as I know, it's a private customer. We're not told the sender, just asked to deliver 'em, see?'

He held out a clipboard with a sheet on it. Sarah took a quick look and saw that, indeed, there was no sender listed, just her name, and the office address. 34 red roses in two bouquets. Sarah thanked the man, sighed, and returned upstairs.

At 4.00 pm, Sarah was sitting in a coffee bar across the street from the office. She had been wracking her brain for who might be behind this, but to no avail. Further calls to Carl had produced no admission of guilt, and he just wasn't a good enough liar ... So she sat and waited and watched. 32 more bouquets arrived, and 64 of them arrived at 5.00. She counted them all as they were carried into her office while she nursed her now-cold coffee.

She became aware of someone standing at her arm. It was the waitress.

'You all right?' she asked. Then she glanced out the window at what Sarah was looking at. 'They've been at that all day. Reckon they have some sort of "do" tonight. Why else would they want all those flowers?'

Sarah nodded absently, and asked the girl if she would get her another coffee.

When the waitress had gone, Sarah suddenly realised that she had wished for someone to send her flowers that morning and it had happened. But why? Why should her wish on this day come true …? She often wished for things. New shoes, a holiday, a pay rise … Why should it work on useless flowers but not on anything else? This was crazy. She had to stop it. Sarah closed her eyes and concentrated and wished with all her heart that she didn't have any flowers. That they would be gone.

She cracked open one eye and looked out across the road. No vans. Leaving her drink, she crossed the road and looked into the reception area. No roses. Wow. It worked. Maybe this was her day. Her special birthday. Maybe this was the day when her wishes actually came true. She smiled.

Sarah Howard opened the door of her Porsche, and sat in the leather seat. Her Prada-covered feet touched the pedals, and the engine hummed into life. Now … who would she like to be waiting for her when she got there? Brad Pitt perhaps … or that hunky chap from IT … and how much money would she like in her bank account …

Sarah felt that on this day … on this day of all days … that she had somehow beaten fate. And it felt wonderful.

With 'It Started With A Rose' I wanted to write something short and simple, but romantically inclined. I didn't intend it to be even remotely fantastical, but being as it is me, it ended up being slightly in that vein. I liked the idea of a simple wish coming true, but then the wish continuing on and on, doubling each time …

Susan

I was walking to my club when I first saw her.

Me in my tailored shirt, jacket casually thrown over one shoulder, and a twinkle in my eye. She was wearing a colourful pair of patterned leggings and a loose T-shirt top cinched tight with a wide belt. Her curly blonde hair cascaded down her back like golden rain, and her strappy high heeled shoes accentuated her legs to the extent that my eye was drawn to travel the length of her in one hypnotic swoop.

I was instantly captivated.

Her name was Susan (well, of course I spoke to her … some things just have to be done) and she was apparently a secretary for one of those insurance brokers in the City. Although I live in London, I have no idea of how it all works. One of the perils of being financially secure. I didn't have to work, and so I didn't. I spent my time travelling and just living the life … often lonely, endlessly wanting companionship, but eventually … every time … everyone I found left me, moved on to other things, to other experiences. Women can be such fickle creatures.

Susan arrived during one of my lean patches. I'd not had companionship for perhaps a year, during which I had sated my need for friendship, intelligent discussion and fine dining through a succession of casual acquaintances, all of which ended badly, and which increasingly left me feeling worn out and desperate for something better.

Susan was also on her own. Her last boyfriend had left her under somewhat strange circumstances and no matter how I tried I couldn't get her to explain the details. Maybe it was too painful for her or something. I could understand that. I too had known pain.

We spent that first evening at my club, and she proved to be a most entertaining and witty conversationalist. We seemed to have a lot in common. Strange when you consider that she was a secretary and I was a … what? I've never been sure how to describe myself. A playboy perhaps? Or a man about town? Certainly not a gigolo or a Romeo, a Casanova or a player … such things were far too crude.

Thankfully she seemed to accept me, and our conversation ranged from the state of the government to horse breeding in Iceland via ice cream flavours, how the American health system worked and which were the best sort of prawns to use in a curry. I was entranced. Her blue eyes would open wide as she explained the finer points of culinary curry making, and her delicate hands would flutter and move as she mapped out the contours of an Icelandic hillside that abutted a slowly encroaching icy glacier. Or at least she said it did. Iceland was somewhere I had yet to visit. Much too cold for me.

As the evening drew on, alcohol turned the discussion to men and sex and magic. We were secret collaborators. Giggling over our overpriced drinks as we discussed her past boyfriends. I, for my part, was as gentlemanly as I could be, not kissing and telling, but smiling with her. Letting my hand rest near hers on the table so that when her butterfly gestures faded she could alight on my hand. I felt her heat pressing into me, sending tingling sensations up and down my body.

I retired to the bathroom at one point to freshen up. To splash a little water on my face and cool my hands a little. When I returned to the table, she had folded one of the napkins into a tiny swan! Looking at me all innocently from under her eyelashes, she claimed ignorance and that the piece of tissue had somehow created the bird-shape all by itself. When I opened it up, however, there was a red kiss-mark there from her lips freshened by scarlet lipstick while I had been away.

Susan enlivened me like no other.

As the evening bled away into night, and the other patrons in the club drifted off to whence they came, it was our turn to bid farewell to the amiable barman, and to step out into the night air.

It wasn't cold, but Susan pressed herself into me. Holding my waist and stepping along in time with me as we sauntered down the deserted sodium-lit street towards my apartment. Solitary figures heading towards a destiny.

It was late. The trains had long since stopped running. The underground was now the domain of drunks, the unwanted and the unloved, and there were no buses heading anywhere close to her own place. So the answer was obvious.

I unlocked the door and we tumbled in, drunkenly shushing each other as we clattered about in the hallway. I gently closed the door so it wouldn't slam, and Susan slipped off her shoes, steadying herself against the wall as she did so.

I went to the kitchen to make some coffee, while Susan headed to the bathroom, trying all the doors along the way as she refused to ask me which was the correct one.

I stood in the kitchen waiting for the kettle to boil. Smiling to myself at my luck in finding Susan that evening.

My internal thoughts were interrupted by her appearance in the doorway. She had found the bathroom, and was now standing there grinning drunkenly at me. All she was wearing was one of my shirts. It was unbuttoned, and I could see the edges of her pert breasts peeping out. She sashayed towards me, hands stroking the front of my own shirt. Deft fingers unbuttoning it, freeing it from my trousers, and then cool palms stroking my skin, fingers caressing and touching. Rubbing gently over my nipples as she raised herself on tiptoe to kiss me oh so gently.

Fuck the coffee.

That first night with Susan was amazing. She was as considerate and experienced a lover as a man could possibly want. Sensitive to my needs, she always knew when to be firm or when to be compliant. She knew when to relax and enjoy, and when I needed some release.

Afterwards, I was exhausted.

So tired I could hardly think straight. My eyes were glued together. My teeth itched. My hands were shaky.

Susan seemed fine. She sprang from my bed around 8 am and headed to the bathroom, humming to herself. I couldn't move and so lay there with my eyes closed.

I heard her come back into the bedroom. The bed moved as she sat on it to put her shoes back on. I felt her _ _ _ _ on my forehead and I swear I felt whatever remaining energy I had pass through into her.

She kissed me on the cheek and said that she'd see me later.

Then, with a clatter of heels and the slam of the door, she was gone.

Silence.

I lay there for maybe another hour, drifting in and out of sleep. Eventually, I cracked open my eyes and looked at the clock. It was 9.15 am. I sighed and stumbled out of bed. The light from the window hurt my eyes so I adjusted the curtains to block it.

In the kitchen, nothing to drink. I was all out. I remembered that I had fully intended to stock up the previous night before I had been distracted by Susan, and now it was too late.

I looked around the kitchen hopelessly. Why didn't I have some emergency backup for the emergency backup that I had used the previous night! Note to self.

On the table was a note written in lipstick. *See you tonight x S.* So maybe she would come back.

I staggered back to my room and buried myself under the covers. In the dark I settled back to exhausted sleep like some sort of hibernating bear.

Susan returned that evening.

I finally woke as the light was fading, my tired eyes blinking in the gathering gloom. I staggered to the bathroom and splashed my face with water again. I felt a little better, but still very drained.

The buzzer sounded on the front door to the apartment. It was Susan. I buzzed her up and shrugged on a lounge suit while I waited. Then she was there.

It was as though my finger had been plugged in a light socket. Her smile lit up my hallway, and as she came in, her scent swirled around me and made my head spin. It was one of the more modern perfumes. Issey Miyake for women perhaps. Or something by Jean Paul Gautier? She filled my world and I took in the close-fitting, short floral dress she was wearing. Her hair was pinned up, make-up subtle, and eyes and mouth smiling at me.

She drew me to her and kissed me. I was lost again.

We spent the evening walking the streets, hand in hand. I was showing her all my haunts. Where I liked to go, stories of places I had been. Susan was a tremendous listener, always prompting with a word and a smile, remembering everything I said and then later on questioning and linking together stories and places with enthusiasm.

We skimmed stones across the mud. We hugged each other on the banks of the river, watching the illuminated boats roll past. We kissed under the rainbow lights of Piccadilly.

She was my world. Totally.

The following morning, I felt worse than ever. I had again completely forgotten to eat, but moreover, I was starting to look quite uncomfortably worn.

Lying in bed, I looked at my hands. They were wrinkled and old-looking. There were some dark moles that hadn't been there before, and the faint markings of some liver spots. My normally immaculate nails were chipped, and the quick was splitting around the base of them. I felt my face. It seemed ancient and tired.

What was happening to me?

As I lay in bed I considered that perhaps the lack of food was a cause. But I had gone without before, and not with such drastic and immediate consequences.

My thoughts turned to Susan. Amazing Susan. I smiled at her memory. But then I started to wonder.

I consider myself a man of experience. Well travelled. And in the free time that being a man of leisure brings, I had made study of many things. I had always had an interest in the supernatural. The creatures and denizens of those stories and fabrications, as well as some of the more truthful manifestations, had always held a fascination for me. Among them, of course, was the vampire. The creature of the night as popularised by Bram Stoker and then bastardised by every film maker ever since. However my studies also extended to other forms of vampirism, to the conceptual ideas and conceits of succubae and incubi. Among this genus there was persistent talk of creatures who fed off energy, who could sap the life from a room of partying folk just by stepping through the door … Could I have stumbled across such a creature? Could the lovely Susan be some demonic creature in disguise? I shook my head to myself. I couldn't really see how that could be possible. It seemed insane. Though the more insane the idea appeared, the more I resolved to be alert next time she came over. Just in case.

She arrived at around 7 pm that evening. Darkness had fallen and I had taken the opportunity to tidy up a little. The apartment was never really messy, but things have a habit of starting to look out of place if you don't straighten the magazines, replace the books in their rightful places and ensure that the DVDs are nicely in alphabetical order.

When the buzzer sounded I was ready, but my heart thumped with an emotion I had never felt before. Fear. She came in, and if she was surprised by my somewhat haggard appearance, she didn't show it. Instead we sat and talked, watched a film – some sort of crazy chick flick about a woman who gets it on with her office manager and then discovers that he likes large underwear, or something like that anyway – sipped a bottle of fine red wine, one of the good vintage ones with body that I keep in reserve, and finally retired to bed.

The lovemaking was again spectacular, but I was tired. So, so tired. I did my best to keep up with her, but she was so demanding and amazing and sensual that by the time I emptied myself for the second time, I felt as though I had nothing more to give.

She skipped back home again, heels clattering. Door slamming.

Silence.

I lay there, moaning quietly to myself. I needed something. My mouth was dry and flaky, my hands trembled. I closed my eyes in exhaustion. The room seemed to whirl around me, patterns blossoming behind my eyelids and lights flashing.

In a moment of horror I realised that I still had not got any food in, but when I tried to make my legs move, maybe to head on out into the night to see what I could find, they refused to obey me. I slumped. One arm fell over the side of the bed and hung there, uselessly.

I swallowed and felt the dryness of my throat catch. Oh for a touch of liquid. Instead I let my weary stupor overtake me, and I fell into a dark, dreamless sleep, disturbed by my restless movements, and the aching, gnawing, paralysing exhaustion that overtook me.

It was not until the following day that I woke. My clock said 14.05, and I had to look at it uncomprehendingly for a few moments before I could figure out what that meant. I had slept all night and all the following morning.

I raised my arm and flung it over my forehead. Something didn't feel right.

I cracked open my eyes and listened intently.

There was no sound inside the apartment.

My eyes scanned the room. Nothing. The curtains were closed, no sunlight was coming through, but I could hear, faintly, the sound of cars on the road outside, and children playing.

I moved my arm and went to run my hand over my face.

But my hand wasn't there!

I blinked, stupidly.

My arm was there. But at the end, where my hand should have been, was just thin air.

I looked closer. Tried wiggling my fingers. Nothing.

There was no pain, nothing to suggest that my hand had vanished in the night. I pushed myself up in bed, noting the aches and pains that accompanied the action, and brought my missing hand closer for inspection.

I tentatively raised my other arm, wondering if that would also be incomplete, but my hand was there. Or was it my hand? It was old. Older than old, it was ancient. My nails were yellow and broken, my skin pitted and dusty. I raised it up in front of my eyes and looked closely. When

I moved my fingers, the fingers of this crone's hand also moved. It had to be mine.

I turned my attention to my missing appendage. I gently pushed back the sleeve of my silk pyjama top and saw crumbling bone. The skin dangling and loose, and grey, powdery dust all over the tissue.

I leaned over the side of the bed and looked at the floor. Below where my arm had been hanging was a small heap of grey dust with what looked like fragments of bone in it. That was my hand!

I closed my eyes, and if I could have cried, I would have, but I was so dry

All I could think of was Susan and how she must have somehow sucked the life from me. Drained me of all my moisture. I held my ruined arm to my chest and rocked gently in the bed. As I did, I could sense my flesh crumbling, falling from me in clouds of grey power. I wondered if I could get out of bed at all. When I used my remaining hand to push back the sheets, I could see that my feet had gone the same way as my hand ... they were no longer there, just heaps of dry powder filling the bottom of the bed.

I screamed. My lungs heaved, dry and rasping for every fragile breath. There was nothing more I could do. I couldn't move. I couldn't speak. So, I resolved then to wait. Susan would be back, and when she arrived, well then ...

The door opened with a click and I was instantly alert.

Susan had obviously found the spare key in the kitchen drawer and had used it to let herself in.

I had been dozing fitfully, unable to do much but listen to the rustle of my crumbling flesh, which fell with a haunting whisper onto the crisp cotton of the bedclothes.

The door to my room cracked open, and Susan peeked in.

She smiled at me, and entered the room fully.

As usual, she was radiant, looking even younger than she had before, if that was possible. She was wearing a smart pair of tight skinny jeans and a plunging T-shirt that displayed her cute breasts to their best advantage.

God save me, I wanted her.

A breeze brought her scent to me, and it tasted like heaven. A stray part of my brain reasoned that perhaps it was laden with pheromones, and this was what had snared me, but there was a reptile, animal side to my mind that still wanted her despite my fear.

I also knew that unless I did something I was going to die. I would be the loser in this battle. I was crumbling to dust before my very eyes. I knew what had to be done to stop it, but did I have the strength to resist her?

Susan came to my bedside, smiling. She was so beautiful, and so unaware.

I raised my good hand and, without allowing her a look at it, cupped it around the back of her head. She dipped towards me, going for a kiss. I can only assume that the creeping grey rot had not yet wholly touched my face.

I brushed her lips with mine. Still so dry.

Then I held her to me. Briefly.

My face pushed into her neck, smelling her sweet scent, filling my mind with the rush.

I felt my teeth itch again, and then that wondrous sensation that I had suppressed for so long, the feeling of sharp canines growing long.

I nuzzled her and she hugged me back.

I licked her neck with my dry tongue, sensing the vein humming and throbbing below the skin.

I couldn't wait any longer. I had denied myself for too long.

I bit.

She screamed.

I fed.

Blood is an incredible substance. I could tell you the chemical make-up, how the red and white blood cells operate in tandem to keep a human body alive. How the plasma binds them, and how the heart pumps this amazing liquid around the body.

I could explain how the taste of blood on my tongue invigorates me. How I could feel Susan, the very essence of Susan, pour into my mouth, down my throat and into my parched and aching stomach. Her essence fed me, invigorated me. As I lapped at her punctured throat, and her cries turned to moans of pleasure, I could see my skin bloom with colour.

I caressed her slim, white neck and drank from her now-willing throat, and I felt better than I had in months. She shuddered under me. They always orgasm as I drain them. I don't know why. *La petite morte* just before the main event. Her movements subsided and she made no attempt to stop me as I buried my fangs into her, seeking out every drop of blood. I lapped and whimpered like an animal, feeling the strength return to me. Susan's strength, unwillingly given, but enjoyed nonetheless.

I changed position, holding Susan's body to me as I suckled on her like a baby. My missing hand was repairing itself. I could see the bone now, my fingers re-knitting like some fantastic visual effect from the films. My skin forming. Nails growing. Perfect once more.

I felt vibrant and full of life. I was wholly me.

I gently removed my fangs from the vein in Susan's leg. She was dry. I had sensed her little heart give up a few minutes ago, and her blood slowed in its pulsing flow into my mouth. I had sucked the last dregs from her key veins, ensuring that none was left.

She lay on my bed, a porcelain doll. Perfect. White. Dead.

I looked around. Very neat, I congratulated myself. Couple of spots on the sheets, but nothing that the laundry couldn't cope with.

I stroked the blonde hair from her face. She looked so still and beautiful.

A pang of remorse shuddered through me. It was always like this. I tried and tried to live a normal life. To enjoy the fine things, the culture, companionship and love. I would drink blood obtained from blood banks, or taken from the street trash of London. I would deny myself for as long as I could.

But then, always, someone would come along. Someone I just couldn't resist.

Susan was no monster. I had realised that as her memories and experiences flooded me through her blood. She had not drained me.

I had done it all to myself. Denial for too long. Failing to get the sustenance I needed because I had been beguiled by love.

And Susan had paid the price.

She wasn't the monster.

I was.

'Susan' was written as a performance piece for the annual Gallifrey convention in LA. There was a reading slot booked at the convention for the Friday night. Actor Frazer Hines was reading from his autobiography, horror author Sam Stone was reading from her new novel, but I had nothing! So I wrote a vampire tale.

Reaction from the event was great – many people

wanted to know when it would be printed and where – and so when we returned to England, I sent it off to an audio magazine that was starting up. They loved it, and it appeared in their fourth edition. You can listen to this story told on their website online at:

www.darkfictionmagazine.co.uk/episode-4/story-susan/

Night Terrors

I don't really like the dark. Can't think why … As a grown man, you'd think I'd have got that sorted by now.

Except I haven't.

It's always at night. You know that moment in the depths of the night when *something* awakens you. You lie in bed and listen. Eyes shut. Totally still. Just listening. And there is nothing. Complete silence. So you crack open one eye, and see … nothing. Just the blackness of the room. Slowly you start to make out shapes and sounds, illumination from the clock perhaps, or maybe the internet router, perhaps a charger for laptop or phone, maybe the single red eye of the television or DVD player on standby … These days there's usually some light even in the darkest of rooms.

Listen. Unmoving. Waiting to see if whatever the sound was that woke you will come again.

For most of you I expect they don't. That is the end of it. You slowly drift off back to sleep, and the dreams return, carrying you away until morning.

But for me, there is always something more.

I think it's this house. It's an old place and so subject to more creaks and groans than usual perhaps. But then again, perhaps there is something here with me.

In the passage between the bedroom and the bathroom there are three doors. Three rooms to pass by before one can get into the bathroom and the toilet, which so often calls in the night.

I have a habit of ensuring that all three doors are closed before I retire for the night. They must be shut firmly, and I push on them as I pass to make certain that this is the case.

In the middle of the night, with eyes glued closed by tiredness and sleep, stumbling from the bedroom to perform ablutions, it is safe to pass along the passage as long as the doors are closed. For if they are not, then I am painfully aware, as I walk in total darkness, eyes still shut, that I am passing a void. An inky black space where anything could lurk. The head of the staircase is at the end of the passage as well, and this too is a well from which something could emerge. So I stumble along the passage, trailing my hand on the wall, happy that the doors are closed. Then into the toilet, and I stand there, exposed, my eyes shut and my mind telling me that there really is nothing creeping slowly up the stairs from below. That there really is nothing standing silently behind the toilet door. There is a corridor that leads further away into the depths of the house, lit by the slight green gleam of light from a smoke alarm in the ceiling, but which throws the end of the passage into complete darkness. And in that darkness anything could be hiding ... Some ghoul or shrouded grave monster.

I take a deep breath before heading back to my bed. I have to turn my back on the stygian corridor, ignore the pit of darkness at the head of the stairs, past the three closed doors, and only release my breath when I am safely in my room again. But then … what might have entered my room when I was gone? Would I slide into bed only to find some rotting corpse lying there beside me, or something cold and slimy, wormed into the warmth of the bedclothes, just waiting for me, for my warmth, for my soul.

And so I lie in bed, my mind playing over what has not just happened, and convincing me that actually it had. That there was indeed a shadow standing behind the door in the bathroom, reaching out a hand to clutch my shoulder as I stood there. I remember shifting my body at the last moment so that the skeletal fingers just missed me as it swiped.

And then, as the dreams start to take hold once more, my bedroom shifts and changes, the bedcovers seem to move of their own volition. A shapeless, formless entity comprised of dust motes and blackness is in the room. I sit up and peer closer through the silent darkness, but there's nothing there. No movement. No bedclothes standing erect as though to lovingly wrap me and hold me while I sleep.

I open my eyes again and see something moving across the ceiling above me. Slowly and carefully it comes. What it is I have no idea, but it stops above me, and then starts to smoothly descend towards my face, getting closer and closer. I don't want to move as I don't want it to know that I am there. That I have *seen* it. So I freeze, eyes open and staring as the shadow creature resolves into some form of face, snake-like with yellow eyes and fanged mouth. One part of my mind connects it with an old film: Jacqueline Pearce transformed into a hideous snake-woman. The other freezes in terror. It silently observes me and fixes me with its hypnotic eyes, like Kaa attempting to bewitch Mowgli.

It sways in the air … I am frozen in terror. And then … it swoops and I'm pitched up and off the bed, waving my hands before my face, swatting away the shadows … My heart is pumping, my breath coming in great gasps … and there's nothing there. I look around. Darkness. Nothing.

There is no snake creature. But it was so real. So *there*.

Eventually, I lie back, close my eyes, and try to rest. Listening to my heart thumping and pounding.

But what is that? Is that the sound of one of those closed doors gently opening? The slightest click of a handle, the soft swish of a door against carpet. Or is it a foot gently dragging along the corridor?

So I lie and I listen, and all the night terrors and horrors crowd around me once more.

All my monsters and demons. Ready to torment me.

'Night Terrors' is another mood piece, written to try and elicit some of the things that cross people's minds when they venture out in their own houses in the middle of the night. What is normally familiar territory gets upset by imagination and fear into a place teeming with terrors and monsters.

It doesn't matter how brave we think we are, there's always a place buried deep in our subconscious, where a small child is hiding under the covers, wishing that the lights would come back on ...

Novel Ideas

When I was considering what to include in this collection, I was uncertain if I should add in the following two novel extracts. However my editor, having read them, felt that they stood alone in their own right, and so should be included. So here they are.

Barkio has perhaps the longest gestation period of anything I have written. The initial inspiration for a boy who has an imaginary family of dogs as friends came from my eldest son, who did exactly what Ben does at the start of the story – invented a family of dogs who then came on holiday with us … Having thought that this was quite an interesting concept, I then wrote the prologue. Then, the story was more fully developed as a possible entry in Virgin Publishing's New Adventures series of original *Doctor Who* novels. The basic idea was that the seventh Doctor and Ace were trying to stop an invasion of Earth by these dog-like creatures, but the problem was that in the dog universe, time ran in the opposite direction to our own … so that the first time that humans are attacked by the dogs, is the final attack from the dogs' point of view. I had the whole timeline for this worked out, how Ace (in the dog world) would interact with the Doctor (on Earth) and how as the novel progressed, certain events would seem very different depending from which angle you viewed them.

Ultimately though, the range editor rejected the story,

finding fault with every aspect of it. I'm not precious about my writing, and I'm not suggesting that this would have been a world-changing book, or even that it was brilliantly written, but I suspect that he didn't want me to write fiction when I was working on factual *Doctor Who* titles for them at the same time. Much later on, while researching for something else, I found a memo in Virgin's files that said they wouldn't commission me for some other project because I was 'doing too much' … not because I couldn't do it or anything, but just because I was in their view too busy. I wasn't best impressed, as you can imagine.

So *Barkio* lay fallow for a few years, and then I picked it up again, dusted it off, and reworked it as an urban horror type story – still with the invasion element as the dogs arrive and infiltrate our human society. I think I sent the outline to a couple of publishers and agents, but there was no interest whatsoever. So it again got put back in the proverbial drawer. This is the first outing for the opening section …

The Cemetery is a horror story through and through, and looking at it again, it would probably make more of a novella than a novel. The idea came about because I went on holiday to Portugal and discovered that there are vast plains of salt flats there, where sea salt is harvested for sale. Furthermore, there are miles and miles of scrubland with only a few olive trees to break up the landscape. A wonderful setting for a horror novel. I seem to recall I initially toyed with a group of people being picked off by a Portuguese version of Chupacabra – the South American goat-sucking monster – but this developed into something more of a cross between the 'Blind Dead' movies of Amando de Ossorio and the horror film *Jeepers Creepers* (which actually came out after I had started playing with the ideas).

I won't say any more as there is always the possibility that I will find time to work on and finish this story ... It's one which I keep coming back to. I don't think that *The Cemetery* is the right title for it overall, but hopefully it works for this opening extract.

Barkio

Prologue

The Hound

The small boy stood in the middle of the forest and looked around. The trees stretched up into the sky around him, forming a lush green canopy, and the bushes and shrubs that surrounded him almost reached his head. He knew what the names of some of them were: the trees were horse chestnut and apple. But others eluded him, especially the shrub with the nice flowers that his mummy called rododrodro or something silly like that.

He moved on through the forest, listening to the birds. Down by his feet he spotted a worm and crouched to look at it. He poked it with his forefinger and wrinkled his nose. His daddy sometimes claimed that he had eaten worm pie for dinner, and that slug soup was his particular favourite. His daddy was weird, but he loved him anyway. The worm blindly made its way across the forest floor, looking for a hole or wherever it was that worms lived.

Crouching by the worm and totally absorbed in its progress across the forest floor, the small boy was completely oblivious to the fact that he himself was being observed.

The hunter was crouched ten yards or so away. It was still and quiet, but it watched the boy intently through slitted eyes. As it breathed, its whiskers trembled slightly, and its sides gently and rhythmically pulsed as air was drawn into its massive lungs and then expelled silently. The smell of human wafted into its sensitive nostrils and it sniffed tentatively. This was a young one for sure. The hunter would enjoy playing with this piece awhile.

The boy lost interest as the worm struggled beneath a leaf, and he stood up again. His gaze alighted on a broken branch of wood that was shaped a little bit like a gun. He ran to it and grasped it firmly in his pudgy fingers. Now he had a weapon, nothing could stop him.

The hunter shifted slightly as the boy moved closer. The muscles in its powerful haunches bunched as it gently rocked from side to side in preparation for the pounce. Its green eyes narrowed further and it stood stock still as it mentally weighed up the distance of the boy from where it was crouching, the velocity it would need to reach him, and the power it would then need to bring him down. The boy came closer and the hunter instantly recalibrated. Soon. It would be soon.

The boy suddenly looked up, hearing his name.

'Ben …'

The familiar voice of his mummy carried through the air. He took a look around the forest and shrugged. He was on the trail of something exciting here, and his mummy could wait.

He spotted something in the bushes nearby.

The hunter knew that it had been seen. It had to

act now or the moment would be lost. It prepared to pounce.

'Ben …!'

The tone was sharper now, and Ben sighed. 'Sorry, Doggy Barkio, I've got to go now. We can play again later.'

Ben ran out of the bushes and down the garden towards his mummy, who was waiting at the back door of his house.

The hunter shrugged its powerful shoulders. Ben was its friend and called it Doggy Barkio.

Ben watched through the window as the huge hound loped up the garden and came through the now-closed kitchen door. Doggy Barkio could do that sort of thing, just as he could make himself invisible to everyone but Ben. Doggy Barkio was his own special friend and it didn't overly concern him that his mummy and daddy couldn't see him. It just didn't seem important.

Ben settled down to his tea, and Doggy Barkio settled down by the fire. Ben smiled. It was good to have friends.

PART ONE

Loss

Chapter 1

Christmas Shopping

'Christmas,' complained Natalie, 'is one never-ending shopping trip.'

She dumped the plastic bags containing the results of her latest outing on the floor of the hallway, whilst struggling to close her umbrella and shut the door at the same time.

Mike stuck his head out of the kitchen. 'Be with you in a moment.'

Natalie finally managed to get the door closed as Ben came careering down the stairs. 'What've you got? What's in there?' he cried as he fell upon the bags.

Natalie squealed. 'Oh, no you don't. Mike – give us a hand please.'

Mike came from the kitchen and scooped Ben up in his arms. Ben, kicking and struggling, complained vociferously as he was unceremoniously dumped in the living room and the door firmly closed.

'What's in there? What's in there?' echoed Mike, pretending to rummage through the bags.

'You'll just have to wait and see,' said Natalie, planting a quick kiss on the end of his nose. She struggled out of her coat and threw it on the post at the bottom of the stairs. Mike stopped his pretend search for presents and grasped her round the waist, lifting her feet onto the bottom step. Now her head was level with his.

'How was the traffic?' he asked, nuzzling her neck with his lips.

'Not bad.'

Natalie extricated her arms and put them round Mike's neck. She looked at him and then melted into a big hug. After the hug came a big sloppy kiss. All tongues and small moans of appreciation as Mike's left hand caressed her neck, her throat, finally coming to rest on her right breast, the thumb gently stroking the slight bulge of her nipple through the material of her jumper.

'I should really put these things away before Ben decides to rejoin us,' she smiled.

She hopped off the step and picked up the bags, taking them upstairs. Mike went into the living room to find Ben happily watching for the three millionth time a copy of Walt Disney's *Robin Hood* on video. He had been given that last Christmas and never seemed to tire of the animated adventures of a fox, a bear and assorted other animals as they played out the age-old story of taking from the rich and giving to the poor.

He went to slump in his favourite chair.

'Not there, Dad! Doggy Barkio's sitting there and he's comfortable.' Ben had learned the word 'comfortable' recently and took every opportunity to use it.

Mike grimaced. *Not Doggy Barkio again.* 'I thought Doggy Barkio had gone to live in a shop?'

Ben had announced this latest fact in the complicated

lifestyle of Doggy Barkio and the Barkio family the other week.

They had all been on holiday to Italy, and it was here that Ben had apparently invented this strange family of invisible dogs. They had apparently lived on the cliff beside the hotel, and parachuted down to play in the swimming pool each day. When Mike, Nat and Ben had returned home, Ben had told them that the dogs had stayed in Italy, but that then, all ten of them had come back to England to live in a shop. Quite where all these invisible dogs had come from was not a subject upon which Ben had dwelt, they just appeared over the course of the holiday. Insofar as invisible dogs could appear.

Ben shook his head. 'He came back because it's Christmas and the shops are shut.'

Mike couldn't fault that logic. 'Well, do you think you could get him to move, as I'd like to sit in my chair.'

Ben tore his eyes from the video for long enough to glance at the chair. 'He's gone now anyway.'

Mike dropped into the chair. Natalie stuck her head round the door. 'Who's going to make me a nice cup of tea?'

Mike sighed and got up again. Oh well. He didn't want the rest anyway. On the way to the kitchen he stole another kiss from Nat. He then happily filled the kettle while she bustled away upstairs. Tomorrow was Christmas Eve and the hectic preparation time was over. Anything that wasn't done didn't matter, and all there was to do was to sit by the television, eat chocolate, and go to bed early. He smiled. He was particularly looking forward to the last one, especially as he had wrapped up some rather spectacular underwear for Nat this year. Stockings, he thought. Nothing like having something nice in stockings for Christmas.

Upstairs, Natalie finished putting away in her wardrobe the last of the gifts she had bought. She tucked her little finger in her mouth and sucked on it as she mentally ticked off all the bits and pieces. Damn! Damn and blast. She knew she'd forgotten something. Mike had his heart set on getting the latest *Doctor Who* videos, and she knew that none of the local shops stocked them. Oh well, there was nothing for it but to head up to London on Christmas Eve.

She sat on the bed and looked at her reflection in the mirror. Thirty-something. Still good looking. Her hair was short and dark, and it framed an elfin face with ears that were slightly pointed on top to add to the impression. Body slim. Hips okay. Breasts, a little on the small side, but Mike liked them just fine. She smiled. *Listen to me, worrying about my appearance when downstairs is the most mouthwatering man I've ever seen.* Well, okay, perhaps not *the* most mouthwatering, but the only one to have married her! And he was all hers.

And then there was Ben. Her pride and joy. Same dark hair as her and Mike, with a button nose and a cheeky grin that made your heart melt. Her little four-year-old monster.

The doorbell rang, and with a final check that everything was hidden away from the prying eyes of husbands and children, Nat headed downstairs.

Ed and Jane Thompson were standing on the step, and as Natalie started to open the door they launched into an off-key rendition of 'Good King Wenceslas'.

Natalie laughed as Jane elbowed Ed in the ribs as his face creased in laughter.

'Ed …! This is meant to be a serious song!'

Ed apologised and tramped into the house as Natalie held the door. 'All ready for the big day?' he boomed, his voice filling the hall.

'Just about. Go through.' Janet ushered them into the front room. 'Tea?'

'Please,' they chorused, and then looked at each other again. This time it was Jane's turn to collapse in giggles as Ed stuck out his tongue at her.

'Two more teas, Mike!' Nat shouted through the hall.

Robin had just performed an impressive feat of marksmanship on the television, firing an arrow straight through another. 'Merry Christmas, Ben,' said Jane to Ben's back.

Predictably Ben ignored her, so she crept up behind him and repeated the greeting into his ear. He still ignored her, so she grasped him firmly round the waist and started to wiggle her fingers. This got his attention and he collapsed, screaming and laughing on the floor.

The door opened and Mike delivered two cups of tea

into the room. 'That's enough now, Ben,' he admonished. 'Hot tea's here.'

He returned to the kitchen for his and Nat's tea and joined the others.

'No tree yet?' asked Ed.

'No. We'll get it sorted out tomorrow,' explained Mike. 'I see you had yours up early again.'

Ed and Jane lived next door, and each year they were the first in the street to have a tree up in the front window. This was a source of some amusement to Mike and Nat, and they tended to think that the Christmas season had not yet started until Ed and Jane's tree was up.

'Done all the shopping?' asked Jane, knowing full well that Natalie would have left it all to the last minute as usual.

'In fact, I have,' said Nat proudly. 'All bar a couple of bits I'll get up in London tomorrow.'

'Tomorrow,' exclaimed Mike. 'But you promised we'd choose a tree tomorrow.'

Natalie leaned across and pecked him on the nose. 'Sorry, hon.'

Mike looked at Ed. 'I don't suppose you could lend a hand?'

'Of course. Where and when?'

As Mike and Ed made arrangements to pick up a tree, Natalie smiled. She was actually looking forward to Christmas this year. *There's a turn up for the books*, she thought.

Chapter 2

London

Shopping was invented by a sadist, thought Natalie as she pushed her way through the thronging crowds of London's Oxford Street on Christmas Eve.

All this just to get a couple of sodding video tapes that she had forgotten. She only hoped that Mike appreciated all this effort she was making on his behalf. She paused to look in the window of one of the many clothes shops that lined London's most famous shopping street. It appeared to her untrained eye that the punk fashions of the mid-'70s were back in. The window display consisted of several female shop dummies attired in flowing velvets and chiffon, finished off with string vests. They were all wearing crucifixes around their necks.

A sudden movement in the glass made Natalie spin round. Behind her was a shambolic remnant of a man. His matted beard was crusted with dirt and other indefinable substances and his rheumy eyes swung restlessly from side to side. One hand had a plastic bin liner hanging from it while the other scratched at a worn patch on his baggy trousers. He wore several threadbare scarves, at least two battered jackets, and his feet were enclosed in two carrier bags tied at the top with string.

'Merry Chrithmuss,' he spluttered to no-one in particular, and Natalie noticed the green neck of a bottle poking out from one of the jacket pockets. The tramp staggered to a nearby rubbish bin and started rummaging through it with his free hand, all the while muttering to himself. Passers-by gave him a wide berth as he stopped his frantic search and staggered upright again.

'You know,' he said, pointing a finger straight at Natalie, who was still standing by the shop window, mesmerised by this hellish apparition. 'Gotta watch those doggies. Gotta watch 'em. They'll get'cha every time.'

He sighed, shook his head and muttered something unintelligible before shambling out into the road. A black cab roared past, its driver shouting abuse at the walking disaster that he had just missed.

Natalie watched the tramp cross the street and enter an alleyway between two buildings. She clutched her bag to her and resumed her journey towards Centre Point and from there down Charing Cross Road to Waterloo.

As she came closer to the footbridge over the Thames by Charing Cross station, she noticed that the number of tramps and vagrants was increasing. She was sure that she had not noticed this many the last time she was in the City. Perhaps it was something to do with Christmas; that all the homeless flocked to London hoping for the chance of some charity – even if it was only a hot bowl of soup from one of the mobile canteens that toured the capital at this time of year.

Rather than take the overground from Charing Cross to Waterloo, she decided to cross the footbridge and make her way to Waterloo through the concrete jungle that was the National Film Theatre complex on the South Bank of the Thames. She always enjoyed the stark contrast of the cement slabs with the modern statuary that populated it: a large bust of Nelson Mandela, a copper shape courtesy of Henry Moore, and all the posters for weird and wonderful plays long past or coming attractions at the NFT itself.

As she moved through the complex she spotted more and more tramps. Some were shuffling about, others were just sitting, and most had small dogs with them. There was an old, old man with more wrinkles than skin, busking with a penny whistle to an audience of none. Natalie found herself wondering if the instrument had been designed to play more than the one note it seemed capable of.

Leaving the complex, she headed along a raised walkway alongside the Archduke wine bar and restaurant. She had once enjoyed a very nice sausage dinner with Mike there – sausage was all they had had on the menu at the time. She smiled at the memory of Mike's face as she bit into her sausage in a very suggestive and unladylike manner.

Just past the Archduke, the walkway descended to street level and she could see the impressive Victory Arch entrance to Waterloo station ahead of her. To get there she had to walk past what could only be described as a permanent home for several 'homeless' people.

The road went under the railway line, and in one of the arches, a dwelling of sorts had been erected from lumps of plywood, corrugated iron and old sheets, all hung up to form a surround for an ever-present fire. There were normally one or two men standing in the tunnel cajoling passers-by for money, but this time the tunnel was deserted. Still thinking of sausages, Natalie adjusted her step to allow a couple of other travellers *en route* to the station to catch up with her, and then she headed off through the tunnel.

Mid-way across, she noticed that a lone tramp was propped up against the wall opposite the ramshackle dwelling. A small black dog was curled up by the pathetic figure, and the animal raised its head to look up at her as she passed.

'Merry Christmas, govn'r,' wheezed the creature in the filthy coat as she passed, and the dog whined exactly on cue. Natalie stopped. It was Christmas, and she hadn't given anything to any of the other vagrants she had passed. She smiled at the human wreck before her and rummaged in her pocket for her purse. Pulling out a five pound note, she bent and pressed it into the tramp's hand, which she noticed with distaste was tattooed on the palm.

'Thangoo kindly miss,' muttered the man.

Natalie was about to move off when the dog whined again. Poor little mite, she thought. Unlike Mike, she had always had a soft spot for dogs. She reached out and

218

touched the animal on the top of its head, rubbing the fur gently with her thumb.

She was immediately standing on a vast green plain. Thunder and lightning rolled around her. Dog-like creatures scurried underfoot. There was the sound of human crying and screaming.

Natalie spun round in a daze. The screaming grew louder. A sense of human sweat and fear reached her. There was blood on her hands. Something bad was happening. Something was coming. Something …

Natalie felt as though a bomb had exploded in her head. Thoughts, words and images ricocheted around her mind and she recognised only some of them as hers. The feeling subsided and she realised that she was back in the tunnel still touching the dog. She pulled her hand back sharply. A sense of bloated goodwill filled her, and she had the strangest feeling that something barbed had lodged itself in her brain. It was sinking into her being. Becoming a part of her. In a second the feeling was gone.

Natalie pulled herself together. 'Merry Christmas,' she muttered to the tramp, who smiled a ruined and toothless smile back at her. Without looking back she headed off towards Waterloo station.

Had she looked back, she would have seen two figures detach themselves from the shadows at different points in the tunnel. From inside the dwelling stepped someone bulked out with clothing. The being seemed to be made from material, and bright eyes glinted in a bearded face perched atop the bloated body. After a second or two watching Natalie's retreating back, the figure returned to the dwelling.

Moments later another shape detached itself from the shadows by the tunnel wall further back. Lithe and agile, it crept forward, checking whether the coat man had gone. Confident that he had, it jogged across the road to the tramp lying where Natalie had left him. From within a black windcheater over black leggings, a knife flashed quicksilver. There was a muffled yelp.

'Now you can rest,' whispered a female voice to the old tramp, whose face was a beaming picture of joy. The figure ran lightly back the way it had come, leaving a happy old man and a dog with its throat cut beside him.

The Cemetery

Chapter One

It was going to be one of those days. Robert Coleborn had the mother of all hangovers. The blackness behind his eyelids sparkled. His head was throbbing, sending fine needles of pain through his forehead, but something else was wrong. Robert tentatively opened his eyes a fraction, revealing blue sky, bright sun and brown earth. The pain intensified and he rapidly squeezed his eyes shut. Then he realised what was wrong. The blue sky had been underneath him.

He was hanging upside down. In a jeep. His head was tilted so he could see out the window. And he could smell petrol. Memories flooded back. The holiday. The jeep safari. The drunken driver and the crash.

Petrol.

I have to get out of here, Robert realised, and started struggling . He quickly found that he was held fast. He relaxed as his mind ran through the possibilities … He was trapped in a crashed jeep … possibly paralysed … his legs crushed beyond repair … maybe even his legs missing.

He opened his eyes a fraction once more. Then, as he became accustomed to the sunlight, he opened them all the way, with a wince as the throbbing in his head intensified. He couldn't move, because he was still wearing his seat belt. He looked down at his legs. They were both still there. He gently moved his arm down his body towards the lock on the seat belt. Looking down, he braced himself against the canvas ceiling with his other arm.

He released the catch on the seat belt and fell into an ungainly heap on the ceiling of the jeep. He turned himself over and sat for a moment breathing in the petrol fumes before his brain once more suggested that it might be a good idea to get the hell out of there. He looked around and realised that the jeep's driver, a swarthy, unshaven man, was still in his seat. His arms were hanging down and a large pool of blood had formed on the ceiling under him. Robert gently lifted one of the arms and fumbled for a pulse. After a few moments of feeling different parts of the man's wrist and finding nothing, Robert gave up and eased himself across the roof towards the open window. Pushing his feet through, he pulled himself shakily upright and stood in the blazing sunlight.

It was cooler outside, but only just. They were at the Spanish end of the Portuguese Algarve in mid-Summer and the sun was high in the sky. The heat beat down upon the blasted landscape unremittingly. The only things that grew here were cork trees and assorted stubby bushes with sharp, needle-like thorns. The ground was dusty and dry and the heat stifled everything as there were no breezes to stir the hot air. The silence was also crushing. No birds cried out, no insects buzzed and hummed. It was a dead place.

The path the jeep had taken was pretty obvious. A line of bushes had been wiped out in a gouged-out path down a ravine from the dirt track that they had been travelling on. Robert had a flashback of the jeep tumbling over and over several times, and he noted there were bits of debris scattered to either side of the furrow in the dry earth.

'No wonder I'm dizzy,' he said to no-one in particular. His voice sounded strange in the silence.

Robert staggered around the jeep. Leaning his hand on the metal, he quickly pulled it away as the chassis was red hot. Another moment and he would have been burned. Distracted by his hand, he looked down and found himself looking at a body, a middle-aged woman, lying half under the jeep. She seemed to be peacefully asleep and Robert didn't need to check whether she was alive or not as it was obvious that she had been crushed under the vehicle as it came to rest. Around the base of the jeep the ground had turned a deep red as her blood soaked into the parched soil. Robert wondered idly if she had thought herself lucky to have been thrown clear before the rolling jeep toppled onto her.

Robert had been sitting up front with the driver as he found that travelling in the open back with the others made him feel sick. Now he wondered how many of the others had been thrown clear as the jeep tumbled down the ravine.

A groan from a bush nearby made Robert turn.

The bush started to thrash, and a man in a once-smart safari suit hauled himself upright.

'Shit.'

Robert moved across to the man. 'You're bleeding,' he said.

The man lifted a scratched hand to his head and found the blood.

'Shit,' he said again.

'I don't think it's that bad,' said Robert. 'Looks like a flesh wound.'

'Feels like someone's taken a hammer to my head,' said the man. 'Gotta sit down.'

He stumbled to a nearby rock and sunk down onto it. He peered up at Robert. 'What the hell happened? One minute we're driving along, and the next I'm upside down in a frigging bush!'

Robert looked back at the upturned jeep and gestured. 'We crashed,' he said. 'Badly.'

The sound of sobbing broke through the silence and Robert headed off to the other side of the jeep.

A young girl was standing, looking at the jeep. She was cradling her left elbow in her right hand. She glanced at Robert as he came towards her.

'I … I think I've hurt my arm,' she stammered.

'But otherwise you're okay?' Robert asked, wondering what he would possibly be able to do if she wasn't. He knew the girl. At least by sight. On this holiday he had found himself surrounded by married couples and geriatrics, and the sight of a pretty, apparently single young girl around the hotel had drawn his attention like a magnet. Until now, however, he had not plucked up courage to talk to her, and he had been almost ecstatically pleased when she had turned up for the same safari drive he had booked for. He had thought it might be fate that had thrown them together, but hadn't realised just what fate had had in mind.

The girl nodded. 'There's a body back there,' she said, gesturing with a nod of her head. Robert dragged his attention away from the way her short blonde hair bobbed as she nodded.

He walked past her and found the unmoving body of a youth of about 18. He was lying face down on the earth, and Robert crouched to see if he was alive. He shook the boy, but there was no reaction, and so he turned him over. The boy's face was scratched and bleeding, but the front of his T-shirt was ripped open, as was his belly. He had landed on a sharp, skyward-pointing boulder that had simply punctured a hole right through him. Robert gagged and quickly pushed the body over onto its front once more.

'Is he okay?' asked the girl.

Robert stood and shook his head. This kid had been chatting with the girl on and off ever since Robert had arrived. Bizarrely, he found himself pleased that the competition had been removed and was amazed at his own reaction. Perhaps it was shock.

'We ought to see if anyone else is alive,' he said. 'Do you remember how many people were in the jeep?'

The girl thought for a moment, her brow furrowing as she rubbed her elbow gently. 'There were eight, I think. Not including the driver.'

'Well, he's dead,' said Robert. 'There's our friend in the bushes there, a lady under the jeep and a chap in a suit …' the girl nodded, 'over the other side of the jeep,' Robert continued. 'He's made it as well. That makes four.'

'Hey dudes!'

Robert and the girl both swung round as the shapes of two black men emerged over the lip of the track above them.

The men were both aged about 25. One wore a battered pair of dark glasses while the other chattered incessantly to his friend as they made their way down the slope towards the jeep.

'See, man, I told you we'd be all right. Everything's fine … Watch your footing there … There's people here.'

He looked up at the girl, 'You're okay? We're a bit battered … Grazed my knee up there … but Jones here's like a cat. Nine lives, I tell you. Always lands on his feet. Ain't that amazing …'

'Why were you up there,' asked the girl, interrupting him, 'when we're all down here?'

The man stopped and grasped Jones's hand in his own, waving it in the air. 'See, this is my insurance. My man Jones here may not be able to see, but he's got this grasp of what's happenin' better than most folks. Says he felt something was wrong … and man was that driver weaving about something bad … and the second that jeep left the road, me and my man here was jumpin' off the back for our lives.' He burst into laughter. 'We done saved our asses.'

Robert smiled despite himself. 'Good for you.' These two were real characters. Robert had seen them about the hotel, chatting good-naturedly to all the other guests and staff. The man that could see was the 'helper' of the blind man, and they had come on holiday together. There was a phrase that summed them up: life and soul of the party. Though Robert found all the banter a little wearing, he couldn't help but smile at the antics.

The man suddenly frowned. 'But what about the rest of them. Where's the other guys.'

'Well, I'm here,' said the safari-suited man, standing up from his rock to peer at the others across the shattered hulk of the jeep.

'We'll have to search,' said the girl. 'And listen,' she added with a sidelong glance at Jones's friend, who hurriedly closed his mouth as he had been about to launch into another monologue.

Robert sniffed the air. The smell of petrol was getting stronger in the oppressive heat and his head was really starting to ache. 'We'd better make it quick,' he muttered.

Jones was helped across to the rock and sat down, and then the four survivors started to move through the bushes surrounding the jeep, looking for the remaining two passengers. Before long, the man in the safari suit called out that he had found someone. Robert, who seemed to have taken the lead in events so far, moved quickly across.

The body was slumped across another rock, and was twisted at an unnatural angle. Robert remembered that this was the husband of the lady lying under the jeep. 'Dead,' he said, and turned away to continue looking.

Once again they fanned out, but no-one else could be found.

'I think we ought to get away from the jeep,' suggested Robert. 'Smell that petrol … In this heat, anything could happen.'

He helped Jones to his feet and the party limped and walked towards another outcrop of rocks about a hundred metres away. The sun beat mercilessly down on them and the air around the rocks shimmered. They circled the rocks until they reached the shaded side and sank down to the ground. The heat was less intense in the shade, but Robert was sweating, as were, he noticed, all the others.

'What should we do?' asked the girl. 'Does anyone know where we are?'

'Someone will come looking for us,' said the safari-suited man with certainty. 'For God's sake, we're here on holiday, and when that jeep doesn't appear back at the hotel tonight, they're sure to send someone to look for us.'

'I dunno,' said the black man. 'That driver, he sure didn't seem to know where the hell he was. How do we know he was even on the right road for the safari?'

'Whatever,' said Robert. 'For the moment, we'll stay here, get our strength back, and then decide what to do.'

He turned to the girl. 'How's your arm?'

'It'll be okay,' she said, giving her elbow a final rub and flashing him a smile that lit up her face. 'If we're going to be stuck here, then we might as well get to know each other.'

She stuck out her right hand towards Robert. 'I'm Maria. Maria Saarinan.'

Robert smiled and grasped her hand. 'I'm Robert Coleborn. Pleased to meet you. You're … you're not English, are you?'

'The accent's that obvious?' Maria smiled again. 'I'm Finnish, but I've been studying in England for several years. Let's put it this way … I learn fast.'

As he released her hand, it seemed to him that Maria held onto it and held his gaze for a fraction of a second before letting go. As she did so, he noticed that the upper joint on her right little finger was missing.

'I'm Walker. Peter Walker.' The man in the safari suit interrupted Robert's contemplation of Maria's hand.

'Jaz,' said the black man with a beaming smile. 'And my man here's Jones.'

Jones stepped forward and held out his hand. Robert

grasped it and shook it firmly. 'Pleased to meet you, Jones.'

'Likewise,' said Jones. His voice was surprisingly soft after the loud bonhomie of Jaz.

'So,' said Peter, looking round at the others. 'What do we do now?'

'It's a shame we couldn't find the other guy … The guide, wasn't he?' said Robert. 'He'd be pretty useful to have around.'

'If you wanted to know all about cork trees,' said Jaz. 'That guy was amazing. Knew all about the rings of cork, the growing conditions, the uses … Man, I bet he could find his way out of here.'

Robert wiped his forehead with the front of his T-shirt. 'I think the first thing we've got to do is find some water. In this heat we're not going to last until evening without a drink.'

'There should be some at the jeep,' said Maria, turning to head back that way.

'I'll come with you,' said Robert, jumping to his feet. 'The rest of you stay here. We'll bring back whatever we can find.'

Robert set off after Maria, who was some metres ahead. He was reluctant, now, to let her out of his sight, which was strange considering he'd only just met her. *I should know better,* Robert thought. He had taken this holiday after a very acrimonious split with his fiancée and was feeling wounded both in pride and in self-esteem. Maria seemed to like him, and she was simply gorgeous. Here they were, stuck in the middle of nowhere, but Robert was sort of enjoying himself. And it was all because of Maria.

'Hold up,' he called, hurrying forward to catch up with her.

Ahead of them, the jeep lay like a beached dinosaur amid the bushes and rocks. The air around it shimmered both with heat and petrol fumes, which were, by now, very strong indeed.

'Smell that?' commented Robert.

Maria sniffed and wrinkled her nose. 'Mmm.'

'Just don't do anything that might make a spark.'

They approached the jeep and looked around. Amid the debris scattered up the bank was a large plastic water bottle, thrown clear as the jeep had tumbled. Robert headed for it and hefted it up. It was half full. He opened the cap and sniffed.

'A bit stale,' he called. 'But beggars can't be choosers.'

Maria smiled. 'What does that mean? Beggars can't be choosers.'

Robert grinned at her pronunciation. 'Choosers. With a "zed" sound. It means that we have to make do with what we can find.'

He swung the canister down by his legs and trotted back to the jeep. 'Your English isn't that good, then.'

Maria aimed a gentle kick at his leg. 'You.'

'So, find anything else?' he asked.

'No. We weren't exactly expecting this to happen, you know.'

'I remember someone had a rucksack with a bottle of something in it. It was that kid back there,' Robert gestured to where the dead teenager lay. He put the canister on the ground and walked over to the body. There was no sign of a rucksack.

Maria, meanwhile, was exploring the upside-down cab of the jeep. 'Maybe there's a map or something here.'

Robert, with his back to her, grunted. 'I doubt that. These guys know the terrain so well that they don't need a map.'

He returned to the jeep as Maria backed out of the cab. 'It stinks in there,' she commented. Robert glanced at the hanging body of the driver. Something seemed odd about it.

He bent and took a closer look. The skin was dry and taut across the corpse's face. Robert reached out and prodded one of the hanging arms. It did not move and his finger rasped as it pressed against dried skin the consistency of old leather.

'What the ...' The blood below the man's head had dried up as well, leaving a crusty stain.

'What is it?' asked Maria.

'This man,' said Robert. 'When I was in the cab with him before, he was normal. Well ... he was dead, but as normal as a dead person presumably is ... but now, he's completely dried out.'

Robert took a breath and reached for the man's hand. As he applied pressure to try and move it, the leathery fingers started to crumble under his touch.

'Shit!' Robert pulled his hand away quickly and banged his head on the rim of the door. 'Ow!'

'Are you okay?' asked Maria. Robert was aware that she rested her hand on his shoulders. Rubbing his head, he looked back at her and smiled a pained smile. 'Fine.'

He turned back to the corpse. 'Look at that.'

Maria leaned in past his head to get a better look and Robert caught a smell of her cologne. Fresh and summery, with a hint of her sweat.

The hand that Robert had grasped had partially disintegrated under his touch, and a small pile of dust had gathered below it. A trickle of dust was still spilling from the arm.

'He's completely dry!' said Maria. 'Is that normal?'

'I don't think so,' said Robert. 'Sorry.'

He pushed himself backwards and Maria removed her hand from his neck. As she did so, she gently stroked the hairs there. Robert stood and looked at her. Maria looked innocently around.

'So where can we get more water?' she asked.

Robert roused himself and brushed the dust off his knees. 'I'm not sure. Maybe there's enough here for all of us.'

He breathed in and immediately started coughing. 'These petrol fumes are really getting to me. We'd better get back to the others.'

He turned and headed back to the rocks where they had left the others. Maria fell into step beside him. Robert looked around as they walked. Nothing to see but the edge of the ravine, and miles of trees and shrubs stretching off into the distance along the crevice in which they were walking.

Suddenly, Robert caught a glimpse of movement out of the corner of his eye, and he spun round. Blurred by the heat haze, he thought he saw a large animal of some description disappear behind some trees beyond the crashed jeep.

Maria stopped and turned. 'What is it?'

'I don't know. I thought I saw movement.'

Maria scanned the area. 'I don't see anything.'

Robert nodded. 'Not any more … Maybe it was the guide.'

He continued to gaze at the bushes, but nothing else moved. Maria gently tugged on his arm to get him moving again and, after a moment, they continued back to the rocks.

As they drew closer, they could hear Jaz talking. No surprise there, thought Robert.

'… then my man here said to these ladies, "I can do that even without a hat," and they screamed with laughter. Anyway, later on, one of the girls comes up to me all friendly like …'

'Don't let me stop you,' said Robert as he and Maria

rounded the rock.

'Yo, man!' exclaimed Jaz in delight. 'D'you find some water?'

Robert hefted the water bottle. 'Some. It's about half full so should last us a couple of days or more if we're careful.'

'A couple of days!' exclaimed Peter. 'I'm not planning to be here a couple of *hours* let alone a couple of days.'

'Be that as it may,' said Robert calmly, 'we don't know what's going to happen, how long we're going to be here or anything. It's best to assume the worst and to try and preserve what we have.'

'So what happens now?' Maria seemed edgy.

Robert looked at the sky. 'The sun's moved over that way, so that gives us a sense of direction, at least. If we head south, then, eventually, we're bound to hit civilisation. The whole coast along this part of Portugal is populated with tourists.'

'So what are we waiting for?' asked Peter.

The others looked at each other.

'Don' ask me, man,' chipped in Jaz. 'I'm just looking after Jones here.'

'Well, Robert seems to have had all the ideas so far,' said Maria, flicking a smile in his direction. 'Perhaps he should decide what we do next.'

Robert grimaced at her. 'Thanks a bunch. No pressure then.'

He looked around at each of them in turn; his eyes

lingered longer on Maria, but only by a fraction of a second and he was sure no-one noticed.

'I think we should stay here for the moment and see if anyone else comes by looking for us. If no-one has appeared by the time night falls, then we start to head south. It'll be cooler at night and easier to travel.'

Peter narrowed his eyes. 'So you just want us to sit here?'

'It was your idea originally,' retorted Maria. 'You said that someone would come and find us if the jeep did not return to the hotel.'

Robert smiled at Maria's pronunciation of 'hotel', as 'hot – el', with the emphasis on the 'hot' rather than on the '– tel'.

Peter exhaled noisily in disgust. It was obvious that he wasn't in any mood to be argued with. 'Fine. Just fine.' He looked at the others. 'Well, if we're going to be stuck here, then I need my cigarettes. Did anyone see them by the jeep?'

There was a general shaking of heads as the others started to ponder on the long, hot wait ahead of them. Jaz and Jones sat down cross-legged on the ground while Maria turned her back on the group and wandered away a little to gaze at the shimmering horizon.

'Fine.' Peter stood up and headed off around the rock. 'Fuck you all!' he muttered. Robert and the others watched him go.

'Leave him, man,' said Jaz. 'Guy's got a problem. He'll

get over it.'

'I'm more worried about the water,' said Robert. 'It may look like a lot, but it's not going to last that long between five of us.

'I think that if no-one comes, then the first priority is going to have to be finding a fresh supply. And some food. I don't know about you guys, but I skipped breakfast because … you know … I'm not good on jeeps … and I'm feeling pretty peckish right now.'

Maria wandered back over to join them. She gracefully sank to the ground, legs folding under her, just behind Robert. 'Don't worry,' she said, her hand gently stroking up Robert's back. 'Someone will come along.'

'I wish I shared your optimism,' muttered Robert.

They sat in silence for a few minutes. There was no sound except the gentle rustling of the surrounding bushes as gentle eddies of air scooted around the rock in whose shade they sat. Robert enjoyed Maria's closeness more than he'd like to admit.

Suddenly, the air was rocked with a huge explosion, closely followed by a piercing scream.

The group leaped to their feet and Robert and Maria raced around the rock to see that the jeep was ablaze and Peter was staggering towards them, his hair and clothes ablaze. He was making the most horrific keening and screeching sound.

Maria raised her hands to her face in horror, and seemed incapable of moving. Robert, however, recovered his composure and raced towards the smoking figure of Peter.

'Roll on the ground! Roll on the ground!' he shouted, but Peter was obviously too much in pain to hear him.

'Shit.' Robert ripped off his T-shirt and bundled it around his hands. He lunged at the flaming figure and knocked him over, then started to kick him over and over in the dust. This seemed to work, and the flames that surrounded him died down rapidly. The next thing Robert knew was Jaz standing beside him with the water bottle. He upended the canister and splashed water over Peter's smoking hair and face.

The man was shuddering and shaking, obviously retreating into shock, and his blackened hands were clenched tightly into skeletal fists. He breathed in long, shaky fits. Jaz splashed more water over him and it sizzled and steamed as it hit the worst affected areas of his body.

Maria appeared over Jaz's shoulder. 'Oh my God!' she breathed as she saw the state that Peter was in. 'How …?'

Robert gestured to the gold glint of a lighter tightly clenched in Peter's right hand. 'Seems the stupid bugger couldn't wait for his fag, and decided to light it before he was far enough away from the petrol fumes.

Robert, Jaz and Maria silently regarded the shaking figure for a moment. 'Jaz, help me carry him into the shade,' said Robert.

The two men gently took hold of Peter's arms by his shoulders and hauled him upright. A thin keening noise was coming from his throat, and Jaz and Robert frogmarched him as quickly as possible back to the rock.

'There.' Robert bunched his T-shirt on the ground as a makeshift pillow, and he and Jaz laid Peter down as gently as they could. Peter's breathing was laboured and his body was still twitching and jerking.

'Where's the water?' asked Robert.

Jaz hurried back to where he had left the canister and returned with it. The bottle was now only a quarter full.

'Brilliant,' said Robert through gritted teeth. 'All the water we have and this son of a bitch decides to go and get burnt up.' Realising what he had said, Robert glanced at the others apologetically. 'I … I'm sorry. I didn't mean that. It's …'

'Doesn't matter,' said Maria gently. 'How do you say? You did what you did.' She placed her hand on his arm and looked into his eyes. 'Doesn't matter,' she said again.

Robert smiled thinly. 'That's easy for you to say.'

He motioned to Jaz to bring the water over. Jaz produced a large and colourful handkerchief from his pocket and, placing it over the end of the bottle, wetted it thoroughly. He then carefully wrung some drops into Peter's mouth and used the edge of the cloth to gently dab at his face.

'It's not as bad as it looks, man,' he said. 'Lot of this dirt is just that, dirt from rolling on the ground.' Jaz winced as

Peter's skin cracked and split as he dabbed it.

Robert, who had seen enough to know that Peter was, in fact, quite severely burned, nodded. 'Maybe. All we can do is try and keep him comfortable until help arrives.

'This rather scuppers the plan to move south if all else fails.'

Maria knelt down by Peter and took over dabbing at his black and bleeding face from Jaz.

Robert leaned back against the warm rock and stared into space. The hot air smelt of burning rubber and petrol, and Peter's whimpering slowly subsided as the man fell unconscious.

Robert closed his eyes against the glare of the sky. It was definitely one of those days.

Chapter Two

Robert woke to find that the sun was now hanging, hot and red, just above the horizon. He blinked and took in the others. Jaz and Jones were snoozing to one side of him, while Peter was still lying unconscious on the floor. Robert wondered briefly where Maria was, but then realised that she had snuggled up close to him and had her head on his shoulder. He gently flexed his arm and eased it into a different position around her shoulders. His hand tingled as the blood flowed through it.

He shook Maria gently.

'Hey you.'

Maria stirred and raised her head. Realising that Robert was awake, she quickly settled herself upright and moved away from him. 'Oh ... I'm sorry,' she murmured. 'I didn't think you'd mind, and I was getting cold ...'

Robert smiled. 'Now why don't I believe that ...?' he asked, brushing beads of sweat from his brow with his hand. Come to think of it, Maria was not sweating at all. He remembered the feel of the top of her shoulders. She had been cool.

He caught her eye. 'A Finnish ice maiden, eh?'

Maria dipped her eyes to the ground. Then she abruptly stood up and, brushing the grit from her bare legs, took a couple of steps away before stretching like a cat.

Her movement disturbed Jones and he sat up. 'What's going on? Anyone there?'

'It's only me, Jones,' said Maria. 'Sun's nearly gone.'

Robert stood up and moved around the rock to look back at the jeep. The flames had died down and now there was only a thin stream of black smoke rising, almost in a straight line, from the burnt out wreck.

He returned to the others. 'There's no sign of any movement there, and it must be several hours since we crashed. I suggest that we get our stuff together and move off south.'

'I don't know, man,' said Jaz. 'What about Peter here? We can't leave him.'

Robert regarded the motionless form of Peter. Maria was crouched by him, feeling his pulse.

'He's still alive,' she said. 'There's still a pulse, but it's not strong.'

As if in answer, Peter stirred and moaned gently in his sleep. Motioning to Jaz to dampen the handkerchief once more, she allowed a few drops to fall into his mouth. His tongue wetted his lips in a reflex action. Maria dabbed his face with the damp cloth.

'He can't walk,' she said. 'If we're going to move, then we'll have to carry him.'

Robert nodded. 'That's going to be tricky, the state he's in.'

The light was growing dimmer and Robert looked about. 'I think that Jaz, you and I should make a final check around the jeep to see if we missed anything that might be useful. Maria, you stay here with Jones and look after Peter.'

Robert moved off with Jaz around the rock and together they made their way through the twilight and lengthening shadows towards the gently smoking wreck of the jeep. They circled it, scanning the ground for anything they might have missed before.

Jaz pounced on a thermos flask half-hidden under a bush. He shook it. 'Got sommat in, man!' he declared and opened the top. He sniffed the contents tentatively. 'It's orange juice.'

'Well done!' congratulated Robert. 'Anything like

that'll be of use.'

After several more minutes searching around in the increasing gloom, their haul had come to the thermos, a tattered blanket and the rucksack belonging to the teenager, which Robert had spotted hanging in the branches of a cork tree some way away. The rucksack did indeed contain a bottle of mineral water, as well as some biscuits and a bar of chocolate.

Their inspection of their findings was interrupted by a piercing scream from behind the rock. It was Maria.

Robert and Jaz raced back to their makeshift camp to find Maria standing over Peter's body, sobbing fitfully.

'What's the matter,' asked Robert, to be rewarded by Maria throwing her body into his arms and burying her face in his shoulder. A distant part of his mind noted that her skin was still very cool. He grasped her by the shoulders and pulled her away from him.

'What is it?' he asked again.

The girl glanced at him and then down at Peter. 'It's … it's …' she stammered.

Jaz, who had crouched to see how Peter was, looked up at Robert.

'I've never seen this before,' he said solemnly, and moved to allow Robert to see Peter's body.

Just as with the driver of the jeep, Peter's flesh had sunken in on itself. His lips were drawn back over his teeth in a rictus scream of pain and, although his eyes were wide open, the sockets were empty apart from a small shrivelled ball of matter resting at the back. His cheeks were pulled in and the bones of his skull were clearly outlined. His hands too were skeletal and clenched and, where Jaz had touched his skin, it had disintegrated into a loose grey powder.

Robert reached out his forefinger and gently pressed on Peter's cheekbone. There was a sharp crack and a hissing sound, and Robert's finger pushed right through the skin and bone, which simply turned to powder around it.

'But I hardly pressed at all,' Robert said, removing his finger from the corpse's cheek.

He stood up and grasped Maria again. 'Can you tell us what happened?'

Maria was still sobbing and looked at Robert blankly.

He shook her gently. 'Come on. Maria. Maria? Can you hear me? Listen. We have to know what happened.'

Jaz looked at Jones, who was sitting where he had been left. 'Do you know what happened, man?' he asked.

Jones shook his head. 'Actually, I'd be obliged if someone could tell *me*,' he said. 'I've just been sitting here, minding my own business as usual, and then, out of the blue, that crazy woman shrieks loud enough to wake the dead … excuse my bad taste there … and then you come running.'

'Peter's dead,' said Robert. He turned back to Maria. 'Well?'

She stopped whimpering and took a couple of gulps of air.

'After you and Jaz had gone,' she said, wiping her nose with her hand, 'I stayed with Peter for a moment, and then went back to wet the handkerchief. When I came back, Peter was like this.'

She pushed herself into Robert's arms again. 'Robert, I'm scared. It's just like the driver.'

'What about the driver?' said Jaz.

Robert explained, and Jaz whistled through his teeth. 'Strange, man. Strange.'

'So, what're we going to do?' asked Maria.

'I suppose we set off south,' said Robert.

They had been walking for about half an hour when Jones suddenly stopped.

'C'mon, man,' said Jaz. 'What've you stopped for?'

'I heard something,' said Jones quietly.

The others stopped walking and stood in silence. They could hear nothing except the sighing of the breeze through the trees.

'You sure?' asked Robert, walking back to where Jones was standing.

'Sure,' said Jones. 'I might not be able to see, but I hear things pretty well.'

'What was it you heard,' asked Maria.

'Breathing. And footsteps. Something was walking alongside us.'

Robert peered into the blackness all around them. The night was clear, but the starlight was weak and all he could see were the inky shapes of the trees nearest them looming out of the night. Suddenly, he saw a black blob move behind one of the trees.

'Stay here,' he whispered to the others. 'And keep talking.'

As Robert circled back along the trail, the others stood in a huddle. 'Where's he gone,' asked Maria calmly.

'He'll be back,' said Jaz. 'He's just gone to lose a little water, if you know what I mean.'

'Well I don't like it,' Maria said. 'Leaving us alone like that.' So far on their night-time trek, she had made sure that she was within touching distance of Robert, a fact that had not gone unnoticed by Jaz. 'You like him ...' he chided.

'So ...?' challenged Maria. 'If it had escaped your attention, we're all in this together.' She stepped away from Jaz and Jones.

'Don't go too far now,' said Jaz with a smile in his voice. 'Wouldn't want to have to go looking for you.'

The silence around them was broken by the sound of a muffled cry, and string of curses. Jaz, Jones and Maria hurried across to where the sound was coming from and found Robert sitting on the back of another man. Robert had his arm locked behind his back.

'What have we here?' said Robert. 'Are you going to behave yourself?' he asked, giving the man's arm another twist.

The man uttered another babble of Portuguese before breaking off with a cry. 'Yes! Yes! I'll be good. I'll explain. Just don't hurt me.'

Robert jumped from the man's back. 'There are more of us than there are of you, so don't try anything funny. Why were you following us?'

'You're the guide from the jeep!' exclaimed Maria. 'Where have you been?'

The man looked from one to the other. 'I was thrown from the jeep when it crashed,' he explained in halting English. 'I hit my head, and when I came round, I didn't know where I was. I've been wandering around here for hours, and then I heard you coming along. I was just going to call out to you when this *imbecile* jumps on my back, scaring me half to death.'

'Sounded more like you were keeping watch on us,' said Jones. 'Why would you want to do that?'

'I wasn't,' the man insisted. 'Anyway, what would the point be?'

'Maybe you wanted to steal our water,' said Maria. 'Or kill us as we slept.' Her eyes glinted in the darkness. 'Or maybe even worse!'

'That's enough,' said Robert. 'The question is, what do we do now? Can we trust him?'

Jaz smiled. 'Don't matter if we do or don't. He's either gonna come with us where we can keep an eye on him, or he's gonna make his own way. Don' forget that he's a local.

Might do us good to have someone who knows the area.'

'I don't know *this* area,' said the man. 'Fool Carlos, he had too much firewater at our last stop. He always does. But this time he gets it into his head to try a different route back. I've got some idea where we are, but not much.'

'Well, not much is better than none at all,' said Robert. 'We'd better get walking again.'

He prodded the guide with his finger. 'I think our friend here would like to lead the way.'

The man mumbled something under his breath and started walking. Behind him followed the others, with Maria skipping forward to walk alongside Robert as before. Robert glanced at her. Despite all the exertion so far, she still seemed quite fresh, whereas Robert was just feeling knackered. He shook his head and concentrated on the bobbing back of the guide in front of him.

They had been walking for around an hour when the bushes and trees suddenly thinned out around them. In front of them a large whitewashed building loomed, its shape materialising out of the darkness as they approached.

'What's this place?' asked Robert.

'I ... I'm not sure,' said Miguel, the guide. Some small-talk had established his identity as they walked along.

Maria ran forward a few paces and stopped. 'I think it's a church ... or something,' she called back.

The others advanced to meet her and found themselves

at a large porticoed entrance. Two old and battered wooden doors leaned at odd angles in the doorway, and a line of dilapidated picket fencing ran from either side of the stone edifice into darkness.

A word was carved into the top of the stone arch: *Cemitério*

Seeing this, Miguel stopped walking and hurriedly struck his head, chest and shoulders in quick succession.

'*Mãe de Deus*,' he muttered. '*Não*.'

'What is it?' asked Robert.

'No,' the man said again. 'Not here.'

Jaz moved in and grasped the man's upper arm with his meaty fist. 'Not thinking of running out on us, were you?'

The man gulped. His face had gone pale and beads of sweat stood out on his brow. 'No. *Não*. It's just … this is *cemitério* … a *cemetery* … place of *morto* … the dead. We shouldn't be here. We should go around. *Sim*?'

Robert moved closer to the doors and peered through the large crack between them. 'Place seems deserted,' he said. 'These doors haven't been touched in years.'

'Maybe there's somewhere to rest in there,' said Maria. 'We've been walking for ages and my legs are getting tired.'

Robert couldn't help but glance at her legs. She had very nice legs. She certainly hadn't seemed tired moments ago, but then perhaps appearances were deceptive. Smiling to himself he returned to the doors and gave one of them an experimental push. It was wedged solid. He pushed the other one and it gave slightly. Bracing his arms against the door, he shoved, and the wooden panel swung inward a couple of feet with the jarring screech of protesting hinges and the scrape of wood against grit on the floor.

He stepped through the entrance. 'Come on,' he said, and vanished from their sight.

Maria hurried forward and eased her lithe form through the gap, followed by the guide, Jaz and finally Jones.

Beyond the gate it was even quieter than it had been outside, if that were possible. All around them, chipped and broken headstones disappeared off into the blackness.

Scripts

Doctor Who fans are nothing if not creative and enterprising, and among my friends is a wonderful chap called Keith Barnfather who runs Reeltime Pictures, a small, independent film company that has specialised in corporate video for a variety of clients. Keith is also a big fan of the show, and has produced and released a large number of interview videos, and now DVDs, associated with it. Keith actually made and released the first ever fan drama, a video called *Wartime*, starring John Levene as Sergeant Benton. Since then he has gone on to produce and release many more dramas containing themes, characters and ideas inspired by the adventures of the good Doctor.

For *Doctor Who*'s fortieth birthday in 2003, with the show off the air and no sign of it ever returning, Keith decided that he wanted to make another video to celebrate the anniversary. He had, I think, been chatting with Miles Richardson, who had played a UNIT soldier called Cavendish in an earlier drama, and whose wife, Beverley Cressman, had also appeared as Kate Lethbridge-Stewart, daughter of the Brigadier (a character played by the superb Nicholas Courtney in the show).

Keith wanted these characters to be included, and he had an idea for something using the Sea Devils (marine reptiles from a Jon Pertwee story) and set by the sea. As I had worked with him on several previous releases, he asked me if I would be interested in scripting the drama, and of course I agreed – opportunities like that don't come along very often! So the long process of developing the story started.

When writing a script for a no-budget drama, it's important that you know what limits you are working to. For this script, Keith was pretty sure he could get use of a cottage to shoot in, and also some caves, and possibly some sea front ... so a rough outline was created using those elements. Then news came through that the Sea Devils were not available ...

Luckily, I had just confirmed the use of the Daemons (alien devil-creatures) with owners Barry Letts and Robert Sloman for Telos Publishing's range of *Time Hunter* novellas, so I suggested to Keith that we could create something that tied in with that range, and that used the Daemons as well. This seemed to be liked, and so I came up with the ideas and concepts that eventually developed into the final script.

Among the influences were the *Doctor Who* stories 'Day of the Daleks' and 'The Daemons', but also in my mind were certain scenes from a favourite *giallo* horror film called *Suspiria* ...

The production was taped over the autumn of 2003, and released on DVD in 2004, and even today I'm astounded at how good it all looks. The production values were very high considering it had to be a very low budget production, and Keith really knew how to make the most of what little money he was spending on it. He even managed to persuade Miles's father – the amazing actor Ian Richardson – to do the voiceover at the start and end.

After we had finished making *Daemos Rising*, Keith wanted to do a sequel, and he again asked me to script it. This time I took my lead from another *Doctor Who* story, 'Image of the Fendahl', a Tom Baker tale, and combined this with the location that Keith had in mind – an intact but deserted castle on the coast of Cyprus. Keith's partner was Cypriot, and she knew that permission could be obtained to use this location, and also had contacts to obtain technical equipment like lights and cameras on the island …

So *Face of the Fendahl* was born as another low budget, small cast production, bringing in motifs both from *Doctor Who* and from another low-budget master, Roger Corman, specifically his 1964 film with Vincent Price, *The Masque of the Red Death*. I even made reference to this in the script.

The idea was that Miles, Beverley and Andrew Wisher (son of noted *Doctor Who* actor Michael Wisher) would reprise their roles from *Daemos Rising*, and that this would be a great little horror/thriller set in a deserted castle.

Unfortunately Miles and Beverley split up as a couple and went their separate ways, and Keith's enthusiasm for the project waned … and so it never happened.

The script was completed, though, and so here it is for all to enjoy ... an untold chapter in the *Time Hunter* history, and a glimpse of how the Fendahl could have been developed ...

Daemos Rising

PROLOGUE/TITLES

1. INT: A DARKENED ROOM

It is dark and musty. The floor has a crude pentacle drawn on it. There are black candles at the points of the symbol.

CAVENDISH is lighting the candles one by one. He is wearing a pair of combat trousers but is stripped to the waist. His body is sweaty and glistens in the dim light. He mutters incantations as he moves around the candles.

CAVENDISH (under his breath)

> Hear me oh mighty ones. Hear my call. I summon your power to help me here on Earth. Know that I will use them wisely and knowledgably. Hear me oh mighty ones.

In the centre of the pentacle is the book – a large leather-bound tome covered in runes.

When he has finished lighting the candles, CAVENDISH sits cross legged in the centre of the pentacle and picks up the book.

The camera slowly zooms into his eye as close as we can go ... and we mix to ...

2. EXT: MONTAGE/TITLES

... a montage of ancient sites, Stonehenge, Aldbourne, standing stones, brooding skies, eclipse ... images to suggest ancient rites and activities over which we get the narration.

NARRATOR (over)

Aeons ago, a mighty race toyed with life as children might play with ants. Earth was one such playground, but an emissary to that world became trapped. Blind and ignorant people with a lust for power released the sleeping devil and demanded of him a final judgement. But Azal was destroyed. His energies turned inward ... dissipating deep into the Earth and in time luring the ambitious, the greedy and the broken. In the void between time the devils waited ... patiently ... to be summoned

again … to pass judgement on
the Earth …

Overlaid on the latter part of this sequence after the
narration has finished are the titles:

DAEMOS RISING

*

BY DAVID J HOWE

*

STARRING
MILES RICHARDSON
BEVERLEY CRESSMAN
with
ANDREW WISHER

*

DIRECTED BY KEITH BARNFATHER

ACT ONE

3. EXT: STATION – DAY

Mix to the sun in the sky and pan down to reveal a railway
station. A train is just pulling out.

KATE walks from the station out to the forecourt. She is

carrying an overnight bag and is dressed in jeans and a T-shirt with a jacket over the top. She has her hair down, loose around her shoulders. Smart casual.

There is no-one in sight. She looks left and right.

KATE (to herself)
> I might have known there'd be
> no taxis. Oh well …

She pulls from her pocket a hand-drawn map. She studies it and sets off in a direction.

4. EXT: ROADS AND FIELDS – DAY

A short montage of KATE walking from the station, along a road, over a stile, by a river … a series of locations to suggest getting further and further from civilisation.

This sequence leads into …

5. EXT: FOREST AREA – DAY

Mix between different areas of forest. There is birdsong.

Bring up the sound of KATE making her way through

the forest.

Pick up KATE walking through the woods. She seems concerned about something, looking about from time to time.

Suddenly, there is a cracking noise and KATE stops to look around.

She sees brief, quick movement, the fraction of a person's body as they are hidden behind a tree.

KATE
>Hello?

She moves to where she saw the movement and looks around

KATE
>Anyone there?

She can't see anyone. She catches another movement out of the corner of her eye and just glimpses someone else.

KATE
>Who's there?

There's no answer, so with a shudder, she continues

through the woods.

6. EXT: CLEARING – DAY

KATE emerges into a small clearing where a large statue is visible in the middle. It is hunched and deformed but is clearly a humanoid shape. It's about the size of a crouching adult, covered with moss and lichen as though it has been there for some time. There is no sound in the clearing.

KATE moves closer to the statue and looks at it.

KATE (to herself)
> God, you're ugly, aren't you.

She catches more movement out of the corner of her eye and just glimpses someone.

KATE
> Hello?

KATE looks round in exasperation.

KATE (to herself)
> I don't need this. What am I
> doing here …?

She turns on her heel and heads off back the way she came. We follow her for a few moments and then cut back to a shot with the statue in frame. Kate re-enters the clearing. She stops dead and stares at the statue, clearly not believing her eyes.

She carefully turns 180 degrees, and, with a glance back at the statue, walks away out of the clearing again.

Fade to a different shot of the clearing, but still with the statue in shot. Kate re-enters the clearing. She stops. She is now very puzzled indeed.

KATE (to herself)
>
> So I *can't* just leave, is that it?
> We'll see about that.

She pulls her mobile phone from her pocket and dials a number.

KATE (into phone)
>
> Hello? Dad? Hello …

She pulls the phone from her ear and looks at the display.

KATE (to herself)
>
> No signal.

KATE stuffs the phone back in her pocket and looks at the statue, moving closer to it.

KATE (to the statue)
> Are you doing this?

KATE reaches out to touch the statue, and there's a momentary tingling sensation in her hand. She pulls back and rubs her fingers together thoughtfully.

KATE (to herself, thoughtful)
> There's something …

Then she reaches out and touches the statue and …

7. INT: VOID

… KATE is standing in a smoke-filled black void. Coloured lights play about and the air is filled with the sounds of crying and screaming. People shouting 'No', moaning and so on.

There is an eerie whizzing twittering sound. These are the psionic forces and we'll hear this sound whenever there is power building, and psionic force being gained.

A deep, grating, asexual voice is chanting words that have

no meaning. We can only just hear them.

VOICE (oov)
>   Eco eco dah a elttil bmal … eco
>   eco dah a elttil bmal … eco eco
>   dah a elttil bmal

KATE looks around, wide-eyed …

8. EXT: CLEARING – DAY

… and takes her hand off the statue.

KATE stands for a beat rubbing her fingers together. She's very puzzled. She looks around herself somewhat alarmed and scared.

KATE (to herself)
>   So if I can't leave …

She looks around and sees the cottage ahead through the woods. She walks off towards the cottage.

9. EXT: COTTAGE – DAY

KATE is walking down towards the cottage, when

suddenly a grimy hand grasps her arm from behind. She jumps in fright.

KATE
What the –

The hand belongs to CAVENDISH. He is dirty and his hair is somewhat messy and unkempt. He's dressed in what might once have been a smart trousers and shirt arrangement – very public school – but which is now quite grubby and slept in.

While he is talking, CAVENDISH is a mass of tics and nervous energy. He keeps glancing around, and occasionally will hear himself (though KATE cannot hear these interjections) talking in a suave accent as though he is arguing with another part of him. These asides are indicated here with (over).

CAVENDISH
Thank goodness you came …

KATE (recognising him)
Douglas?

CAVENDISH (over)
She knows him.

KATE

> Douglas? It's me, Kate … You called me …

CAVENDISH

> Glad I got you. Nearest phone? Miles away. Had to walk. Transport all up the creek.

KATE

> What … what's been happening?

She looks him up and down.

KATE (cont)

> Why are you all …

Realisation dawns.

KATE (cont)

> Have you been sleeping rough?

CAVENDISH

> Had to. Couldn't stay in the cottage. Too much happening. Too much going on.

CAVENDISH (over)

> Get her away from here.

CAVENDISH

> I can't. Need her.

CAVENDISH (over)

> Get a grip man.

CAVENDISH (to Kate)

> I ... I'm sorry ... a lot has been happening ... I'm finding it hard to cope. I get confused on my own. Not sure who I am. There are ... voices ... voices in my head ...

KATE

> I'm not sure I know who you are either. Why did you ask me to come here? You said it was something to do with Dad ...

CAVENDISH

> You were the only person who might understand.

KATE (derisory)

> Understand …?

CAVENDISH nods. He starts to wander towards the cottage, distracted.

KATE (cont)

> But you nearly killed us all! Everything …

CAVENDISH

> I know … I know …

KATE

> So why should I trust you? What's this got to do with Dad?

CAVENDISH stops and turns to face KATE.

CAVENDISH (defeated)

> You were the only one who visited me, Kate. The only one who cared. (HE TAKES HER HAND) When it was all over … when I was taken to … to … hospital. Severe mental and nervous burn out. Nothing left.

But you …

KATE

Dad told me you had been a good friend to him. Before. I felt I owed him that.

CAVENDISH

But you were there, you saw …

KATE (quietly)

I know. I wouldn't have believed it myself …

She shakes her head.

KATE (cont)

… and Dad said he had seen much, much worse in his time … but, Douglas, you were discharged. No blemish on your record. None of it was your fault …

CAVENDISH (exhausted)

Burn out. That's what they called it. Fine young officer. Prime of life. Excellent UNIT material … and then just put out to roost.

No regard for what I wanted.

CAVENDISH (over)

Not finished yet.

CAVENDISH (cont)

Kate. You came. I didn't think you would. You'll help me? Help me sort it before anyone finds out?

KATE

Of course I will … if I can …

KATE (cont, kindly, realising the ruse)

You'd have said anything to get me to come, wouldn't you? (SHE DROPS HIS HAND) Look … I've just walked miles from the station. It's the end of October … I'm tired … I'm cold … my feet hurt and I'm dying for a cup of tea.

She looks around and shivers again.

KATE (cont)

And that clearing … back there in the woods? I saw someone. Something happened and …

silly really, but every path I took
led back to the statue …

CAVENDISH
>Clearing? Statue?

He moans a little and hugs himself

CAVENDISH (over)
>(CHUCKLES) We know *all*
>about the statue …

CAVENDISH (to Kate)
>Don't want to go there.

KATE gives CAVENDISH a long hard look. She's suspicious.

KATE
>Why?

CAVENDISH
>It's not safe.

CAVENDISH moans again and shakes his head. KATE looks back towards the cottage and makes a decision.

KATE

> Well if you'd rather go to the
> cottage …?

CAVENDISH looks at the cottage and back at Kate. He's clearly disturbed at the thought of either option.

KATE takes him gently by the arm.

KATE

> Tell you what, let's look at the
> statue first, and then I'll make
> you a nice cup of tea … How
> does that sound?

KATE and CAVENDISH move off towards the clearing

10. EXT: CLEARING – DAY

KATE and CAVENDISH enter the clearing.

CAVENDISH is shaking his head. He's a little agitated. CAVENDISH hangs back as KATE tentatively approaches the statue and bends to examine it. She goes to rest her hand on it, but holds it just above the stone, without touching it.

KATE

> Something happened when I
> touched it before …

She looks at CAVENDISH.

KATE (cont)

> What do you know about it?

CAVENDISH (quickly)

> Nothing. Nothing at all.

He looks around nervously. There is no sound in the woods here at all.

CAVENDISH (cont, uneasy)

> We'd best get back. Be dark soon.

KATE (thoughtfully to herself)

> Well there's nowhere else to go.

With a final look back at the statue, and a suspicious look at CAVENDISH, she and CAVENDISH head off.

CAVENDISH is almost pulling her away.

We stay in the clearing and see mist start to pool around the base of the statue.

11. EXT: COTTAGE BY WINDOW – DAY/DUSK

KATE and CAVENDISH are standing by the front/back of the cottage. There is a window behind them. In the window we can see the figure of someone standing, watching them. This is the GHOST. He is wearing a dark coloured Nehru jacket and trousers.

KATE (in mid argument)

> … if you think I'm staying outside, then you're sadly mistaken!

CAVENDISH (very nervous)

> But we can't stay inside … It's … it's dark and …

KATE (interrupting authorititively)

> … and you can stop that right now! There's nothing to be scared of. Look, you asked me to come here, right?

CAVENDISH nods, childlike, eyes wide.

KATE (cont)

> And now I'm here. I've got no choice but to stay, so let's go and

see what's got you so upset, eh?

CAVENDISH seems on the verge of tears.

KATE (comforting)
>   It's all right. Honestly it is. We
>   can't make tea out here now can
>   we?

She looks at him worriedly, as if he might suddenly attack her.

KATE
>   Are you sure you're okay? I
>   could phone for someone.

CAVENDISH
>   No ... no ...

KATE
>   ... a doctor ... to come and
>   check you're okay?

CAVENDISH (recovering himself)
>   I'm fine. Really.

KATE gives him a last worried look and then moves to enter the cottage, followed a moment later by

CAVENDISH.

The GHOST just stays where he is, watching them.

Through this sequence, although in some shots we can see the window and the GHOST, no attention must be drawn to him either by CAVENDISH or KATE, or by the camera.

As they head for the door, we fade to black.

ACT TWO

12. INT: COTTAGE LOWER HALL – DUSK

Fade up from black inside the cottage. The front door swings open to reveal CAVENDISH and KATE standing there.

They stand and listen. Nothing.

KATE
            Nothing.

She glances at CAVENDISH who is inscrutable at the moment. Blank. He's bottling up all his emotions.

They step into the cottage and look over the hallway. All the doors leading into the hall are closed. There is an open archway leading to the dining room. KATE moves to the stairs and starts up, she peers up to the top. Nothing. She looks back at CAVENDISH, who is starting to crack.

KATE moves back down the stairs and to the archway. With another glance at CAVENDISH, she peers into the room beyond.

13. INT: COTTAGE DINING ROOM – DUSK

It's a perfectly normal dining room. Table, sofa, fireplace, television … nothing unusual at all. Except that we can see the shadowy outline of GHOST. We don't get a good look at him, however.

KATE steps into the room, and a second sweep by the camera shows the GHOST has gone. She frowns and steps out again.

KATE
> Nice room.

14. INT: COTTAGE LOWER HALL – DUSK

KATE moves down the hall to the next door, one leading under the stairs. Behind her on the stairs, the shadowy GHOST can be seen, just for one shot. Next time, it's gone again. KATE finds that this door is locked. She cannot open it.

KATE

     Locked?

CAVENDISH pushes her out the way and, gently touching the door, makes sure it is closed.

CAVENDISH

     Locked. Yes. Keeps him at bay. But sometimes (HE LEANS FORWARD CONSPIRATORIALLY) he comes out.

CAVENDISH (over)

     It will be opened soon.

CAVENDISH

     No. It must stay locked.

CAVENDISH (over)

     Soon …

CAVENDISH looks at KATE with pleading eyes. She smiles at him but she looks worried.

KATE (gently)
>Keeps who at bay, Douglas?
>Why must it stay locked?

CAVENDISH (startled)
>There's … a person. A figure. I
>don't know. Honestly.

KATE heads upstairs, leaving CAVENDISH alone. He looks around himself nervously, then he checks that the door is closed. He pulls on the handle, turns it a couple of times. Listens at the door, then turns the handle again, pulling against the handle while he does so – ensuring that the door stays closed – before gently letting go and backing away as though the handle might explode.

KATE (coming downstairs again)
>Nothing up there either …
>Whatever it is that's going on in
>this house, it's being pretty quiet
>about it.

KATE's tone here suggests that she is humouring him and that she thinks he might have lost his marbles.

We see a shot of KATE with the stairs leading up behind her, and standing on the stairs is the part-transparent GHOST again.

KATE (eying CAVENDISH carefully)
> Are you *sure* you're all right? It *is*
> a bit cut off out here, and you're
> only just out of hospital. At least
> let me call for a doctor.

KATE pulls her mobile phone from her pocket, and looks at the screen.

KATE (to herself)

> Still no signal …

KATE moves to the doorway and checks the phone again.

KATE (puzzled and thoughtful, to herself)

> Mmm …

She replaces the phone in her pocket, and with another wary glance at CAVENDISH, moves to the next door downstairs. This leads to the living room.

15. INT: COTTAGE LIVING ROOM – DUSK

KATE, followed by CAVENDISH, enters the room.
The room contains a table on which is the large book from the opening sequence. There's also a large manila envelope with 'UNIT CLASSIFIED' and a code number: '05-06/71 JJJ' printed/written on it. There is also a large mirror somewhere in the room.

They look around, and KATE turns to CAVENDISH.

KATE

> You're going to have to open up
> a little, Douglas. As far as I can
> see, this is a perfectly normal
> cottage, but with some heating
> issues, and a little dry rot in the
> walls …

While the following discussion is taking place, CAVENDISH goes over to a dresser, gets two glasses and a bottle of something out, then returns to the table and sits.

CAVENDISH

> I wasn't sure you'd believe me.

KATE

> I came, didn't I? I'm not in the

habit of dropping everything to run off somewhere, you know. You're lucky that Beth was available to look after Gordy …

CAVENDISH looks puzzled.

KATE

> Gordy … my son!

CAVENDISH

> Oh … oh yes …

KATE

> … otherwise there's no way I could have come.

CAVENDISH

> And I'm grateful.

KATE

> So …?

CAVENDISH (after a deep breath)

> I think this place is haunted.

KATE (wait a beat before replying)

> By this person you've been

seeing?

CAVENDISH nods.

KATE (cont)

Haunted? Douglas, you're a UNIT operative –

CAVENDISH (interrupting)

Ex-UNIT operative …

KATE (sighs)

Okay … *Ex*-UNIT operative … and you're telling me that you're afraid of the ghost of Aunt Mable!

CAVENDISH (mumbling)

It's not as simple as that.

KATE

I should hope not.

CAVENDISH

I've seen things in this place at night. Heard things too. Crying and screaming. Souls in torment.

KATE (thoughtful, remembering the Void earlier)
>Souls in torment …

By this point CAVENDISH is sitting at the table. He has shakily poured himself a drink, and offered one to KATE who declines.

CAVENDISH
>At first I thought it was the drink – after I was discharged from the hospital, I hit the bottle quite hard. Trauma can do that to a chap (laughs), they say. But when the voices started, I gave it up, but it wasn't the booze at all. By then it was too late …

CAVENDISH's eyes flick to the large book on the table. He reaches out and touches it reverentially.

KATE
>What's that?

She pulls the book over to her and flicks through some of the pages, revealing runes and writing and various images of devils and demons.

From her POV we see the words moving around slightly,

blurring and hard to read.

She looks up at CAVENDISH.
KATE (slightly sneering)
>   Devils, demons and spells?

CAVENDISH pauses, unsure of what to say. Then he seems to crumple and blurts out the next line.

CAVENDISH
>   It was meant to be my pension.
>   UNIT looks after its own ... they
>   said. Only while you're useful to
>   them.

KATE
>   But Dad always said –

CAVENDISH (interrupting)
>   – It's fine for your father ...
>   (SARCASTIC AND BITTER)
>   Brigadier Alistair Gordon
>   Lethbridge-Stewart gets a much
>   better deal. But for an unknown
>   Second Lieutenant ... forget it.

CAVENDISH moves the book back in front of him and turns the pages.

CAVENDISH (cont)

>(REMEMBERING) I once asked your father if he had ever taken any 'keepsakes' from his time with the Taskforce ... the irony is I did just the same.

KATE

>I was as surprised as anyone when we found that he had ... Sorry ... go on.

CAVENDISH

>UNIT has a secure facility. Just outside London. Vast warehouse-like place, covered with alarms and barbed wire. They keep all their 'treasures' in there. Strange alien objects ... guns ... pieces of equipment ... crates of shop dummies ...

KATE (amused)

>Why would they keep crates of shop dummies ...

CAVENDISH gives her a stern look.

KATE

>Fine … Okay … go on …

CAVENDISH

>So I was down there with Virtual Ordnance to check out some files, and I found this book. Ancient-looking thing, isn't it?

KATE squints at the book. The words and pictures are blurring again.

CAVENDISH (cont)

>Chipper Norris, an old friend from Oxford, was really into old parchments and manuscripts. Worth a fortune he once told me, so I took it.

KATE

>You stole it.

CAVENDISH

>It was quite easy, really. Just slipped it in my bag and walked out with it. No-one questioned VO staff, security getting a bit lax and all that.

KATE pulls the book back towards her and gently plays with the cover.

KATE

> But what's it for?

CAVENDISH

> For? It was a means. A way out. Something I wanted. After I took it, I kept it hidden for months. Then, after my … my …

CAVENDISH cannot complete the memory and he trails off. After a beat he shakes his head and continues.

CAVENDISH (cont)

> When I first tried to read it, I couldn't make any sense of the words, they all kept jumping and moving. But then, I found I could read sections. Strange words, poetic …

KATE (alarmed)

> So you've been reading from this book?

CAVENDISH nods sheepishly.

KATE (cont)

> And that's when things started to happen to you?

CAVENDISH

> I thought I could control it. I thought it would be a way for me to get some power, some respect. To *be* someone. But it started to read itself. To control me!

CAVENDISH has a drink from his glass.

CAVENDISH (over)

> But not totally in control. We need more power, the final incantations …

CAVENDISH

> Which is when I started to hear voices in my head, to see things … people … Kate … I … I …

CAVENDISH starts to break down. KATE moves to comfort him.

KATE (eying the book nervously)

> Maybe we need that tea now …

leave that book alone.

CAVENDISH (recovering slightly)
>I intend to. But you'll see, Kate.
>You'll see what we're up against.

KATE (taken aback)
>We?

16. EXT: COTTAGE – NIGHT

Establishing shot of Cottage at night.

17. INT: COTTAGE BEDROOM – NIGHT

The door to the room opens and CAVENDISH shows KATE into the room. She has a cup and saucer with her, just finishing her tea.

CAVENDISH
>You can sleep here.

KATE enters the room.

KATE
>Are you sure you'll be all right?

CAVENDISH

> I'll be fine. Just fine.

KATE (concerned)

> Okay then. But just shout if you
> need me. If anything happens?

CAVENDISH smiles a brief hard smile and leaves the room, closing the door behind him.

KATE stands in the room and sighs, shaking her head. She shudders and hugs herself.

18. INT: COTTAGE LOWER HALL – NIGHT

CAVENDISH descends the stairs. Part way down, he stumbles.

CAVENDISH (to himself)

> Not again … not now …

CAVENDISH (over)

> Time for a bedtime story …

CAVENDISH

> No. Kate's here to help …

CAVENDISH (over)
>   You invited the woman here
>   because you think she likes you
>   … and you certainly like her …

CAVENDISH
>   No …

CAVENDISH (over)
>   (chuckle) I know you better
>   than that. So we can use her to
>   get what we want …

CAVENDISH
>   I won't … won't.

CAVENDISH (over)
>   You can't stop us!

CAVENDISH straightens and smiles an evil grin. The suave persona has taken over. He continues down the stairs and enters the dining room.

19. INT: COTTAGE LIVING ROOM – NIGHT

CAVENDISH sits at the table and opens the book before him. He runs his finger over some lines of text and starts muttering to himself.

CAVENDISH

>Snub ssorc toh ynnep a owt ynnep a eno snub ssorc toh snub ssorc toh

20. INT: COTTAGE BEDROOM – NIGHT

KATE is sitting on the bed and she feels that something is watching her. Her teacup is on a bedside table. She looks around the room and her gaze alights on the darkened pane of the window. She gets up and moves towards it.

21. EXT: CLEARING – NIGHT

In the forest clearing, the hunched statue is wreathed in mist and fog.

22. INT: COTTAGE LIVING ROOM – NIGHT

CAVENDISH continues to chant.

CAVENDISH

>Regnam eht ot emoc emoc emoc …

23. EXT: CLEARING – NIGHT

In the forest clearing, the hunched statue is wreathed in mist and fog. The camera swings around the clearing to show the bones of the trees standing around. When we return to the statue, it has gone leaving just swirling mist.

24. INT: COTTAGE BEDROOM – NIGHT

KATE moves closer to the window and peers out.

25. EXT: OUTSIDE COTTAGE – NIGHT

We can see KATE's bedroom window in the distance, with KATE standing in it looking out. The camera starts to track in closer and closer.

26. INT: COTTAGE BEDROOM – NIGHT

KATE looking out the window. She can't see anything.

27. EXT: OUTSIDE COTTAGE – NIGHT

The camera slowly closes in on the window.

28. INT: COTTAGE LIVING ROOM – NIGHT

CAVENDISH continues to chant

CAVENDISH
>Wons sa etihw saw eceelf sti
>bmal elttil a dah yram

29. INT: COTTAGE BEDROOM – NIGHT

KATE still looking out the window. She can't see anything. We can see her reflection in the glass.

30. EXT: OUTSIDE COTTAGE – NIGHT

The camera slowly closes in on the window and comes right up to KATE looking out.

31. INT: COTTAGE BEDROOM – NIGHT

KATE still looking out the window. There is a sudden bang on her door, and she starts away from the glass to look back at the door. Her reflection in the glass, however, stays where it is, looking in.

KATE moves to the door, and listens. She sees mist creeping under the door, before gently turning the handle and opening the door.

32. INT: COTTAGE UPPER HALL – NIGHT

KATE peers from her doorway up and down the hall. There are tendrils of mist all along the floor, and something flits away from her sight down the stairs. She moves down the hall to the stairs and starts down.

33. INT: COTTAGE LOWER HALL – NIGHT

KATE creeps down the stairs. The locked door has mist and pulsing light pooling under it, coming from whatever is beyond it. She goes to the door and listens at it. Nothing.

There is a sudden noise from the living room behind her, and she turns and goes in.

34. INT: COTTAGE LIVING ROOM – NIGHT

KATE enters the room to find CAVENDISH sitting at the table, eyes wide open and staring straight ahead. The book is open in front of him.

KATE

>Douglas?

CAVENDISH

>I'm sorry … I'm so sorry. The voices … they took control again, completed the incantation. Now they have enough power to start the next stage …

KATE gently closes the book, and picks it up, looking around for somewhere to put it safely away from CAVENDISH. She ends up leaving it on the table. She helps CAVENDISH to his feet. He is muttering that he is sorry as they leave the room.

35. INT: COTTAGE LOWER HALL – NIGHT

They stop in the hallway.
KATE

>It's so cold …

KATE breathes out and we see her breath steam.

KATE and CAVENDISH both stand still as they suddenly see the GHOST right on the stairs in front of them. He is talking to them and gesturing, but they cannot hear a thing.

The GHOST walks past them, and looking back impatiently, walks through the locked door.

KATE looks alarmed at CAVENDISH.

CAVENDISH (whispering)
> He's back …

KATE
> Who *was* that?

CAVENDISH
> A ghost? You saw him too? I *knew* it wasn't just me …

KATE (to herself)
> But I don't believe in ghosts …

KATE goes to the door and tries it. It is locked.

KATE
> There's no way he could have got through here … unless there's a

secret opening …

She starts to feel around the door, looking for some other way through. CAVENDISH watches her for a moment, then sits on the stairs.

CAVENDISH

> There's no point. There is no hidden door. I did the same thing the first time I saw him.

KATE

> But people can't just walk through walls. It's not …

CAVENDISH

> … human?

KATE stops checking the door and wall and goes over to where CAVENDISH is sitting.

KATE

> Why do you say that? I was thinking 'natural'. What was that you said about them having enough power? Who are 'they'?

CAVENDISH

> I'm not sure. I think they're from another place … maybe another time. They promised me power if I'd help them. At first I was sceptical, but working with UNIT gives you … insights … into what's going on.

KATE

> I could have guessed. Why did you say that this … this ghost thing … was not human?

CAVENDISH

> In UNIT's secure facility I saw the files. Everything neatly labelled and locked away as if that would help control it.

CAVENDISH becomes more agitated, and grasps KATE's hands in his. He gets to his feet, and starts pulling her towards the door.

CAVENDISH

> Come … come see …

As he talks, they leave the house.

36. EXT: SHED – NIGHT

CAVENDISH pulls KATE along while talking animatedly to her.

CAVENDISH (cont)

>   … you do know Kate, we're not alone here. Earth has been visited many, many times, but UNIT hushes it up. The things I saw … photographs … witness reports … crates of equipment like something out of a science fiction film … and then there's the specimens.

KATE (shocked and a little disbelieving)

>   Specimens? They have real live aliens?

They reach the shed and CAVENDISH pulls open the door.

CAVENDISH

>   Not live … not that I saw anyway … but one of the vaults is floor to ceiling with bell jars and other glass containers. Some of the things there – tentacles, lumps

301

> of flesh, foetuses, alien shapes
> and forms all sitting silently in
> formaldehyde ...

KATE (revolted)
> What ... like Damien Hirst?

CAVENDISH
> Take a look.

37. INT: SHED – NIGHT

KATE looks in the shed. There on a shelf, amid the clutter, is a large jar in which is floating a decidedly alien-looking life-form. KATE is amazed.

KATE
> What is it?

CAVENDISH
> No idea. It was there in the store.

CAVENDISH comes up the other side of the shelf and taps the jar.

CAVENDISH (cont)
> Ugly, isn't he.

KATE

>Why did you take it?

CAVENDISH

>Because I could. UNIT didn't know everything about me. When I came out of hospital, I bought this place. I felt drawn to it. No-one knows I'm here, so no-one can come and debrief me.

CAVENDISH pauses and looks at the thing in the jar.

CAVENDISH (cont)

>I wanted a slice of power ... and then I started seeing ghosts. I'm not stupid. I can put two and two together ... ghosts don't exist ... but other things do.

KATE (confused)

>But what? I saw him too. A man. He walked past me, and through a locked door ...

There is a crash from outside.

KATE

>What was that?

CAVENDISH shakes his head.

KATE moves to the door of the shed.

CAVENDISH

>What are you doing?

KATE

>Going to look? Coming?

38. EXT: SHED – NIGHT

KATE peers out. There is nothing to see, just mist swirling.

KATE, followed by CAVENDISH, leaves the shed and looks around.

KATE (whispering)

>Where do you think it came from?

CAVENDISH (retreating slightly into himself)

>No idea.

KATE moves off along the side of the house.

KATE (whispering)
>> Come on!

CAVENDISH, with worried looks all round himself, follows.

39. EXT – COTTAGE – NIGHT

They move around the cottage, but there's nothing to be seen. As they draw close to KATE's window, however, there's a swirl of mist on the path ahead. It clears to reveal the hunched statue on the pathway.

KATE and CAVENDISH stop dead.

KATE (whispering)
>> Now, that wasn't there before!

They approach the statue gingerly. CAVENDISH looks all around, hugging himself.

CAVENDISH (whispering)
>> Can we go back inside now?
>> There's nothing here.

KATE (whispering)

> I want to know how this statue
> got here from the clearing.

KATE looks at CAVENDISH.

KATE (uneasy)

> But then again … a ghost …
> spells …

KATE moves around, peering into the darkness around the cottage. She returns to the statue and regards it.

KATE

> Last time I touched this thing,
> something happened. I was
> … somewhere else. It was
> terrifying. But maybe … maybe
> we can learn more about what's
> happening.

KATE looks up at CAVENDISH.

KATE (cont, apprehensive but decisive)
> I'm going to touch it again.

KATE goes to touch the statue, but pauses at the last moment, remembering what happened last time. She looks over to where CAVENDISH is standing.

KATE

> If anything happens ... anything
> at all ... you will help me won't
> you?

CAVENDISH gives a quick sharp smile and a nod.

KATE reaches to touch the statue ...

40. INT: VOID

... and as before, there is a flash of light and sound and she's back in the dark, smoky vortex with lights shining around.

She hears a voice. Asexual and deep.

VOICE (oov)

> The portal is now open. Psionic
> science is superior. We can start
> the ritual.

KATE looks around herself, but there is nothing to be seen, just light and smoke.

CAVENDISH (oov)

      Kate? Kate?

KATE reaches out her hand into the void. There's a shadowy form just visible in front of her.

KATE

      Who's there? I can't see you.

VOICE (oov)

      We no longer need the man …
      now as the power builds, we
      will animate the totem … The
      movement was successful …
      next will be transformation …

As the voice speaks, someone cowled like a monk, the face bowed and hidden from view, emerges from the mists. The camera tracks behind the figure and picks up KATE, who looks at the figure. It slowly raises its head, and KATE's eyes open wide in horror. She screams …

41. EXT – COTTAGE – NIGHT

… and is back by the statue. She's lying on her back, and CAVENDISH is sitting over her.

CAVENDISH (Worried)
> Kate! Kate!

KATE

> I'm … I'm okay. Would it be daft
> to ask what happened?

CAVENDISH (with a glance at the statue)
> You touched it, and then went
> rigid … Then I panicked and
> ran at you, knocking you away.

KATE and CAVENDISH get to their feet. KATE looks
closely at the statue. It's the same as it was before.

KATE

> I don't know what that thing is,
> but I'm not touching it again!
> Let's get back inside.

KATE and CAVENDISH move away from it back towards
the front door of the cottage. KATE looks back at the
statue sitting on the ground outside her window.

Fade to black on KATE's face

ACT THREE

42. EXT: COTTAGE ESTABLISHING SHOT – MORNING

Fade up from black onto the exterior of the cottage. It's morning.

43. INT: COTTAGE LOWER HALL – MORNING

Inside the cottage, KATE and CAVENDISH are sitting huddled at the foot of the stairs. They wake up and groan – they have been there all night.

KATE

> Oh, my back … That's the last night I ever spend scrunched up on some stairs!

CAVENDISH stands and stretches.

KATE

> At least nothing else happened … did it?

CAVENDISH

> I don't think so.

CAVENDISH listens for a moment.

CAVENDISH

> The voices ... in my head ...
> they're not there anymore.

KATE

> When I touched the statue I saw
> someone else ... someone dark
> and hooded ... They said they
> didn't need you any more ...

CAVENDISH

> What did they look like?

KATE

> I only caught a glimpse.
> Deformed ... twisted.

CAVENDISH

> Not our ghost then.

KATE

> No ... no ... this was someone
> else.

CAVENDISH

> I think our *friend* has been

trying to talk to me.

KATE

What does he say?

CAVENDISH

Don't know. Can't hear what he's saying. Then he vanishes.

KATE

Convenient.

CAVENDISH (starting to crack again)

You've got to help me. He's following me. I can't get away. I can't –

KATE (interrupting)

We'll have a proper look around. For starters, what's through that door? A basement?

KATE gets up and goes to the locked door. CAVENDISH looks panicked.

CAVENDISH

I don't know … That is, I've never been down there … It's locked.

312

KATE

> I know it's locked. Where's the key?

CAVENDISH looks guilty.

CAVENDISH

> I threw it away.

KATE (exasperated)

> You threw it ... So how do we figure out what's going on?

CAVENDISH

> I don't want to know ... I just want it to stop.

CAVENDISH holds his head in his hands.

CAVENDISH (cont)

> I want it to stop ...

KATE (gently)

> Then we've got to find out what's happening here. Look, before that ghost appeared, there was some sort of mist coming from under this door. There was a mist

around the statue, and in that …
that other place I went to.

CAVENDISH
You think they're connected?

KATE (gives him a look – it's obvious!)
We *really* need to see what's on
the other side of the door.

KATE lets go of CAVENDISH and moves off.

KATE (cont)
I'm going outside to see if I
can find some tools, or maybe
another way under the cottage.
It should be safe enough now it's
daylight. Will you be okay?

CAVENDISH just sits there.

KATE (insistent)
Will you be okay?

CAVENDISH looks towards the living room. The book
sits on the table.

CAVENDISH
> Yes ... I ... I'll be fine.

KATE sees what he's looking at. She goes into the living room, picks up the book and returns. She smiles at CAVENDISH.

KATE
> Just in case, eh?

As KATE leaves through the front door with the book, CAVENDISH sighs deeply, stands and goes into the living room, shutting the door behind him.

44. INT: COTTAGE LIVING ROOM – DAY

CAVENDISH closes the door and looks at the bottle and glasses on the table. He sits. He's obviously trying not to decide to get blindingly drunk. He rocks a little.

His eye is caught by a calendar on the wall, it's showing October.

CAVENDISH
> Today ... October 31st ... All
> Hallows Eve ...

He thinks he hears something. He goes to listen at the door.

45. EXT: PATH – DAY

KATE eyes the statue on the path. She edges warily round it and heads for the shed.

The statue's head slowly turns to follow her. Its eyes start to glow.

We faintly hear the sound of psionic forces building.

46. INT: COTTAGE LOWER HALL – DAY

The camera prowls the hallway. There is mist pooling under the locked door again. All is otherwise quiet.

47. INT: COTTAGE LIVING ROOM – DAY

CAVENDISH moves from the door back to the table and looks at himself in the mirror, running his hands through his hair. Suddenly, the GHOST fades up in the mirror. CAVENDISH whirls and looks behind him but there is nothing there. He turns back to the mirror and the GHOST is still there.

GHOST

> No, don't run. Please don't run.
> Can you hear me?

CAVENDISH (puzzled)

> Yes … I … I can … but …

GHOST

> There's no time. It's the mirror,
> reflects and conserves power.
> I'm trapped, trapped in time …
> you have to help me … us.

CAVENDISH

> Help you? How?

GHOST

> I know you think you caused
> all this, but you're not to blame.
> Trust me.

CAVENDISH

> Trust *you*?

CAVENDISH shakes his head and balls his fists into his eyes.

CAVENDISH (cont)
>I'm really cracking up now.

GHOST
>There isn't much time left …
>You have to listen …

48. INT: SHED – DAY

KATE places the book somewhere safe in the shed, and starts to sift through the items on the shelves. There's a mixture of garden implements, bulbs, seeds, tools etc, plus bits and bobs of electrical equipment and so on.

She senses something and shivers.

She looks up at the alien in formaldehyde.

We start to hear the twittering of psionic forces. The whole shed starts to rattle.

Staring through the window at KATE is the face of the statue.

49. INT: COTTAGE LIVING ROOM – DAY

CAVENDISH is looking in the mirror at the GHOST. As they talk, CAVENDISH is fascinated by the mirror and reaches to touch the image from time to time.

GHOST

> I come from the future. Your future.

CAVENDISH

> Mine?

GHOST

> And Hell is on Earth. A powerful faction of revolutionaries called the Sodality seized power. They'll kill anyone who stands in their way. They're committed to control and corruption. They use the science of an ancient race of beings called Daemons, and they're unstoppable.

CAVENDISH

> But who are you?

GHOST

> In my era, we were called 'Time Channelers'.

319

As the GHOST speaks, the mirror image fades and we see a montage of images showing what the GHOST is saying. His voice continues as a voice over these images.

50. INT: VOID

We see the hooded monks chanting, smoke wreathed about. This is the Void we have seen before.

We see the GHOST and a female FRIEND running from the monks, before coming right up against one of them. They turn and run again, but are blocked again. The monk points and chants an incantation, and the GHOST twists and falls in pain, unable to breath. The same thing happens to the FRIEND.

GHOST (oov)

> With the aid of our Time Sensitive companions, we roamed history. But the Sodality killed me, destroyed me with psionic power. Now I have only this wretched half-existence, living in the past times I have visited. But it's not all lost.

51. INT: COTTAGE LIVING ROOM – DAY

GHOST (cont)
> This time – this day – is key.

CAVENDISH
> All Hallows Eve.

GHOST
> It's a crucial nexus point. With your help, we can frustrate the Sodality's plans and start to give the future a chance.

CAVENDISH
> You said the Sodality controlled the future …

GHOST (shaking head)
> There are key moments where conditions are right to summon the Daemons themselves. They've opened portals back through time. That's where they'll gain the greatest power of all.

52. INT: SHED – DAY

The psionic forces are in full flow. Things rattling. Stuff thrown about. KATE crouches on the floor, hands over her head.

The bottled alien falls to the floor and smashes. The creature lies in an oozy, giblety mess at KATE's feet – It is dead, so doesn't need animating.

The psionic onslaught dies.

KATE looks up in fright as the door slowly opens.

We see a 'statue' leg step into shot (a human female leg wrapped in plaster bandage), followed by a wholly human female leg, then a second human female leg. The creature is transforming as we see it, at ground level, feet/legs only, approach KATE.

NOTE: The statue is duplicating KATE, so the legs should be the same as KATE's legs, with the same clothes etc. It would be nice if this can be done with bare legs first, then morphing clothes onto them.

53. INT: COTTAGE LIVING ROOM – DAY

CAVENDISH is looking in the mirror at the GHOST.

GHOST

> There are other Time Channelers, people like me who can avert the death of the future before it becomes irreversible.

CAVENDISH

> Am I one? Am I a Time Channeller?

GHOST (smiling wanly)

> No. You're a vessel, someone weak and broken enough to be controlled by the Sodality. They used you to help open the way, but it's not too late!

CAVENDISH

> Tell me –

GHOST (interrupting)

> Where is the book? It has power we can use.

CAVENDISH

> Kate … she took it. She –

There is a loud scream (KATE), and CAVENDISH turns from the mirror. When he looks back, the GHOST has gone.

CAVENDISH heads for the door, and, opening it, peeks out.

CAVENDISH
> Kate?

54. INT: COTTAGE LOWER HALL – DAY

CAVENDISH emerges from the room and peers up the stairs. Nothing.

The front door slowly starts to swing open. KATE (2) is standing there, smiling. She saunters into the cottage. She is looking very sexy and very alluring. Her hair is up in a single ponytail.

KATE (2)
> Hi there ... I'm bored with this.
> Can you come and play awhile?

She giggles.

CAVENDISH

> Kate? What happened, I heard
> you scream.

KATE (2)

> Scream? Did I?

CAVENDISH

> Well *someone* screamed.

CAVENDISH moves past her to the door and checks outside. As he moves past KATE (2), she reaches out and strokes his arm.

KATE (2)

> You know, Douggie, we just
> spent all night together here
> … and you never once really
> noticed me.

> CAVENDISH closes the front
> door.

CAVENDISH

> What do you mean?

KATE (2) (very suggestive)
> Well …

CAVENDISH

> Well ... I ...

KATE (2)

> Come on ... I *know* you like me.

CAVENDISH

> I do ... but ...

KATE (2) (teasing)
> What?

CAVENDISH

> I never get what I want ... but I like you, Kate, I really do ... but ...

KATE reaches out and strokes his face

CAVENDISH

> You're so cold ... so cold ...

CAVENDISH takes her hand in his.

KATE (2)

> Maybe I need warming up?

KATE moves in on CAVENDISH and he backs away.

CAVENDISH

> No … it's not … I'm not …

KATE (2)

> What, Douggie? Don't you want
> me?

CAVENDISH

> Yes … no … I … I don't know
> … keep away.

CAVENDISH backs away, hugging his body with his arms.

KATE (2)

> Aww. Doesn't Douggie want to
> play? What a spoilsport.

KATE (2) is right up to him. Staring him in the eye, she starts on one of the incantations.

KATE (2) (smoochy)

> Wons sa etihw saw eceelf sti
> bmal elttil a dah yram …

CAVENDISH (realising)
> You're not Kate!

KATE (2)
> I could be. Bmal elttil a dah yram …

CAVENDISH
> No!

KATE (2) (suddenly cruel)
> No matter. It's time. You've been struggling far too much …

KATE (2) moves closer to CAVENDISH and he pushes himself up to his feet.

ACT FOUR

55. INT: SHED – DAY

KATE is lying on the ground. The GHOST suddenly appears beside her, growing solid. He kneels and looks over her body.

GHOST

> You have to wake up.

The GHOST places his hand over her head, not quite touching her. KATE stirs and groans.

KATE

> Oh … my head.

GHOST (urgent)

> Come on … while there's still time …

56. INT: COTTAGE LOWER HALL – DAY

CAVENDISH backs away from KATE (2).

CAVENDISH

> No. You're not Kate! Not Kate!

KATE (2) laughs.

KATE (2)

> Of course I'm not Kate! I'm here to give you what you want … and in return, I just need to take a little from you.

57. INT: SHED – DAY

KATE pushes herself up, and looks around groggily. She starts when she sees the GHOST, and backs away.

GHOST

>Don't be afraid. I won't hurt you.

KATE

>Why should I trust you?

GHOST

>I'm an echo, that's all, a living echo of a possible future.

KATE

>I've heard crazier things today …

KATE starts struggling to her feet.

GHOST

>Then listen. The power is building. The portal from the future is opening wider and wider. We can use that power.

KATE

>We? That's as in 'us'?

GHOST

> But the Sodality are strong. They're intent on summoning the Daemon.

KATE

> Whoa ... no, no, no. Hang on. Daemon? Portal?

GHOST

> A passage between times.

KATE (not convinced)
> Oh. Right.

GHOST

> The Sodality used that to influence your friend to fetch the spell book.

KATE looks uncomfortable.

GHOST (cont)

> They used psionic power from the incantations to animate the statue. Here, in this time.

KATE shudders.

KATE

> I think I got in the way of that.

GHOST

> We must hurry. The statue has shifted. It's hunting the final power to secure the Sodality's future.

58. INT: COTTAGE LOWER HALL – DAY

CAVENDISH

> What are you? Are you a Daemon?

KATE (2) laughs.

KATE (2)

> You want to see the form of the Daemons?

KATE (2)'s form ripples and starts to change into something else, something devil-like comprised of smoke and fire. We only briefly glimpse it at this point, mixed in with the form of KATE (2). The creature approaches CAVENDISH, an arm outstretched. CAVENDISH slides around the hall, trying to keep away from the creature.

KATE (2)

> Scary, aren't they.

Suddenly the creature is KATE (2) again, and she takes hold of CAVENDISH's hand. He starts to slump as he feels the energy start to drain from him.

KATE (2)

> *I* am controlled by the Sodality, rulers of Earth. Their power is older than time itself, *from* the shapers of Humanity. But you … with your inquisitive mind and acquisitive nature …

KATE (2) breaths in as though smelling a flower.

KATE (2) (cont)

> That's right … let the power flow through me … *you* who were led to remove an ancient tract of summoning from where it had been secured … *you* have helped us release *their* power … and now … we want to reward you.

59. INT: SHED – DAY

KATE is rummaging through the chaos of the shed, looking to see if CAVENDISH has any other useful things from his time at UNIT stored there.

KATE

> Must be something ... But all he steals are pickled aliens. (TURNS TO THE GHOST) So if these Daemons interfere with Earth's development...

GHOST (nods)

> They are scientists and explorers. They dabble when it suits them ... they've no specific agenda to cause destruction.

KATE

> You come from the future?

GHOST

> Where the Sodality rule using the Daemon's powers.

KATE

> And they've followed you here.

334

GHOST

> Not really. They have limited
> control over time and space.
> They enslaved other Time
> Channellers. But I refused to
> cooperate. That's why they
> killed me.

KATE uncovers a Dalek exterminator on one shelf, but fails to understand its significance.

GHOST (cont)

> I still exist in the times I visited.
> And I can try and disrupt their
> plans. When I saw you arriving,
> I couldn't let you just walk away.
> I need your help.

KATE

> I figured that. (SHE GIVES
> UP HER SEARCH) No good.
> Nothing to use here anyway.
> Unless we're going to throw
> daffodil bulbs at them.

GHOST

> You have the book.

KATE (cagey)
>
> Well, I …

GHOST
>
> I saw you take it.

KATE reluctantly admits defeat. She gestures to where the book was left when she first entered the shed.

KATE
>
> I had to get it away from Douglas.

GHOST
>
> Good. Its power is not easily read.

KATE
>
> Don't look at me. I don't want to read it all.

KATE picks the book up, and looks at it thoughtfully.

KATE
>
> Can't we get rid of it?

GHOST
>
> Better that we use it. Good or
> bad. You can use it for either.

KATE

>Me? (Laughs) You're joking. I
>don't do spells.

GHOST (smiles grimly)

>Who else is there?

60. INT: COTTAGE LOWER HALL – DAY

KATE (2) is still holding CAVENDISH's hand, he has slumped against the wall as the energy is drained from him.

KATE (2)

>Now we need the Horned Beasts
>to grow.

CAVENDISH (exhausted)

>No …

KATE (2)

>We need life force to summon
>them. Their experiment was a
>triumph. *We* are the result. And
>this place shall be our temple to
>them …

As she has been speaking, CAVENDISH's hand and face have grown grey and slack.

CAVENDISH (exhausted)
>You're insane.

KATE (2)
>Not insane … we will have what we always deserved … *total* control … *total* power.

KATE (2) drops his hand and he slumps back. He manages to lift his head, and his eyes open wide looking at the doorway.

Standing in the doorway behind KATE (2) is the GHOST and beside him is KATE. She has the book in her hands.

KATE (2)
>You cannot stop us.

GHOST
>Now I think you can hear me …
>We have the book …

The GHOST indicates KATE standing beside him, holding the book.

KATE (2)

> The book is ours by right.

GHOST

> But it's not in *your* hands.

The GHOST nods to KATE. She raises the book up. The two of them start to walk slowly down the hall. One step at a time.

KATE (2) steps out aggressively to block their way and raises her hand.

KATE (2) (under her breath)

> By the power of the Sodality ...
> regna ni kcab kool tnod ...

The book held by KATE starts to glow slightly. KATE looks surprised, but holds it up determinedly.

GHOST

> Don't stop ... Keep going.

The book glows brighter. It is absorbing the power from KATE (2).

KATE

> It's getting hot.

KATE (2) starts to gasp for air and sway.

GHOST
> Hold on to it. Keep going.

KATE (2) (very unsteady)
> ... regna ni kcab kool tnod ...

KATE (2) moves forward.

CAVENDISH weakly kicks out, hitting KATE (2) in the legs. KATE (2) falls to the ground, allowing KATE and the GHOST to hurry past to the locked door which swings open, smoke billowing around it, and light pulsing brightly from below.

KATE (2) (grovelling on the ground)
> No!

The GHOST and KATE descend through the open door into the smoke. KATE (2) looks furious, and with a contemptible glare at CAVENDISH, who is slumped against the wall, she heads to the previously locked door.

61. INT: CAVERN STEPS

KATE, clutching the book, emerges from darkness down a flight of steps and into a vast network of cavernous tunnels. She is unsure of which way to go, and looks back up the stairs to see KATE (2) just appearing at the top. She hurries off down one of the passages at random.

62. INT: CAVERN TUNNELS

KATE walks along the passage, trying to figure out which way to go. She reaches an intersection and stops. Suddenly, the GHOST is there, and he indicates a direction. KATE hurries after him.

63. INT: CAVERN TUNNELS

KATE (2) moves purposefully along the tunnels.

64. INT: CAVERN ALTAR AREA

A vast open space riddled with tunnels. KATE and the GHOST emerge into the area.

We see the remains of a crude altar in an open area, with the trappings of a black mass on it (black candles, red cloth, sacrificial knife). This is all dismantled and shattered, covered in dust and grime. It's obvious that no-one has been down here for a long time.

KATE

>What is this place?

GHOST

>It's long been a magnet for those
>who would try and gain power.

KATE and the GHOST move towards the broken altar. They look back as KATE (2) emerges from a tunnel across the cavern from them.

KATE (2) eyes them carefully, and like some sort of predator, starts to close in.

KATE (2)

>The time is right. We shall
>summon the Daemon *now* …

KATE (2) stops and stands still, eyes closed, mouth moving, incanting. (Note: it doesn't matter what she says as no words will be heard)

KATE starts to pull the altar back together again, placing the candles upright, and setting the book in place. She opens the book and flicks through pages until the GHOST indicates for her to stop.

The GHOST indicates a line of text in the book, and KATE starts to read it, stumbling over the unfamiliar words

KATE

> Llams dna taerg serutaerc lla ...
> lla lufituaeb dna thgirb sgniht
> lla.

KATE (2) starts to quiver and shake.

KATE (amazed)

> It's working!

GHOST

> Don't lose it ... don't lose it ...
> The book will help you ...

KATE (2) recovers and continues to chant.

KATE (clearly stressed at this)

> Lufrednow dna esiw sgniht lla
>
> ...

KATE (2) staggers again.

KATE (rising panic)
>Lla … lla … I can't read it! I can't
>see the words!

The words in the book are blurring and jumping again.
KATE (2) stops chanting and looks at KATE. She chuckles
evilly and then resumes chanting under her breath, her
arms coming out from her body.

GHOST
>Come *on* Kate. You can do it. The
>book will channel the power.

KATE (concentrating)
>Lla meht edam dog drol eht …

KATE (2) elegantly drops in a kneel to the ground. KATE
breaks off chanting and stares in astonishment.

KATE
>Look!

KATE (2) transforms into the statue briefly as KATE (2)'s
image starts to decompose, finally transforming into
the smoky devil-like form we saw before. There is a wet,
tearing sound and the form detaches from the statue on
the ground and rises to ripple in the Cavern.

GHOST

> We're too late … the portal is
> widening … the Beast is coming
> through.

KATE (determined)

> Not if I can help it.

KATE approaches the statue, holding the book and
continuing to chant.

KATE

> Llams dna taerg serutaerc … lla
> lufituaeb dna thgirb sgniht lla.

As she nears the statue, suddenly, the rippling black
smoky shape rushes at her, and she screams in surprise
and drops the book. She stumbles onto the statue and …

65. INT: VOID

… and is back in the void. The sounds of crying and
screaming and shouting are still evident.

VOICE

> The Daemon has been
> summoned. Increase the power.

Maintain the connection.

Standing around KATE in the void we see a number of hooded MONKS, we do not see their faces. The camera circles around them, with KATE in the centre. She spins and tries to find a way out of the circle, but there is none.

VOICES (chanting)
> Eco eco dah a elttil bmal ... eco
> eco dah a elttil bmal ... eco eco
> dah a elttil bmal

As the camera spins round, so the MONKS slowly start to raise their heads to look at her. We do not see their faces, but KATE looks from one to the other in horror ...

VOICE
> She knows much, but not enough.

The sounds increase in volume and echo as the power levels increase. KATE claps her hands to her ears, and closes her eyes in pain ...

66. INT: CAVERN ALTAR AREA

… and she is lying on the Cavern floor by the statue. The book is lying nearby. The black smoky being is swirling around.

CAVENDISH stumbles into the Cavern behind her. He is weak, but is managing to pull himself along. He half helps, half drags KATE and the book towards the altar where the GHOST is standing. They look up as the swirling shape finally spins faster and faster and eventually, with a crack of thunder, coalesces into a large horned beast – the DAEMON has arrived.

It stands about eight feet tall, a terrifying demonic presence shrouded in darkness. Its goat-like eyes glow red, and it has curved horns in a ring around its face. It has no mouth, just a pulsing dark set of vertical slits through which smoke is emitted. Despite this, its voice echoes around clearly. It is cloaked in smoke. It sizzles and steams as it moves.

The DAEMON's voice is proclamatory and full of confidence.

DAEMON
> Who has summoned me here?

KATE stares at the DAEMON, her mouth dropping open.

The GHOST speaks, but we can't hear anything. It's like a radio going out of tuning. The DAEMON is drawing energy from the surroundings.

GHOST

> No … (there is an) … energy
> drain …

The image of the GHOST is also starting to spark and fade in and out like a badly tuned television.

The DAEMON looks about inquisitively. Its movements are fast and insect-like – a little like the questing of the Ring-Wraiths in *Lord of the Rings*. It eventually focuses on KATE who is standing holding the book.

DAEMON

> I sense the powers which have
> brought me here. They are from
> a distant time.

KATE continues to stare in shock at the creature.

DAEMON

> You … you have the smell of
> power on you. Why have you
> summoned me? Am I to be
> questioned?

348

KATE (shakes her head and recovers a little)
>   Who … what are you?

DAEMON
>   I am Mastho … from a world
>   many light years distant. My
>   people watch as you puny
>   humans play at life.

CAVENDISH (very upset)
>   Must stop this … must stop. All
>   my fault.

CAVENDISH takes the book, and starts frantically flicking through the pages.

CAVENDISH
>   Where is it … where is it …

As he does this, the DAEMON moves closer to him. KATE realises this, and, with a glance at CAVENDISH, moves in the other direction, distracting the creature.

KATE (to the DAEMON)
>   Who are your people? Have you been here
>   before?

KATE backs away across the Cavern. The DAEMON

follows her.

DAEMON

> We have been summoned many
> times. We are interested in how
> our experiment progresses.
> We like to see how this planet
> responds to our input.

KATE

> But why are you here now?

DAEMON

> It amuses us to indulge the
> whims and caprices of you
> humans. In other times we are
> worshipped as gods … I was
> summoned here by those who
> would perhaps seek to control
> me.

KATE reaches the wall. She looks across to where
CAVENDISH and the GHOST are standing. The
DAEMON, seeing her glance, starts back towards them.

CAVENDISH (rousing himself)
> No. I have it …

He smooths out the pages, and prepares to read the text.

CAVENDISH (cont)
> We must stop this ... this evil!

DAEMON (amused)
> Evil? What evil? We do what we do for the sake of science ... if there is some judgement over our interest, then that comes from the heart of man.

KATE walks back from the wall of the Cavern watching as the DAEMON approaches CAVENDISH.

CAVENDISH
> Emac uoy ecnnehw morf ecalp eht ot nomead nruter nruter ...

DAEMON
> But you, the one called Cavendish ...

CAVENDISH stops chanting and looks up.

DAEMON (cont)
> You have more energy for me ... (SMILES) you are broken, and a broken vessel bleeds faster than

> a sound one … Ahhh …What
> do you seek? What is your
> broken heart's desire?

The DAEMON gestures at the statue, and it flickers back into the form of KATE (2) looking radiant.

KATE (2) walks across the Cavern and approaches CAVENDISH. He backs away, eyes wide. She approaches him. He stops, hypnotised by her gaze, a rabbit in headlights. She gently caresses his face, and he looks deeply into her eyes as she talks to him.

KATE (2) (gently)

> What is it you want? You want
> this form? (SHE SMOOTHS
> HER FREE HAND OVER
> HER BODY) You want
> companionship? An end to
> loneliness? To despair? To feeling
> unwanted, and unloved? Give
> me those feelings, that power.

CAVENDISH's eyes fill with tears and he starts to sob, still looking into her eyes, as KATE (2) speaks to him. Behind him, the GHOST is agitating wildly.

KATE (2)
>That's right, you're a good, good
>man.

CAVENDISH's eyes flicker closed, his face is ashen grey. His mouth hangs slackly open.

KATE (2) kneels by the waiting DAEMON, looking up adoringly at the creature.

DAEMON (whispering)
>Power ... freedom ...

KATE (quiet, but firm)
>... from a good man.

The DAEMON turns and regards her.

It moves towards KATE and brushes her cheek almost tenderly. There's a crackle of energy as it does so.

KATE inhales suddenly as though punched in the stomach as the creature takes a rush of energy from her, and then she staggers back.

DAEMON (thoughtful)
>Your father would know what
>to do ...

KATE (drained)

>My father is a good man …
>as is he (GESTURES TO
>CAVENDISH) and if you feel
>you've won, after having fed
>on his desires and hopes, then
>so be it. But I don't have to stay
>and watch.

KATE turns her back and walks unsteadily away across the Cavern.

DAEMON

>Stop!

KATE ignores the DAEMON and keeps walking towards one of the Cavern Tunnels.

67. INT: CAVERN TUNNELS

The DAEMON follows across the Cavern after KATE. After a moment, KATE (2) stands and follows after them as well. She is looking concerned.

DAEMON

>Explain yourself.

KATE

> Why? Can't you tell when there's more important things at stake than power? Don't you have a heart? Look at what you have taken … perhaps you'll find the answer there. But I doubt it.

KATE keeps walking, steadying herself against the Cavern Tunnel walls.

KATE (cont)

> If you're going to destroy the Earth, or whatever it is you *want* to do, then I *want* to be with the people I love. My son. My dad …

The DAEMON starts to laugh.

KATE

> That's more important than arguing with you.

Suddenly the DAEMON is there in front of KATE.

DAEMON

> That is an interesting observation, human. Power

causes you to react in different ways.

KATE (2) appears behind KATE.

The DAEMON regards KATE (2).

DAEMON (thoughtful)
Ahh ... my channel to the future. What have you to say?

KATE (2)
Power is whatever humanity makes of it. You are simply the catalyst, not the cause or the reaction.

KATE turns and walks off down another passage. It re-emerges into the main area where she sees CAVENDISH collapsed by the altar. She turns on her heel and re-enters the tunnel, but the DAEMON is suddenly there again in front of her.

DAEMON
... the Portal is still open. I can feel the Sodality probing, testing me with their rituals and their bindings ...

KATE

    So what do *you* want?

DAEMON (searching his stolen energy)

    Cavendish was lonely …
    despairing … he wanted … he
    wanted …

KATE

    Love?

KATE (2) laughs loudly at this, and KATE sees her walk
out behind the DAEMON.

DAEMON (thoughtful)

    I cannot recognise that. But there
    is much which interests me.

KATE (2)

    We are taking what is rightfully
    ours. The power to control this
    zone, to extend our worship
    of you through all times. Love
    does not come into it.

KATE

    But power corrupts … Love
    heals. A world without Love is

pointless.

KATE (2) (scornful)

>Love is transient. Humans die every day, love unrequited. Pathetic.

KATE

>But love transcends death. Why do people mourn? Because they have lost something precious and valuable. Because they *continue* to love.

KATE (2) (To the DAEMON)

>Don't listen to her. She's trying to trick you. You have been summoned by the Sodality … you must obey.

The DAEMON regards KATE (2) with interest.

DAEMON (amused)

>Obey? You … what are you? An artefact controlled from the future by those who would seek my power. Do *you* know this thing called love?

KATE (2)

> With power there is no need
> for love.

The DAEMON laughs.

DAEMON

> Power ... power! Is that all your
> puny minds can conceive?

KATE (2) looks concerned. She turns her thoughts inwards, and starts to mutter incantations to herself.

KATE (2)

> Eco eco dah a elttil bmal ... eco
> eco dah a elttil bmal ... eco eco
> dah a elttil bmal

KATE (To the DAEMON)

> So go on then ... do whatever it
> is you were summoned for ...

DAEMON

> The Sodality want my power to
> control this temporal zone. Even
> now they are preparing to take
> it. But I am a Daemon, and they
> *dare* to try and shackle me.

The DAEMON pauses, thoughtful.

DAEMON

> Love ... You humans are fascinating. Three times I can be summoned. This Sodality forgets this. Perhaps they need reminding ... and their portal works both ways ... The experiment continues.

The DAEMON turns to KATE (2) who is still chanting. It lifts its hand and touches KATE (2)'s head. She stops chanting and screams loudly as she and the DAEMON fade away, leaving her screams echoing around the corridors.

KATE turns and heads off back down the Cavern Tunnel towards the main area.

68. INT: CAVERN ALTAR AREA

KATE re-enters the Cavern and hurries to where CAVENDISH is slumped on the floor. The GHOST is still there but very faint now.

CAVENDISH (very weak)
> You managed to distract him.

KATE
> I'm not so sure.

CAVENDISH
> And we're safe …

KATE
> For the moment.

CAVENDISH (relieved)
> Thank you Kate.

KATE
> That … creature, Mastho. It seemed very sure of itself. And three times it said … does that mean it will be back?

CAVENDISH (sleepy)
> Can't see the future.

KATE
> Pick a future. Any future at all.

KATE looks up and sees the GHOST staring back at her.

He's very faint and faded. He lowers his eyes and fades completely.

KATE

    Does that mean we won … or …

KATE's eyes drift to the book which is lying open on a page. We slowly pan to the book and zoom in on an image of death and horror pictured therein.

Bring up the sounds of screaming and torture

Crash to black

END CREDITS

Face of the Fendahl

CHARACTERS

BARNABY TEWKES

Time Channeller and 'Ghost' from last film. He was in Antioch with his Time Sensitive companion, drawn there by the power from the mythical Spear of Longius. They have been able to use some of the residual psychic energy from the First Crusade to give Barnaby a body, however when trying to get to the spear, they became trapped by Vincente in his castle outside Antioch. Barnaby's motivation is to get back Catherine and to gain enough power to time-jump back to the future to share the knowledge they have.

COSTUME: Same as the first film – black and silver trousers suit outfit.

CATHERINE

Barnaby's Time Sensitive companion. She is young and very pretty, however this belies a great strength inside. She has been taken over by the Fendahl in preparation for it using her as its core, and Vincente has been summoning the Fendahl using the 'spear', which is in fact a fragment of bone imprinted with the Fendahl's DNA codes. She is in thrall to Vincente, and he is using her to kill his enemies and the resultant psychic shockwaves (and from the Crusade massacres at Antioch itself) are bringing the Fendahl into existence.

COSTUME: Either a female equivalent of Barnaby's outfit, but sexy with cleavage and looking faintly period. OR: A period outfit in velvets with a corset and so on.

VINCENTE

Think Vincent Price in *The Masque Of The Red Death*. A totally corrupt man, seeking ultimate power. He has found he can summon 'Death' – his master – in the form of Catherine to kill his enemies, and Barnaby he sees as a helpless fly against his might. He intends to sacrifice Cavendish, Kate, Barnaby and anyone else he can muster in a final summoning of the Fendahl. He is also a Sodality agent from the future …

COSTUME: Period outfit typical of the old Corman films. Jerkin and leggings, but rich-looking, befitting someone who thinks they are a Prince.

IBRAHIM

A deserter from the Turkish armies besieging Antioch. He does not understand most of what is happening, but can see that Catherine is in danger and wants to help. He does not trust Cavendish and Kate, seeing them as agents of the Crusade.

COSTUME: Robes with a rope belt.

CAVENDISH AND KATE

Our heroes from *Daemos Rising*. They are brought to this place by Barnaby as he wants to sacrifice them to get Catherine back. Barnaby realises that Cavendish may be susceptible to the Fendahl as well and so wants to use him. Kate won't allow this of course.

COSTUMES: CAVENDISH: as from the first film – a rumpled shirt and black trousers. KATE: a summer dress.

Face of the Fendahl

1. INT: CASTLE CORRIDORS AND ROOMS

A castle, camera prowls around. Wisps of smoke here and there, to create an eerie atmosphere. We hear whispered voices, but we can't really make out the words. It's too echoey and distant.

This sequence is fast cut into a montage of images of the castle leading to:

2. INT: CASTLE CORRIDORS

We hear footsteps. Running. A GIRL of about 21 years old comes into view and runs along the corridors. She is terrified by something and keeps looking behind her as she runs. She is wearing a period costume a la *Masque Of The Red Death* – a tight corseted top and a light flowing skirt beneath. Her hair is a mess.

She runs down some steps and to a door. It is locked. She turns and regards the stairs, where a BLACK CLOAKED FIGURE is descending. We don't see its face.

Cut to

The FIGURE moving jerkily as though all its bones have been broken.

Cut back to

The GIRL shaking her head in denial. She screams, and the scream ends with a gargle.

Cut to

Blackness. We hear a sucking sound. Camera pulls back to reveal the figure in black moving away from a mummified corpse, which is all that is left of the GIRL.

TITLES

FACE OF THE FENDAHL

By David J Howe

ACT ONE

3. INT: CASTLE CORRIDORS

Castle corridors as before. We hear footsteps and a man walks into view. This is BARNABY (our time travelling ghost). He looks around and continues walking. He's wearing his outfit from the first film.

Tracking shot as camera follows him.

4. INT: MAIN HALL

We follow him into a main hall. It is very run-down and decrepit. There are tattered and faded wall hangings and flags. A long table is covered with a ragged cloth and old candles burn in sticks thereon. At the end of the room is a throne-like chair, and on this sits PRINCE VINCENTE (pronounced Vin-cent-ee) regarding a goblet of wine speculatively. He is a hard-faced man, with a small goatee beard. His whole manner is expansive and full of total confidence.

VINCENTE is dressed in finery; he considers himself to be a Prince and above everyone else and so he dresses and acts accordingly. He is very much based on and played as Vincent Price in any number of the old Roger Corman films of the '60s. Everything he says is with an arch and ironic air.

He turns as BARNABY enters.

VINCENTE

> Ah, Barnaby, how goes the day?

BARNABY

> My Lord.

VINCENTE (slyly – he knows this will get a reaction)

> And your friend … She's a pretty one to be sure. So kind of you to introduce us.

BARNABY looks pained.

VINCENTE: (Pauses a moment to finish his goblet of wine)

> Come.

He stands, then sweeps out of the room. BARNABY follows him, glaring at his back.

5. INT: CASTLE CORRIDORS AND STEPS

BARNABY and VINCENTE head up some steps and arrive at a doorway and VINCENTE breezes in without knocking.

6. INT: CATHERINE'S BEDCHAMBER

Sitting with her back to the camera is CATHERINE, dressed in a sexy period outfit, with maybe a hint of BARNABY's outfit in it as well (to show that they are actually connected).

CATHERINE is a woman of about 25-30 years old, startling to look at, slim and very attractive.

VINCENTE

> Ah, Catherine my dear. How are you this day?

There is no reply or movement from CATHERINE.

VINCENTE breezes around the room and checks the curtains/out the window and generally looks at whatever there is in there.

VINCENTE

> You really shouldn't exert yourself too much, you know, it can be very tiring fighting me all the time … You should relax and let things happen. Much easier in the long run.

BARNABY moves around the room, peering in concern at CATHERINE.

BARNABY (trying to keep his emotions under control)
> What have you done to her?

VINCENTE
> Just a little potion of my own devising, my friend. Nothing to worry about. I find that from time to time my partners need a little … something to relax them and make them better suited to … my enjoyment.

BARNABY (half to himself)
> But what do *you* enjoy?

VINCENTE (overhearing)
> Enjoy, my friend? Enjoy? Why, to try and place measures and balances on simple enjoyment is a near impossible art. I have my vices … and my demons … and sometimes I like to share these with others … Perhaps you will partake with me one time, my friend. After all, you arrived here a mystery to me …

He runs his hand through the unresisting CATHERINE's hair.

VINCENTE (Cont.)
> … and bearing such a pretty gift, that it seems only right that I should repay your generosity

with some of my own.

BARNABY (through gritted teeth)
> You have been *most* generous, my Lord.

VINCENTE
> I have, haven't I? Now we must leave the lovely Catherine here awhile to become accustomed to her new life …

VINCENTE turns and sweeps from the room.

VINCENTE (as he leaves the room)
> Wine, I think, and a little sustenance before I retire.

BARNABY pauses to look worriedly at CATHERINE and then he turns and follows VINCENTE out.

7. EXT: CASTLE EXTERIOR (MONTAGE)

We see some establishing shots around the castle, the views, the sun, the beach and the rocky areas.

8. EXT: HOLLOWED ROCK AREA

We end on the hollowed rock area, and after a moment there is a shimmering of blue light and flashes and sparks of electricity within the centre of the rock. There is a flash and CAVENDISH and KATE step through the rock from nowhere.

As they step through, they are arguing. CAVENDISH is dressed in his customary scruffy suit and KATE is wearing a summer dress.

KATE (section in brackets won't be heard)

> ((He can just summon us and we don't))
> … know where we're going to end up or anything, it's ridiculous …

CAVENDISH

> But you still agree to come along, every time … Sometimes I wonder …

CAVENDISH has a silver hip flash in his hand and sips from it. He seems to take strength from the action.

KATE

> … and you brought that thing with you as well … How many times Douglas …? How many times do I have to …?

KATE suddenly realises where they are and looks around

CAVENDISH (over KATE's reaction to where they are)
It helps me relax … I told you that …

KATE
Oh my word. It's gorgeous.

CAVENDISH eyes the scenery and takes another guilty sip from his flask before stoppering it and shoving it in his pocket.

KATE and CAVENDISH step forward some more and look back at the stone archway, which is now completely normal.

KATE
I suppose we'd better go and find out what trouble our friend has got himself into this time.

CAVENDISH (muttering)
… and what that will mean for us …

They head off.

9. EXT: CASTLE COURTYARD AND DOORWAY

CAVENDISH and KATE approach the main Castle entrance. They are very impressed with what they're seeing.

They arrive at the door and KATE knocks.

There is no answer, so CAVENDISH reaches out and pushes against the door. It swings open, revealing a dark interior.

With a glance at each other, they step through into the Castle.

10. INT: CASTLE HALLWAY

CAVENDISH and KATE enter the Castle and CAVENDISH pushes the door shut behind them.

KATE (whispering)
>   I wonder if anyone's home.

There are footsteps and VINCENTE arrives, sweeping in as usual.

VINCENTE (enthusiastically)

> My friends, my friends, welcome to my humble home. Come in, you are most welcome.

He glances at their attire but makes no comment.

KATE

> Thanks. We're …

VINCENTE

> Introductions can wait, my dear. For the moment, know that you are safe and now under my protection from the war and unrest that sweep this troubled land. Come …

VINCENTE sweeps away towards the MAIN HALL, and CAVENDISH and KATE, with a glance at each other, follow him.

11. INT: MAIN HALL

VINCENTE sweeps in followed by CAVENDISH and KATE. He is talking enthusiastically. The first section in brackets can be overlapped with the end of the previous scene if that works.

VINCENTE

>((Of course this)) castle used to be the centre of life in Antioch, before the Christians came and laid siege to the place. Now no-one can venture here, and all my noble vassals and squires have been seconded to the battles. We are getting by though …

VINCENTE takes two goblets and splashes wine into them from a flagon. He passes one to CAVENDISH who sniffs it experimentally, and one to KATE who sets it on the table.

CAVENDISH (recovering himself)

>Forgive me … Whom do we have the honour of meeting?

VINCENTE

>Oh my good sir, I forget my manners. I am Prince Vincente of this noble land. Protector and friend of all travellers who pass this way.

CAVENDISH

>Oh …

CAVENDISH nods at VINCENTE.

KATE

> This war you speak of … Christians, you say
> …?

VINCENTE

> You have not heard of the Holy War? The
> dictum of Pope Urban to his countrymen to
> oust the unbelievers from the Holy City of
> Jerusalem …?

This next part of VINCENTE's speech is under KATE
and CAVENDISH whispering to each other.

VINCENTE (cont)

> It is a valid and most wonderful crusade,
> bringing justice and right to the lands. As
> Pope Urban himself decreed: 'For your
> brethren who live in the East are in urgent
> need of your help, and you must hasten
> to give them the aid that has often been
> promised them.'

As VINCENTE speaks he parades around the room, and
CAVENDISH and KATE whisper to one another.

KATE

> It's the first Crusade … We're in the middle
> of the siege of Antioch!

CAVENDISH

> Keep your voice down … He may seem friendly enough, but there's something about him …

KATE

> But the year is 1098 or something … We're stuck in the middle ages!

VINCENTE (turning to Kate)

> But, my dear, your clothes are hardly suitable to this environment. Go. Freshen up. And on your return we shall speak more of your travels.

VINCENTE turns to CAVENDISH and eyes his clothes as well.

CAVENDISH (thinking fast)

> Oh, these. These are standard issue. Captain in the … Prussian Army. Here on manoeuvres … Very hush hush.

CAVENDISH taps his finger on his nose.

VINCENTE is puzzled

VINCENTE

> I know not of which you speak, but you have the bearing of a man versed in military matters and I would speak with you further on this.

There is a hammering on the door.

VINCENTE (with a bow)

> Excuse me.

VINCENTE sweeps out of the room.

KATE

> How are we going to get out of this one?

CAVENDISH

> Don't worry. I'm sure our ghostly friend is around here somewhere. Hopefully he can explain what's going on …

VINCENTE returns moments later with IBRAHIM. IBRAHIM is a black-skinned Turk, dressed in robes.

VINCENTE (delighted)

> More visitors. This truly is tremendous news. We are ready for the celebrations. You, my dear, must go prepare, while I must start

supervising the surprises to come.

He sweeps from the room.

KATE

> What was all that about?

CAVENDISH

> No idea. But you've a chance to go and have a look around and see what … and who … you can find. I'll see what I can learn here.

KATE leaves the room through the entry door.

CAVENDISH goes up to IBRAHIM and holds out his hand to him. IBRAHIM looks at the hand and at CAVENDISH and makes no attempt to shake it. CAVENDISH is embarrassed, and covers up, shoving his hand in his pocket.

CAVENDISH

> Cavendish, Captain Douglas Cavendish … UNIT …
>
> ((He breaks off mid way through saying UNIT and changes it))
>
> … Prussian Army.

Behind CAVENDISH, VINCENTE lurks in the doorway. He nods meaningfully at IBRAHIM, who nods back.

CAVENDISH (cont.)

You have me at a disadvantage …

IBRAHIM (Haltingly at first)

You must excuse my bad manners. It is a long time since I have seen, even less spoken to a white man without killing him. My name is Ibrahim, and I am a … a deserter from the Turkish Army of Kerbogha, which even now is being defeated by the white infidel who have taken Antioch.

CAVENDISH

The fighting's been bad then?

IBRAHIM

It was a bloodbath. The Christians were on the run, but then the tide turned, and they surged against our people, full of zeal and religious might. We could do nothing.

CAVENDISH

So you got out …

IBRAHIM (nods slowly)

383

It gives me no pleasure to admit this.

12. INT: CASTLE CORRIDORS

KATE walks down some corridors, looking for whatever she can find, maybe peering into rooms as she passes, and finds herself in a dead end room.

13. INT: CASTLE DEAD END ROOM

Suddenly BARNABY is there behind her (emerging from the darkness).

BARNABY

>Kate?

KATE (swings round in surprise)

>Oh, you! There you are!

BARNABY

>How was the transfer this time? Not too much of a shock to the system?

KATE

>It takes more than that to put off a Lethbridge-Stewart. Besides, when the portal opens, we

don't get a lot of choice.

BARNABY

How's Douglas?

KATE (sniffs)

Him. Pain in the ass. He's turned to drink again. I did what I could ...

BARNABY

I'm so sorry Kate. I hoped with these trips ...

KATE (pulling herself up)

It's okay. I'm just a martyr to a good cause. So ... what have you got yourself into this time?

BARNABY

To coin a phrase, there's good news and bad news.

KATE

Oh great.

BARNABY

The good news is that I've been able to reinstate my body using energy from this era

… I'm no longer a ghost, Kate.

KATE

>Really?

KATE reaches out and touches BARNABY on the arm. Then on the shoulder.

KATE

>That's a difference. It's good to … feel you …

KATE and BARNABY hug.

BARNABY

>But I've lost my companion. And that's where I need your help. She's been taken by Vincente and drugged or mesmerised or something … I don't know. But I have to get her back, otherwise … we'll all be trapped here.

KATE

>Trapped?

BARNABY (nods)

>Yes. We can travel, but it needs our combined abilities to do that.

KATE

> So you finally found yourself a companion.

BARNABY

> Yes. Catherine. She's amazing … I … I'm lost without her.

KATE

> So what can Douglas and I do? You must have a plan … I don't want to end up spending the rest of my life in a godforsaken castle in the middle ages …and I just realised, I don't even know your name!

BARNABY

> (Laughs) It was a bit hectic last time, wasn't it? My name's Barnaby. Barnaby Tewkes. Time traveller, explorer, adventurer. At your service.

BARNABY bows formally and shakes KATE's hand. KATE smiles.

BARNABY

> And a plan? Not really … I just knew that if I had more friends here then Vincente might get distracted enough from his own schemes …

KATE

>Schemes? What's he scheming? It's not the Daemons again, is it?

>((NOTE: Daemons is pronounced: Day-mons))

BARNABY

>No, it's not the Daemons. Not this time.

14. EXT: CASTLE PARAPET

CAVENDISH and IBRAHIM are standing on top of the Castle parapet, looking out over the views. The sun is setting and the scenery is gorgeous.

IBRAHIM

>Somewhere out there, my brothers are being slaughtered like cattle.

CAVENDISH

>Why are you fighting anyway?

IBRAHIM

>It is the infidel from the Christian countries. They think we should not be living in their Holy cities, drinking their Holy wine, and

eating their Holy grain, and they believe they have God on their side.

CAVENDISH

> Why should they believe that?

There is a groan from behind them, and CAVENDISH turns to see a badly injured MAN resting against the wall, just around from them.

CAVENDISH checks the MAN, but he is dying and very nearly unconscious.

CAVENDISH

> I wonder what happened here …

While IBRAHIM and CAVENDISH speak, VINCENTE appears behind them, and stands there listening, unseen by either of the other men.

IBRAHIM

> The infidel were given a sign from God … something that took them into battle again when all hope had seemed lost for them.

CAVENDISH

> What sign?

IBRAHIM

A spear head. Something found by Peter Bartholomew in the Church building in Antioch.

CAVENDISH

A spear head? How can that be inspirational?

IBRAHIM

It is said to be the spear that pierced the side of the Christ as he hung on the cross. But I have done what I can to help my brothers … I have it here …

CAVENDISH

You have it? You mean you stole it?

IBRAHIM

It was not Peter Bartholomew's in the first place, so no theft can have taken place. It is here …

IBRAHIM shows CAVENDISH a pouch he has around his body.

IBRAHIM (cont)

… I was able to remove it during the battles.

Now let us see if God remains on the side of the infidel …

VINCENTE (striding over and making himself known)
My friends. I'm delighted you're getting to know each other. And my dear Ibrahim … you have done as I asked.

IBRAHIM (bows his head)
Master.

VINCENTE
You are a good and loyal servant, as I knew you would be when we first met …

VINCENTE turns to CAVENDISH

VINCENTE (cont)
You see, I leave nothing to chance. When my friend here appeared at my door on the way to Antioch, seeking shelter, I was happy to provide it … on one condition … that he bring me the so-called Spear. And now he has, the celebration can begin.

VINCENTE unsheathes a small knife and, looking at the dying MAN as one might look at a side of beef, gently pokes the MAN with the knife, eliciting another groan.

CAVENDISH does not know what to do.

CAVENDISH (trying to distract VINCENTE)
> You mentioned a celebration before … what
> celebration? What is there to celebrate here?

VINCENTE continues to idly carve at the MAN with the knife as he speaks. The MAN's protestations becoming weaker and weaker. VINCENTE is cutting a pentagram into the man's chest.

VINCENTE
> We are to welcome my Master to this place.
> He will be joining us at last.

CAVENDISH
> Who is your Master?

VINCENTE (smiling cruelly)
> You will find out in good time. You will know
> him when you meet him. And he meets with
> everyone at some stage.

VINCENTE makes a final thrust with the knife deep into the MAN, who dies with a sigh.

VINCENTE (quietly)
> He comes to everyone …

ACT TWO

15. EXT: ESTABLISHING SHOT OF CASTLE

The sun is setting on the castle.

16. EXT: CASTLE PARAPET

CAVENDISH and KATE are kneeling over the dead body of the MAN.

CAVENDISH

> ... and then he just killed him. Without a flicker of emotion.

KATE

> But that's horrible. And look at the symbol ... a pentagram. But Barnaby said ...

CAVENDISH

> Barnaby?

KATE

> That's the name of our ghostly friend. He told me. And he told me that the Daemons aren't involved.

CAVENDISH

> You found him then. (Gestures to the pentagram.) I recognise this from the Book – if it's not the Daemons, then it's probably something connected.

CAVENDISH pulls out his flask and takes a sip of the contents, looking nervously around himself.

KATE

> Must you do that? You know you can't be trusted when you've had too much. And we can't run the risk of you not being able to cope with whatever it is that this Vincente is cooking up.

CAVENDISH

> I'll … I'll be okay. I just need something …

KATE

> You and your nerves. You'd be better off staying sober.

KATE sighs and looks out over the countryside.

KATE (cont)

> It's such a beautiful land, but even here there is so much death and horror. Barnaby told

me about the war, about the Christians being slaughtered by the Turks. He's looking for his companion, Douglas. She's being held prisoner by Vincente.

CAVENDISH

And he wants us to help him get her back …

KATE

Yes … but there was something about him … something I couldn't quite put my finger on. He seemed … guarded about something. As though he wasn't telling me the full story.

CAVENDISH

I guess we'll find out in good time.

VINCENTE arrives on the rooftop behind them and strides over.

VINCENTE

My friends. Everything has been prepared. You are most honoured. You will meet my Master this very night.

CAVENDISH and KATE exchange a worried look.

VINCENTE
>But first I need to be amused.

VINCENTE turns and sweeps away.

VINCENTE (cont)
>Join me in the main hall.

CAVENDISH and KATE exchange another look and follow after VINCENTE.

17. INT: MAIN HALL

In the main hall there are a table, chairs and some bread and wine set out. There's a roaring fire in the grate, and VINCENTE is warming himself by it.

IBRAHIM is lounging on one of the chairs, drinking from a goblet of wine.

CAVENDISH and KATE enter and look around.

VINCENTE (turning from the fire)
>Ah my friends. Kate. Join me by the fire here. The night air is chilly.

KATE moves to stand by VINCENTE and he holds her

face in his hands and studies it intently.

VINCENTE
> You are so beautiful, my dear.

As VINCENTE talks, so BARNABY enters the room and stands by the door, watching.

VINCENTE (cont)
> Beautiful. And so like my darling Catherine ...I can see the lines of power that mark you both.

VINCENTE releases KATE and she steps away, idly rubbing her face where VINCENTE was holding her.

VINCENTE claps his hands together.

VINCENTE
> But I need some sport. Some entertainment to set tonight's events underway.

VINCENTE moves to stand behind IBRAHIM. CAVENDISH meanwhile is looking for some wine he can pour to drink.

VINCENTE puts his hands on IBRAHIM's shoulders

VINCENTE

> What would you say, Ibrahim. What sport can we devise that would involve the fair Kate here?

IBRAHIM starts laughing to himself, and rubs his hands crudely on his tunic. He pushes himself to his feet and moves towards KATE, lust on his face.

IBRAHIM

> I know of one good sport that can be had …

IBRAHIM makes a grab for KATE but she steps out of the way.

KATE

> No … I'm no sport … Douglas!!

CAVENDISH is distracted from where he has been looking for wine, and comes over to where KATE is being herded into a corner by a laughing IBRAHIM

CAVENDISH

> That's not very gentlemanly, old boy.

CAVENDISH grasps IBRAHIM's shoulder and pulls him away from KATE.

IBRAHIM snorts with disdain and tries to get to KATE again, but CAVENDISH insinuates himself between them and pushes him back.

CAVENDISH

  I don't think the lady wants to play tonight. Sorry about that.

IBRAHIM

  No infidel tells me what to do …

IBRAHIM picks a sword up off the table and waves the point at CAVENDISH, who edges around the room so that KATE is not in any danger.

CAVENDISH lunges and picks up another sword.

IBRAHIM and CAVENDISH fight.

As they fight, so VINCENTE claps and cheers them on, thoroughly enjoying the spectacle.

Also, as the fight progresses, BARNABY slinks away out of the room.

18. INT: CASTLE CORRIDORS

BARNABY makes his way through the corridors to CATHERINE's bedchamber.

19: INT: DOOR TO CATHERINE'S BEDCHAMBER

BARNABY listens at the door.

20: INT: CATHERINE'S BEDCHAMBER

CATHERINE is still sitting as she was before. Still and silent.

21. INT: MAIN HALL

CAVENDISH and IBRAHIM fight in the main hall while VINCENTE claps his hands together in glee, and KATE watches in horror.

22. INT: CATHERINE'S BEDCHAMBER

BARNABY enters CATHERINE's room. She is still and silent.

He kneels before her.

BARNABY

>Catherine? Catherine? Can you hear me?

BARNABY starts to break down in tears

BARNABY

>Oh please, Catherine, my love, my life, please come back to me. Whatever Vincente has done, fight it. Fight it my love.

When there is no reaction at all, BARNABY kisses CATHERINE on her unresisting lips and brushes her hair away from her face.

BARNABY

>I will rescue you, my darling. Whatever it takes, and whoever it takes, I will not let this happen to you.

23. INT: MAIN HALL

The fight between CAVENDISH and IBRAHIM comes to an end. CAVENDISH pins IBRAHIM to the floor.

CAVENDISH

    Should I end your life now?

IBRAHIM (with disgust)

    Infidel. ((Spits)) Better you do that, or I will
    surely kill you next time.

CAVENDISH (coming to a decision)

    No.

CAVENDISH removes his sword.

CAVENDISH (cont)

    No. You may live Ibrahim. I have no wish to
    take the life of another man.

KATE looks very impressed with CAVENDISH at this.
She is thinking that maybe she has underestimated him.

VINCENTE (clapping)

    Bravo … Bravo. Such sport for an evening.
    Do you not agree, Ibrahim?

VINCENTE bends and pulls the pouch containing the
spear off IBRAHIM

VINCENTE

    And to the victor … the spoils I think.

VINCENTE unwraps the spear. It is not a spear, but a spear-shaped shard of bone. Very old, and etched with all manner of cabbalistic symbols and designs. Among them is a pentacle. VINCENTE looks upon it almost reverentially.

VINCENTE (whispering to himself)
> At last … the shard of power … after all this time.

VINCENTE suddenly strides over to Kate and grasps her hand in his.

CAVENDISH
> No … stop.

VINCENTE
> Now we shall see if the summoning works …

VINCENTE scratches KATE's left hand with the shard, drawing blood. KATE cries out.

VINCENTE (cont)
> Now we shall see.

The room darkens and a cold wind blows through. There is the sound of rising power.

VINCENTE starts to laugh, placing the shard on the table.

VINCENTE

> See … it begins …

24. INT: CATHERINE'S BEDCHAMBER

Inside CATHERINE's room, BARNABY hears the power start to rise and backs away as CATHERINE's eyes start to glow golden.

CATHERINE stands and leaves the room, heading downstairs in a trance-like state. She is moving in a jerky manner.

25. INT: CASTLE CORRIDORS AND STEPS

CATHERINE, golden eyed and in a trance, heads for the main hall.

BARNABY follows behind her, looking worried and terrified.

26. INT: MAIN HALL

CAVENDISH grabs KATE away from the laughing VINCENTE, looking at the cut on her hand.

KATE

It's all right, it's just a scratch.

CAVENDISH pulls out a handkerchief and roughly wraps it around KATE's hand.

CAVENDISH

I hope so.

VINCENTE

Nothing can stop my Master … even the small sacrifices are sustenance to him.

The doors open and CATHERINE enters. Her eyes are glowing gold, and she has an evil smile on her face. We hear the faint sucking slurping sounds of the Fendahl all around and the whine of power.

CAVENDISH

Oh my god!

KATE

What's happened to her!

VINCENTE laughs with pleasure.

VINCENTE

My Master has power over all death, and his name shall be heard across the land before this night is over.

VINCENTE approaches CATHERINE with deference.

VINCENTE

Welcome. Welcome.

VINCENTE turns to the others.

VINCENTE

Behold, my Master … the Fendahl. And now, with the shard, I have the ultimate power … He comes for those I mark.

VINCENTE looks at KATE and smiles like a hungry panther. KATE cowers backwards.

CATHERINE approaches KATE around the table, but CAVENDISH blocks her way. Behind them, BARNABY enters the room and looks on.

As CATHERINE and KATE start a slow dance around the room, KATE trying to keep out of the way of the possessed woman, BARNABY picks up the shard, which VINCENTE has left on the table, and makes his way towards IBRAHIM.

IBRAHIM is watching and laughing as CAVENDISH and KATE scrabble backwards in an attempt to get away from CATHERINE.

BARNABY suddenly lunges and scratches IBRAHIM on the arm with the shard. Blood runs down IBRAHIM's arm.

CATHERINE stops, sensing the new victim, and moves towards IBRAHIM instead. She leans over him, her hand seeking the back of his neck. He stiffens and screams horribly as the life is sucked out of him – she smiles with cruel pleasure as his life is taken. BARNABY drops the shard in horror as he watches.

CATHERINE lets IBRAHIM's mummified body slump to the ground and turns to face the others. She reverts to human form having fed.

The others are all somewhat shocked, including VINCENTE.

CATHERINE (hollow and slightly distant voice)
        Number 11.

CATHERINE glances at the mummified corpse.

CATHERINE (cont)
> One more and the summoning will be complete.

CATHERINE raises her hand and points at VINCENTE, then swings to point at each of the others in turn.

CATHERINE
> The power is strong now, and the Fendahleen roam the corridors and passages of this place. One more …

CATHERINE turns and walks jerkily away.

VINCENTE (recovering himself and applauding)
> Excellent. Superb.

CAVENDISH
> What do you mean? How can ((he gestures to the corpse)) this be superb?

KATE (checking her hand)
> I think he's insane.

VINCENTE
> Insane? You think so? One more needed

… and I have three guests staying. Nothing could be better.

BARNABY

> You're a madman! What have you done to Catherine?

VINCENTE

> Done? My dear chap I've done nothing. Simply the application of a few herbs and spices in her drink to make her … receptive. That's all. She has a … talent for this, don't you think?

BARNABY (very angry)

> I'll kill you for this!

BARNABY launches himself at VINCENTE and the two men struggle together. At one point they are face to face, and BARNABY's face creases in confusion.

BARNABY (confused)

> But you're not … you're not …

While BARNABY is distracted, VINCENTE pushes him away and, laughing, picks up the Shard and strides from the room.

BARNABY slumps in a chair, and CAVENDISH turns on him.

CAVENDISH

> Time for some answers, I think.

BARNABY (distraught)

> Catherine … my Catherine …

CAVENDISH

> What's happened to her? Why is she like that?

BARNABY

> It's Vincente. We arrived here drawn by the sense of power in this zone, but then Catherine was taken unawares and before I could do anything, he had her controlled and bent to his will.

BARNABY picks up a goblet of wine from the table and studies it for a moment as he speaks. Then he throws it violently across the room.

BARNABY (cont)

> Whatever he's done to her, I can't seem to break through, but without her I can't escape. Vincente is the key to all this, but he's not all

he seems.

KATE

Who ... or what ... is he then?

BARNABY

When I touched him just now, I sensed a great age, stretching into the future.

KATE

He's one of the Sodality?

BARNABY

Yes ... I think so. That twisted cabal of evil men intent on controlling the future. We weren't sure at first, but now I'm certain.

CAVENDISH

What's he doing here?

BARNABY gets up and goes to check on IBRAHIM's corpse.

BARNABY

It's the crusade ... He's using the psychic energy generated by the death and terror to feed this thing he calls Fendahl. But there are peaks and troughs as the battle ebbs and flows. He's been killing people here – he needs 12 ritual deaths before this Fendahl creature can fully manifest, and our friend here was the eleventh …

KATE

I don't like the sound of all this. So one of us is going to be the twelfth victim?

CAVENDISH

Unless we can stop him.

BARNABY

There's no stopping him.

CAVENDISH

Spoken like a true defeatist. Barnaby, I'm surprised at you. There must be something we can do.

KATE

Maybe if we talk to him … Vincente …

BARNABY

We tried that when we first arrived. The man is deranged, insane. All he wants to do is to get this Fendahl on Earth, and that won't be good for anyone living here. In any case, even if we stop him and get Catherine back, someone else could yet be the host for the creature.

KATE

I don't like the sound of that.

CAVENDISH

So what can we do?

BARNABY

The only way to stop this creature is to trap it in a place where time is folded in on itself – we've done something similar before …

KATE

What? When was this?

BARNABY

It's best you don't know. Catherine and I can make this happen, but I can only do it if she is freed. There's a … a ruined temple not far from here. When Catherine and I first arrived, we found that the lines of power were strong there, and we can tap into those to bend time … or Catherine can anyway.

We need to get her there, then I can try and

free her and trap the Fendahl forever.

KATE

What can Douglas and I do? Anything?

CAVENDISH (looking at the wine wistfully)
We could stay here and have a drink?

KATE gives CAVENDISH a dirty look.

CAVENDISH

Joking …

KATE

Well I'm not laughing.

BARNABY

If you can go to the temple and make sure
it's clear, then I'll try and bring Catherine
… Hopefully working together we can put a
stop to all this.

KATE

Right. Come on Douglas. We're off sight-
seeing.

KATE leaves the Hall followed by DOUGLAS. BARNABY
pauses a moment looking thoughtfully at the body of

IBRAHIM then leaves as well.

From the shadows steps VINCENTE, who has been listening. He is stroking the shard of bone, somewhat obsessed by it.

VINCENTE

> So they know about the Fendahl, and my history ... Interesting ... but no matter ... with the shard now in my possession, nothing can stop me. The Sodality shall be triumphant.

> And of course they have to get past the Fendahleen first ...

VINCENTE leaves the room.

ACT THREE

27. INT: CASTLE CORRIDORS

BARNABY is walking carefully along the corridors to CATHERINE's Bedchamber. He hears a sound and stops.

He listens carefully … there's a slow dragging and sucking sound coming from ahead.

BARNABY presses himself into a doorway and stands rigid as something passes by. We don't see exactly what it is, but it's HUMANOID, wearing a cloak, and moving with a slow, jerky gait.

When it has gone, BARNABY emerges from the doorway and quickly hurries up the steps towards CATHERINE's room.

28. INT: CATHERINE'S BEDCHAMBER

CATHERINE is still sitting immobile.

BARNABY enters the room behind her.

BARNABY

Catherine? Catherine? Oh please my darling.

BARNABY shakes her a little. Her head rises slightly.

BARNABY

Come on. We need to go for a walk.

BARNABY puts his arm around CATHERINE and helps her to her feet. She stumbles along with him and they leave the room.

29. INT: CASTLE CORRIDORS AND STEPS

KATE and CAVENDISH move through the Castle.

KATE

> I thought you knew how to get out of here.

CAVENDISH

> I'm sure it's just down here.

They move along the corridor and come to another set of steps.

KATE

> Brilliant. Now which way?

CAVENDISH is standing with his head cocked, listening.

CAVENDISH

> Listen.

KATE
>What?

CAVENDISH
>Something's coming.

They hide by the stairs and try and press themselves into the gloom there.

Down the steps comes one of the FENDAHLEEN CREATURES. It is humanoid and we see a pair of legs lurching jerkily down. It pauses at the bottom.

KATE peeks out of her hiding place, and her eyes open in horror.

KATE (mouthed to herself)
>Oh my God!

We see what she's seeing, a HUMAN FIGURE swathed in a cloak. Its face however is that of a monster – a protruding snout which makes the slurping noises, surrounded by a ring of waving tentacles, and in the middle, a set of sharp teeth set in a circle, a little like a fanged leech. There are no eyes, and the skin is shiny and slug-like.

KATE pushes herself back into the darkness again and closes her eyes tight. CAVENDISH holds her as the creature moves closer.

It pauses just by them, and then moves off again, the dragging and slurping sounds fading as it moves away.

KATE and CAVENDISH relax.

KATE

>What was that thing?

CAVENDISH

>I have no idea, but I don't want to meet it again. This way …

CAVENDISH leads KATE up the stairs.

30. EXT. CASTLE HALLWAY

KATE

>About time … that place is a maze.

CAVENDISH

>The ruins should be over this way … come on.

KATE and CAVENDISH leave the castle and hurry away.

31. EXT. WASTELAND

KATE and CAVENDISH make their way across scrubland towards the ruined temple.

32. EXT. TEMPLE ENTRANCE

KATE and CAVENDISH arrive at the temple entrance. They look around and enter.

33. INT. TEMPLE MAIN AREA

KATE and CAVENDISH enter the Temple, and stand looking at the ruins.

KATE

This is the place? Not much left of it.

CAVENDISH (listening)

Shhh. Can't you feel the power here?

CAVENDISH lays his hand on one of the rocks.

CAVENDISH

Even I can feel it.

CAVENDISH starts looking around the area

KATE

> Douglas?

CAVENDISH stops and looks at her.

KATE

> You ... you protected me earlier ... from Ibrahim.

CAVENDISH

> Yes ... well ...

KATE

> No, I wanted to say thanks. I ... I didn't think you would ...

CAVENDISH

> Well ... despite appearances ... I do quite like you Kate, and didn't want to see you mauled by some Turkish soldier.

CAVENDISH pulls out his flask and takes a quick nip.

KATE

> Can't say the thought appealed to me much either.

KATE wanders around looking at the Temple.

KATE (cont)

>So what are we meant to be looking for here anyway? Maybe some means of tapping the power? An altar or something?

KATE continues to look around, and realises that CAVENDISH has not replied.

KATE

>Douglas?

KATE turns to see CAVENDISH is being held around the neck by BARNABY who has a slim knife pressed to his throat. CATHERINE is standing to one side, immobile and emotionless.

KATE

>Barnaby?

KATE steps towards BARNABY

BARNABY

>Hold it there.

KATE

>What's all this? I thought you wanted our

help?

BARNABY

>I need to get Catherine back, and you'd never have agreed to the terms.

KATE

>Terms? How can you do this Barnaby?

BARNABY

>I told you. I need Catherine back. And this means sacrificing one of you to the Fendahl.

KATE

>I can't believe this.

BARNABY

>I … I'm sorry Kate. But it's the only way.

BARNABY pushes CAVENDISH to the centre of the Temple area. The flask falls from his fingers to the ground as he goes.

We hear the sounds of Fendahl power growing.

BARNABY

>Hear that … the power. It's on the rise again.

Behind BARNABY, CATHERINE starts to come slowly to life like a giant preying insect (think of the movements of the girl at the end of the Japanese version of *The Ring*, like every bone has been broken in her body).

CAVENDISH stands tense, awaiting the moment when he can act.

CATHERINE stumbles brokenly towards them. BARNABY guides her to stand by CAVENDISH.

BARNABY

> The stage is set. The players await. All I need now is the shard of power.

VINCENTE laughs loudly from the entrance and swaggers in, brandishing the shard.

VINCENTE

> Looking for something, my dear Barnaby?

BARNABY

> I knew you wouldn't be able to resist being here.

VINCENTE

> Barnaby … you have done well. Two new sacrifices for my Master.

BARNABY

I'm ready to help you summon the Fendahl.

VINCENTE

And how do you know what I want?

BARNABY

Oh, Vincente. Isn't it obvious. I'm a Sodality agent as well. You tried hard to hide it, but ultimately you can't fool one of your own.

KATE

Barnaby?

BARNABY (glares at KATE)

Be quiet.

BARNABY (to VINCENTE)

So ... is it to be the glorious apocalypse? All we needed was the ancient bone, the catalyst kindly brought by Ibrahim ...

VINCENTE (weighing BARNABY up)

You want to help me? My Master isn't one to be summoned on a whim ...

BARNABY

Oh I know ... an ancient evil, thought to

have been banished forever, but which can be manifested in times and places where we can assemble individuals ((He gestures to CATHERINE, KATE and CAVENDISH)) of the correct genetic make-up.

VINCENTE (delighted)

Oh, you do understand.

BARNABY

So let's do it. Summon the Fendahl here. Now. And then we can travel on in search of ultimate power. But ...

VINCENTE (sighs)

There's always a condition ...

BARNABY

Catherine must go free. We have others we can use now.

VINCENTE (considering)

Very well ... The shape of the vessel is irrelevant. Your friend can go free.

VINCENTE circles CAVENDISH and CATHERINE. CATHERINE is still shaking and CAVENDISH is looking very uneasy.

VINCENTE reaches out and takes CAVENDISH's hand. Using the shard he cuts him on his palm. As the blood flows, so CATHERINE comes to life, and CAVENDISH holds up his hand to ward her off.

As their palms touch, the Fendahl noises and power whine grow and grow and the camera starts to spin around CATHERINE and CAVENDISH.

Slowly CATHERINE is released from the spell, returning to human form, whereas CAVENDISH's eyes start to glow golden as his posture changes to that of the broken-boned, preying Fendahl core.

CATHERINE stumbles backwards, and BARNABY rushes to hold her.

VINCENTE laughs in delight, and steps back, admiring his handiwork. He reaches out and grabs KATE, who is watching in horror.

VINCENTE

> See, my dear. See your friend become the host for the Fendahl.

KATE

> Douglas? What have you done?

VINCENTE

> ... but my Master is hungry for the twelfth victim so he can manifest completely. Come my dear, allow the Fendahl to feed on you. It's the ultimate and noblest sacrifice.

KATE (struggling against VINCENTE)

> No!

VINCENTE starts to manhandle and push KATE across to where CAVENDISH is transforming.

CAVENDISH is flickering back and forth into a blurry half-snake, half-human creature similar to that we saw in the Castle corridor. He is hissing and swaying hypnotically.

VINCENTE

> See, the true wonder of my ... Master my ...Lord ...

VINCENTE's eyes starts to glaze over and his feet drag to a halt.

KATE (struggling)

> No. I can't ... can't move my ... feet. What's happening?

BARNABY has dragged CATHERINE away from the centre of the Temple and she is coming round. She realises where she is and smiles at BARNABY and embraces him.

CATHERINE
Barnaby? What?

BARNABY (crying with happiness)
Catherine. You're back.

CATHERINE looks around in puzzlement.

CATHERINE
But how …?

BARNABY
It was Vincente. He's a Sodality agent. A pawn from our time. The one we were sent to find.

CATHERINE
Vincente? We should have guessed.

CATHERINE struggles to her feet, her true character showing through for the first time. She is fiery and full of energy, totally in control of the situation. BARNABY is somewhat put in the shade by her.

CATHERINE

So what's happening now?

In the centre of the room, the FENDAHL/CAVENDISH has completed transforming and turns to VINCENTE and then to KATE.

VINCENTE

My Master is arising. Take the girl ...

VINCENTE tries to push KATE forward but she throws him off balance. VINCENTE pulls out the Shard and they struggle together, VINCENTE trying to cut KATE and KATE trying not to be cut.

VINCENTE thrusts the Shard at KATE, but she feints, and pushes VINCENTE off. They struggle some more and VINCENTE falls to the ground and when he rises, he has cut his own hand on the shard.

VINCENTE looks from his hand to KATE to the FENDAHL/CAVENDISH.

VINCENTE

No ... no ...

VINCENTE backs away in horror, the shard falling from his hand.

We hear the Fendahl noises grow and VINCENTE's legs start to seize up. VINCENTE makes an effort to move his legs, turns and runs off through the Temple.

The FENDAHL/CAVENDISH lurches brokenly off after him.

KATE is left standing alone in the centre of the Temple. CATHERINE and BARNABY come up to her and CATHERINE puts her hand on KATE's shoulder.

34. INT: TEMPLE CORRIDORS

VINCENTE runs in panic through the ancient temple.

The FENDAHL/CAVENDISH is close behind.

35. INT: TEMPLE MAIN AREA

BARNABY and CATHERINE walk through the main area of the Temple, assessing it as if for a house survey.

CATHERINE

> I think … no … no … yes. Yes. This spot here should be suitable.

BARNABY

>Yes … a good choice.

BARNABY picks up the Shard from where VINCENTE dropped it.

KATE (confused)

>What are you doing? Douglas … what's happened to Douglas?

BARNABY smiles as if talking to a child.

BARNABY

>Don't worry, Kate. We're going to put everything right now.

KATE

>Don't you patronise me! What have you done? I trusted you.

BARNABY

>I had to get Catherine back. Don't you understand? Without her my life was nothing … but with her we have a chance.

CATHERINE

>Barnaby …

BARNABY turns from KATE

BARNABY
> Yes?

CATHERINE
> Concentrate.

CATHERINE's eyes start to flicker with blue lightning as she and BARNABY concentrate and CATHERINE stitches together power from the air and time starts to fold in on itself.

36. INT: TEMPLE DEAD END

VINCENTE runs into a dead end and looks madly around for an exit, but there isn't one. He goes to return the way he came, but the FENDAHL/CAVENDISH is there and slowly approaches him.

VINCENTE
> No ... please no ...

FENDAHL/CAVENDISH (a whispering cadence)
> I thought you wanted to meet your Master
> ...

VINCENTE

Yes, but not like this … not like this …

The FENDAHL/CAVENDISH approaches, raising his hands, the power builds, and VINCENTE cries out and starts to age to a husk as the life is sucked out of him.

He screams.

37. INT: TEMPLE MAIN AREA

VINCENTE's scream echoes around.

CATHERINE is controlling the fold in time, through which we can see elements of the last scene playing out and repeating. Her eyes are blue fire.

KATE

What was that? That scream?

BARNABY

It's the end … We should get out of here.

KATE

What, leave? What about Douglas?

BARNABY (To KATE)
>What about him?

BARNABY (To CATHERINE)
>We should go.

KATE
>No! You can't. After all we've done ... you can't just leave Douglas here and let the Fendahl loose on Earth ...

BARNABY
>It won't happen ... it hasn't happened.

KATE
>What do you mean?

BARNABY
>It's Catherine ... she has looped Vincente's timeline back on itself. He can't ever die now.

38. REPEAT OF 34. INT: TEMPLE DEAD END

VINCENTE runs into a dead end and looks madly around for an exit, but there isn't one. He goes to return the way he came, but the FENDAHL/CAVENDISH is there and slowly approaches him.

39. INT: TEMPLE MAIN AREA

BARNABY

> He is trapped forever in the fold of time that we have created.

KATE

> But how …

CATHERINE (kindly)
> Didn't he explain?

CATHERINE looks sadly at BARNABY who shrugs.

CATHERINE moves to KATE and puts her hand gently on her shoulder again.

CATHERINE (Cont)
> Kate … I can sense the past and future of all things extending away, and I can … manipulate the snakes of time. That man, Vincente, was a Sodality agent from the future, here to carry out some scheme to use the Fendahl to gain power.

BARNABY

> When Catherine was taken from me, I knew
> I had to get her back at all costs as this was
> the only way we could stop Vincente.

KATE

> How do we get Douglas back?

BARNABY and CATHERINE look at each other.

KATE (cont)

> What? We can get him back, can't we?

CATHERINE

> There is a way ... but I need a focus for the
> energy ... something like a flame that I can
> use to momentarily break the time loop ...

BARNABY

> ... but there's nothing here to burn.

KATE is distraught and looks all around her.

KATE

> There must be something ...

KATE chances upon CAVENDISH's flask, which is sitting
on the ground where he dropped it.

KATE picks it up and shakes it.

KATE

What about this?

KATE unstoppers it and sniffs the contents.

KATE

It's whisky … perfect burning material.

BARNABY

Let me see.

KATE hands BARNABY the flask. BARNABY sniffs the contents as well.

BARNABY

It might just work.

BARNABY clears a space on one of the rocks and pours the liquid into a hollow there. He then holds his hand over it and closes his eyes, concentrating.

He mutters a phrase of psionic power

BARNABY

Eco eco elohim.

There is a hum of power and the liquid ignites into pure blue flame.

BARNABY (cont)
>Excellent.

>Now, Catherine, concentrate and extract …

CATHERINE stares into the flame and her eyes start to crackle with blue lightning once more.

CATHERINE (as though she is searching for the moment)
>We just have to find the right moment to separate the human from the Fendahl core …

40. REPEAT OF 36. INT: TEMPLE DEAD END

VINCENTE runs into a dead end and looks madly around for an exit, but there isn't one. He goes to return the way he came, but the FENDAHL/CAVENDISH is there and slowly approaches him.

41. INT: TEMPLE MAIN AREA

CATHERINE concentrates, while KATE looks on helplessly.

42. REPEAT OF 36. INT: TEMPLE DEAD END

VINCENTE
> No ... please no ...

FENDAHL/CAVENDISH
> I thought you wanted to meet your Master
> ...

VINCENTE
> Yes, but not like this ... not like this ...

The FENDAHL/CAVENDISH approaches, raising his hands, the power builds, and VINCENTE cries out and starts to age to a husk as the life is sucked out of him.

He screams.

43. INT: TEMPLE DEAD END

As VINCENTE screams, so time shudders and stops.

There is a rippling in the air and CAVENDISH separates and walks out from the Fendahleen image.

CAVENDISH walks away down the corridor from the frozen moment of VINCENTE's death at the hands of the Fendahleen.

44. INT: TEMPLE MAIN AREA

CATHERINE
> And restart …

CATHERINE's eyes flicker with fire as she concentrates.

45. REPEAT OF 36. INT: TEMPLE DEAD END

VINCENTE runs into a dead end and looks madly around for an exit, but there isn't one. He goes to return the way he came, but the FENDAHLEEN is there and slowly approaches him.

46. INT: TEMPLE MAIN AREA

CATHERINE's eyes return to normal and the blue fire burning on the whisky dies as the liquid is exhausted.

KATE is looking worriedly from BARNABY to CATHERINE.

KATE

>Did it work?

CAVENDISH enters the Temple behind her.

CAVENDISH

>It worked.

KATE

>Douglas!

She runs to CAVENDISH and hugs him.

KATE

>You're back.

KATE (to CATHERINE)
>Thank you.

CATHERINE (Smiles)
>A pleasure.

BARNABY

>I think that was quite successful all told.

CATHERINE

>Yes. The Fendahl manifestation and Vincente are now locked in their time loop – Vincente got what he wanted, to meet his Master, and the Fendahl has what it wanted – an endless supply of terror and the twelfth victim – Vincente.

47. REPEAT OF 36. INT: TEMPLE DEAD END

VINCENTE cries out and starts to age to a husk as the life is sucked out of him.

48. INT: TEMPLE MAIN AREA

CAVENDISH

>I can't say I enjoyed that much – like being a passenger in my own body.

CAVENDISH picks up the flask from the stone and regards it.

CAVENDISH

>A little too close for comfort I think.

CAVENDISH upends the flask and lets the remaining

liquid fall to the ground.

CAVENDISH (Cont)
> I'll try and stay off this from now on.

(TURNS TO KATE)

> If you'll help me.

KATE (holds his hand)
> You know I will …

CATHERINE
> So … farewell for now Kate and Douglas.

BARNABY
> Thanks for your help, and I'm so sorry I had
> to trick you like that.

KATE looks daggers at BARNABY.

KATE
> Just don't do it again … or at least give me
> some warning next time.

BARNABY
> I had to convince Vincente that I was on his
> side …

444

BARNABY hugs KATE. He shakes CAVENDISH by the hand.

BARNABY

> Look after her.

CATHERINE gestures behind them and a rippling portal appears, the same effect as the one KATE and CAVENDISH arrived in.

CATHERINE

> Your portal awaits …

KATE and CAVENDISH step towards it, but KATE stops and looks back.

KATE

> So where does this one go? Where are we going to end up this time?

CATHERINE

> Back in your own time … I hope …

CAVENDISH

> You hope?

CATHERINE smiles.

CATHERINE

    Don't worry.

CATHERINE kisses CAVENDISH on the cheek and he blushes and rubs the spot gently.

KATE

    Come on you.

KATE takes CAVENDISH's arm and pulls him through the portal. They vanish, and the portal shimmers away leaving nothing behind.

BARNABY and CATHERINE hold hands and look into each other's eyes.

BARNABY

    Where to now, my darling?

CATHERINE

    Anywhere you want to go.

BARNABY

    To the future …

CATHERINE

    … or the past?

BARNABY and CATHERINE (together)
>The future.

There is a crackle of blue lightning and they are no longer there. The Temple is deserted.

49. INT: COLLAGE OF TEMPLE CORRIDORS

The camera prowls the corridors. We hear echoes of the earlier voices and dialogue. As we find the dead end area, we see for a final time …

50. REPEAT OF 36. INT: TEMPLE DEAD END

VINCENTE cries out and starts to age to a husk as the life is sucked out of him.

END

CREDITS

Special thanks to George Mann and Jon de Burgh Miller
Based on the TIME HUNTER series of books published by Telos Publishing Ltd

About the Author

David J Howe has been involved with *Doctor Who* research and writing for over 30 years. He has been consultant to a large number of publishers and manufacturers for their *Doctor Who* lines, and is author or co-author of over 30 factual titles associated with the show. He also has one of the largest collections of *Doctor Who* merchandise in the world. David was contributing editor to *Starburst* magazine for 17 years from 1984-2001. From 1994 he was book reviews editor for Shivers magazine until it ceased publication in 2008. In addition he has written articles, interviews and reviews for a wide number of publications, including *Fear, Dreamwatch, Infinity, Stage and Television Today, The Dark Side, Doctor Who Magazine,* the *Guardian, Film Review, SFX, Sci-Fi Entertainment, Collectors' Gazette, Deathray* and the *Oxford Dictionary of National Biography*.

He edited the bi-monthly newsletter of the British Fantasy Society from 1992 to 1995, and also edited and published several books for them, including the British and World Fantasy Award shortlisted *Manitou Man*, a limited edition hardback and paperback collection of short fiction by horror author Graham Masterton. He is currently Chair of the BFS, and edited their fortieth anniversary anthology, *Full Fathom Forty*, published in September 2011.

He wrote the book *Reflections: The Fantasy Art of*

About the Author

Stephen Bradbury for Dragon's World Publishers and has contributed short fiction to *Peeping Tom, Dark Asylum, Decalog, Dark Horizons, Kimota, Perfect Timing, Perfect Timing II, Missing Pieces, Shrouded by Darkness* and *Murky Depths*, and factual articles to *James Herbert: By Horror Haunted* and *The Radio Times Guide to Science Fiction*. He wrote the screenplay for *Daemos Rising*, a film released on DVD by Reeltime Pictures in 2004.

He is currently Editorial Director of Telos Publishing Ltd, a UK based independent press specialising in horror/science fiction novellas, crime novels, and guides to a variety of film and TV shows. In 2006 the company won the World Fantasy Award for their publishing work, and in 2010 celebrated their tenth anniversary while also receiving the British Fantasy Award for Best Small Press. He writes about *Doctor Who* merchandise for *Doctor Who Insider* magazine, and contributes liner notes for AudioGO's range of *Doctor Who* novelisation CDs.

Copyright Details

Copyright Details

Other Telos Titles Available

TIME HUNTER
A range of high-quality, original paperback and limited edition hardback novellas featuring the adventures in time of Honoré Lechasseur. Part mystery, part detective story, part dark fantasy, part science fiction ... these books are guaranteed to enthral fans of good fiction everywhere, and are in the spirit of our acclaimed range of *Doctor Who* Novellas.

THE WINNING SIDE by LANCE PARKIN

Emily is dead! Killed by an unknown assailant. Honoré and Emily find themselves caught up in a plot reaching from the future to their past, and with their very existence, not to mention the future of the entire world, at stake, can they unravel the mystery before it is too late?

An adventure in time and space.

£7.99 (+ £2.50 UK p&p) Standard p/b ISBN: 1-903889-35-9

THE TUNNEL AT THE END OF THE LIGHT by STEFAN PETRUCHA

In the heart of post-war London, a bomb is discovered lodged at a disused station between Green Park and Hyde Park Corner. The bomb detonates, and as the dust clears, it becomes apparent that *something* has been awakened. Strange half-human creatures attack the workers at the site, hungrily searching for anything containing sugar ... Meanwhile, Honoré and Emily are contacted by eccentric poet Randolph Crest, who believes himself to be the target of these subterranean creatures. The ensuing investigation brings Honoré and Emily up against a terrifying force from deep beneath the earth, and one which even with their combined powers, they may have trouble stopping.

An adventure in time and space.

£7.99 (+ £2.50 UK p&p) Standard p/b ISBN: 1-903889-37-5
£25.00 (+ £2.50 UK p&p) Deluxe signed and numbered h/b ISBN: 1-903889-38-3

THE CLOCKWORK WOMAN by CLAIRE BOTT

Honoré and Emily find themselves imprisoned in the 19th Century by a celebrated inventor ... but help comes from an unexpected source – a humanoid automaton created to give pleasure to its owner. As the trio escape to London, they are unprepared for what awaits them, and at every turn it seems impossible to avert what fate may have in store for the Clockwork Woman.

An adventure in time and space.
£7.99 (+ £2.50 UK p&p) Standard p/b ISBN: 1-903889-39-1
£25.00 (+ £2.50 UK p&p) Deluxe signed and numbered h/b ISBN:
1-903889-40-5

KITSUNE by JOHN PAUL CATTON
In the year 2020, Honoré and Emily find themselves thrown into
a mystery, as an ice spirit – *Yuki-Onna* – wreaks havoc during the
Kyoto Festival, and a haunted funhouse proves to contain more
than just paper lanterns and wax dummies. But what does all this
have to do with the elegant owner of the Hide and Chic fashion
chain … and the legendary Chinese fox-spirits, the Kitsune?
An adventure in time and space.
£7.99 (+ £2.50 UK p&p) Standard p/b ISBN: 1-903889-41-3
£25.00 (+ £2.50 UK p&p) Deluxe signed and numbered h/b ISBN:
1-903889-42-1

THE SEVERED MAN by GEORGE MANN
What links a clutch of sinister murders in Victorian London, an
angel appearing in a Staffordshire village in the 1920s and a small
boy running loose around the capital in 1950? When Honoré and
Emily encounter a man who appears to have been cut out of time,
they think they have the answer. But soon enough they discover
that the mystery is only just beginning and that nightmares can
turn into reality.
An adventure in time and space.
£7.99 (+ £2.50 UK p&p) Standard p/b ISBN: 1-903889-43-X
£25.00 (+ £2.50 UK p&p) Deluxe signed and numbered h/b ISBN:
1-903889-44-8

ECHOES by IAIN MCLAUGHLIN & CLAIRE BARTLETT
Echoes of the past … echoes of the future. Honoré Lechasseur can
see the threads that bind the two together, however when he and
Emily Blandish find themselves outside the imposing tower-block
headquarters of Dragon Industry, both can sense something is
wrong. There are ghosts in the building, and images and echoes
of all times pervade the structure. But what is behind this massive
contradiction in time, and can Honoré and Emily figure it out
before they become trapped themselves … ?
An adventure in time and space.
£7.99 (+ £2.50 UK p&p) Standard p/b ISBN: 1-903889-45-6
£25.00 (+ £2.50 UK p&p) Deluxe signed and numbered h/b ISBN:
1-903889-46-4

PECULIAR LIVES by PHILIP PURSER-HALLARD

Once a celebrated author of 'scientific romances', Erik Clevedon is an old man now. But his fiction conceals a dangerous truth, as Honoré Lechasseur and Emily Blandish discover after a chance encounter with a strangely gifted young pickpocket. Born between the Wars, the superhuman children known as 'the Peculiar' are reaching adulthood – and they believe that humanity is making a poor job of looking after the world they plan to inherit …

An adventure in time and space.

£7.99 (+ £2.50 UK p&p) Standard p/b ISBN: 1-903889-47-2
£25.00 (+ £2.50 UK p&p) Deluxe signed and numbered h/b ISBN: 1-903889-48-0

DEUS LE VOLT by JON DE BURGH MILLER

'Deus Le Volt!'…'God Wills It!' The cry of the first Crusade in 1098, despatched by Pope Urban to free Jerusalem from the Turks. Honoré and Emily are plunged into the middle of the conflict on the trail of what appears to be a time travelling knight. As the siege of Antioch draws to a close, so death haunts the blood-soaked streets … and the Fendahl – a creature that feeds on life itself – is summoned. Honoré and Emily find themselves facing angels and demons in a battle to survive their latest adventure.

An adventure in time and space.

£7.99 (+ £2.50 UK p&p) Standard p/b ISBN: 1-903889-49-9
£25.00 (+ £2.50 UK p&p) Deluxe signed and numbered h/b ISBN: 1-903889-97-9

THE ALBINO'S DANCER by DALE SMITH

'Goodbye, little Emily.'

April 1938, and a shadowy figure attends an impromptu burial in Shoreditch, London. His name is Honoré Lechasseur. After a chance encounter with the mysterious Catherine Howkins, he's had advance warning that his friend Emily Blandish was going to die. But is forewarned necessarily forearmed? And just how far is he willing to go to save Emily's life?

Because Honoré isn't the only person taking an interest in Emily Blandish – she's come to the attention of the Albino, one of the new breed of gangsters surfacing in post-rationing London. And the only life he cares about is his own.

An adventure in time and space.

£7.99 (+ £2.50 UK p&p) Standard p/b ISBN: 1-84583-100-4
£25.00 (+ £2.50 UK p&p) Deluxe signed and numbered h/b ISBN: 1-84583-101-2

THE SIDEWAYS DOOR by R J CARTER & TROY RISER

Honoré and Emily find themselves in a parallel timestream where their alternate selves think nothing of changing history to improve the quality of life – especially their own. Honoré has been recently haunted by the death of his mother, an event which happened in his childhood, but now there seems to be a way to reverse that event … but at what cost?

When faced with two of the most dangerous people they have ever encountered, Honoré and Emily must make some decisions with far-reaching consequences.

An adventure in time and space.

£25.00 (+ £2.50 UK p&p) Deluxe signed and numbered h/b ISBN: 1-84583-103-9

CHILD OF TIME by GEORGE MANN

When Honoré and Emily investigate the bones of a child in the ruins of a collapsed house, they are thrown into a thrilling adventure that takes them from London in 1951 to Venice in 1586 and then forward a thousand years, to the terrifying, devasted London of 2586, ruled over by the sinister Sodality. What is the terrible truth about Emily's forgotten past? What demonic power are the Sodality plotting to reawaken? And who is the mysterious Dr Smith?

All is revealed in the stunning conclusion to the acclaimed *Time Hunter* series.

An adventure in time and space.

£9.99 (+ £2.50 UK p&p) Standard p/b ISBN: 978-1-84583-104-2
£25.00 (+ £2.50 UK p&p) Deluxe signed and numbered h/b ISBN: 978-1-84583-105-9

TIME HUNTER FILM

DAEMOS RISING by DAVID J HOWE, DIRECTED BY KEITH BARNFATHER

Daemos Rising is a sequel to both the *Doctor Who* adventure *The Daemons* and to *Downtime*, an earlier drama featuring the Yeti. It is also a prequel of sorts to Telos Publishing's *Time Hunter* series. It stars Miles Richardson as ex-UNIT operative Douglas Cavendish, and Beverley Cressman as Brigadier Lethbridge-Stewart's daughter Kate. Trapped in an isolated cottage, Cavendish thinks he is seeing ghosts. The only person who might understand and help is Kate Lethbridge-Stewart … but when she arrives, she realises that Cavendish is key in a plot to summon the Daemons back to the Earth. With time running out, Kate discovers that sometimes even

the familiar can turn out to be your worst nightmare. Also starring
Andrew Wisher, and featuring Ian Richardson as the Narrator.
An adventure in time and space.
£14.00 (+ £3.00 UK p&p) PAL format Region-free DVD
**Order direct from Reeltime Pictures, PO Box 23435, London
SE26 5WU**

HORROR/FANTASY

URBAN GOTHIC: LACUNA AND OTHER TRIPS edited by
DAVID J HOWE
Tales of horror from and inspired by the *Urban Gothic* televison
series. Contributors: Graham Masterton, Christopher Fowler,
Simon Clark, Steve Lockley & Paul Lewis, Paul Finch and Debbie
Bennett.
£9.99 (+ £2.50 UK p&p) Standard p/b ISBN: 1-903889-00-6

KING OF ALL THE DEAD by STEVE LOCKLEY & PAUL LEWIS
The king of all the dead will have what is his.
£8.00 (+ £2.50 UK p&p) Standard p/b ISBN: 1-903889-61-8

THE HUMAN ABSTRACT by GEORGE MANN
A future tale of private detectives, AIs, Nanobots, love and death.
£7.99 (+ £2.50 UK p&p) Standard p/b ISBN: 1-903889-65-0

BREATHE by CHRISTOPHER FOWLER
The Office meets *Night of the Living Dead.*
£25.00 (+ £2.50 UK p&p) Deluxe signed and numbered h/b ISBN:
1-903889-68-5

HOUDINI'S LAST ILLUSION by STEVE SAVILE
Can the master illusionist Harry Houdini outwit the dead shades of
his past?
£7.99 (+ £2.50 UK p&p) Standard p/b ISBN: 1-903889-66-9

ALICE'S JOURNEY BEYOND THE MOON by R J CARTER
A sequel to the classic Lewis Carroll tales.
£6.99 (+ £2.50 UK p&p) Standard p/b ISBN: 1-903889-76-6
£30.00 (+ £2.50 UK p&p) Deluxe signed and numbered h/b ISBN:
1-903889-77-4

APPROACHING OMEGA by ERIC BROWN
A colonisation mission to Earth runs into problems.
£7.99 (+ £2.50 UK p&p) Standard p/b ISBN: 1-903889-98-7
£30.00 (+ £2.50 UK p&p) Deluxe signed and numbered h/b ISBN:
1-903889-99-5

VALLEY OF LIGHTS by STEPHEN GALLAGHER
A cop comes up against a body-hopping murderer.
£9.99 (+ £3.00 UK p&p) Standard p/b ISBN: 1-903889-74-X
£30.00 (+ £3.00 UK p&p) Deluxe signed and numbered h/b ISBN:
1-903889-75-8

PRETTY YOUNG THINGS by DOMINIC MCDONAGH
A nest of lesbian rave bunny vampires is at large in Manchester.
When Chelsey's ex-boyfriend is taken as food, Chelsey has to get
out fast.
£7.99 (+ £2.50 UK p&p) Standard p/b ISBN: 1-84583-045-8

A MANHATTAN GHOST STORY by T M WRIGHT
Do you see ghosts? A classic tale of love and the supernatural.
£9.99 (+ £3.00 UK p&p) Standard p/b ISBN: 1-84583-048-2

SHROUDED BY DARKNESS: TALES OF TERROR edited by
ALISON L R DAVIES
An anthology of tales guaranteed to bring a chill to the spine. This
collection has been published to raise money for DebRA, a national
charity working on behalf of people with the genetic skin blistering
condition, Epidermolysis Bullosa (EB). Featuring stories by: Debbie
Bennett, Poppy Z Brite, Simon Clark, Storm Constantine, Peter
Crowther, Alison L R Davies, Paul Finch, Christopher Fowler,
Neil Gaiman, Gary Greenwood, David J Howe, Dawn Knox, Tim
Lebbon, Charles de Lint, Steven Lockley & Paul Lewis, James
Lovegrove, Graham Masterton, Richard Christian Matheson,
Justina Robson, Mark Samuels, Darren Shan and Michael Marshall
Smith. With a frontispiece by Clive Barker and a foreword by
Stephen Jones. Deluxe hardback cover by Simon Marsden.
£12.99 (+ £3.00 UK p&p) Standard p/b ISBN: 1-84583-046-6
£50.00 (+ £3.00 UK p&p) Deluxe signed and numbered h/b ISBN:
978-1-84583-047-2

BLACK TIDE by DEL STONE JR
A college professor and his students find themselves trapped by an
encroaching horde of zombies following a waste spillage.
£7.99 (+ £2.50 UK p&p) Standard p/b ISBN: 978-1-84583-049-6

FORCE MAJEURE by DANIEL O'MAHONY
An incredible fantasy novel. Kay finds herself trapped in a strange
city in the Andes ... a place where dreams can become reality, and
where dragons may reside.
£7.99 (+ £2.50 UK p&p) Standard p/b ISBN: 978-1-84583-050-2

HUMPTY'S BONES by SIMON CLARK
Something nasty is found in a village garden by an amateur
archaeologist, something which has lain buried for centuries.
£9.99 (+ £2.50 UK p&p) Standard p/b ISBN: 978-1-84583-051-9

THE DJINN by GRAHAM MASTERTON
Graham Masterton's terrifying 1977 novel is republished by Telos
in a brand new edition, complete with an exclusive introduction by
the author.
£9.99 (+ £2.50 UK p&p) Standard p/b ISBN: 978-1-84583-052-6

RULES OF DUEL by GRAHAM MASTERTON and WILLIAM S
BURROUGHS
A clever and pervasive novel, which turns literature on its head,
and makes the reader work to be part of the evolving plot.
Complete with original introduction by Burroughs, written before
his death in 1997, **Rules of Duel** is a previously unpublished
masterpiece from two of the greatest writers of their generations.
£9.99 (+ £2.50 UK p&p) Standard p/b ISBN: 978-1-84583-054-0

ZOMBIES IN NEW YORK AND OTHER BLOODY JOTTINGS
by SAM STONE
Thirteen stories of horror and passion, and six mythological and
erotic poems from the pen of the new Queen of Vampire fiction.
£12.99 (+ £2.50 UK p&p) Standard p/b ISBN: 978-1-84583-055-7

ART BOOK

ALTERED VISIONS by VINCENT CHONG
Vincent Chong burst onto the horror and fantasy scene several
years ago with a sequence of incredible artworks. Since then he has
gone on to provide cover artwork for authors such as Stephen King,

and has worked with publishers all around the world, as well as providing illustration for record covers and websites. Now some of his incredible artwork is collected in *Altered Visions*.
£30.00 (+ £2.50 UK p&p) Signed Limited Edition Hardback ISBN: 978-1-84583-053-3

TV/FILM GUIDES

DOCTOR WHO

THE HANDBOOK: THE UNOFFICIAL AND UNAUTHORISED GUIDE TO THE PRODUCTION OF DOCTOR WHO by DAVID J HOWE, STEPHEN JAMES WALKER and MARK STAMMERS
Complete guide to the making of *Doctor Who* (1963 – 1996).
£14.99 (+ £5.00 UK p&p) Standard p/b ISBN: 1-903889-59-6
£30.00 (+ £5.00 UK p&p) Deluxe signed and numbered h/b ISBN: 1-903889-96-0

BACK TO THE VORTEX: THE UNOFFICIAL AND UNAUTHORISED GUIDE TO DOCTOR WHO 2005 by J SHAUN LYON
Complete guide to the 2005 series of *Doctor Who* starring Christopher Eccleston as the Doctor
£12.99 (+ £3.00 UK p&p) Standard p/b ISBN: 1-903889-78-2
£30.00 (+ £3.00 UK p&p) Deluxe signed and numbered h/b ISBN: 1-903889-79-0

SECOND FLIGHT: THE UNOFFICIAL AND UNAUTHORISED GUIDE TO DOCTOR WHO 2006 by J SHAUN LYON
Complete guide to the 2006 series of *Doctor Who*, starring David Tennant as the Doctor
£12.99 (+ £3.00 UK p&p) Standard p/b ISBN: 1-84583-008-3
£30.00 (+ £3.00 UK p&p) Deluxe signed and numbered h/b ISBN: 1-84583-009-1

THIRD DIMENSION: THE UNOFFICIAL AND UNAUTHORISED GUIDE TO DOCTOR WHO 2007 by STEPHEN JAMES WALKER
Complete guide to the 2007 series of *Doctor Who*, starring David Tennant as the Doctor
£12.99 (+ £3.00 UK p&p) Standard p/b ISBN: 978-1-84583-016-8
£30.00 (+ £3.00 UK p&p) Deluxe signed and numbered h/b ISBN: 978-1-84583-017-5

MONSTERS WITHIN: THE UNOFFICIAL AND
UNAUTHORISED GUIDE TO DOCTOR WHO 2008 by
STEPHEN JAMES WALKER
Complete guide to the 2008 series of *Doctor Who*, starring David
Tennant as the Doctor.
£12.99 (+ £3.00 UK p&p) Standard p/b ISBN: 978-1-84583-027-4

END OF TEN: THE UNOFFICIAL AND UNAUTHORISED
GUIDE TO DOCTOR WHO 2009 by STEPHEN JAMES WALKER
Complete guide to the 2009 specials of *Doctor Who*, starring David
Tennant as the Doctor.
£14.99 (+ £3.00 UK p&p) Standard p/b ISBN: 978-1-84583-035-9
£30.00 (+ £3.00 UK p&p) Signed h/b ISBN: 978-1-84583-036-6

WHOGRAPHS: THEMED AUTOGRAPH BOOK
80 page autograph book with an SF theme
£4.50 (+ £2.50 UK p&p) Standard p/b ISBN: 1-84583-110-1

TALKBACK: THE UNOFFICIAL AND UNAUTHORISED
DOCTOR WHO INTERVIEW BOOK: VOLUME 1: THE SIXTIES
edited by STEPHEN JAMES WALKER
Interviews with cast and behind the scenes crew who worked on
Doctor Who in the sixties
£12.99 (+ £3.00 UK p&p) Standard p/b ISBN: 1-84583-006-7
£30.00 (+ £3.00 UK p&p) Deluxe signed and numbered h/b ISBN:
1-84583-007-5

TALKBACK: THE UNOFFICIAL AND UNAUTHORISED
DOCTOR WHO INTERVIEW BOOK: VOLUME 2: THE
SEVENTIES edited by STEPHEN JAMES WALKER
Interviews with cast and behind the scenes crew who worked on
Doctor Who in the seventies
£12.99 (+ £3.00 UK p&p) Standard p/b ISBN: 1-84583-010-5
£30.00 (+ £3.00 UK p&p) Deluxe signed and numbered h/b ISBN:
1-84583-011-3

TALKBACK: THE UNOFFICIAL AND UNAUTHORISED
DOCTOR WHO INTERVIEW BOOK: VOLUME 3: THE
EIGHTIES edited by STEPHEN JAMES WALKER
Interviews with cast and behind the scenes crew who worked on
Doctor Who in the eighties
£12.99 (+ £3.00 UK p&p) Standard p/b ISBN: 978-1-84583-014-4
£30.00 (+ £3.00 UK p&p) Deluxe signed and numbered h/b ISBN:
978-1-84583-015-1

HOWE'S TRANSCENDENTAL TOYBOX: SECOND EDITION by
DAVID J HOWE & ARNOLD T BLUMBERG
Complete guide to *Doctor Who* Merchandise 1963–2002.
£25.00 (+ £5.00 UK p&p) Standard p/b ISBN: 1-903889-56-1

HOWE'S TRANSCENDENTAL TOYBOX: UPDATE No 1: 2003
by DAVID J HOWE & ARNOLD T BLUMBERG
Complete guide to *Doctor Who* Merchandise released in 2003.
£7.99 (+ £2.50 UK p&p) Standard p/b ISBN: 1-903889-57-X
HOWE'S TRANSCENDENTAL TOYBOX: UPDATE No 2: 2004-
2005 by DAVID J HOWE & ARNOLD T BLUMBERG
Complete guide to *Doctor Who* Merchandise released in 2004 and
2005. Now in full colour.
£12.99 (+ £2.50 UK p&p) Standard p/b ISBN: 1-84583-012-1

THE TARGET BOOK by DAVID J HOWE with TIM NEAL
A fully illustrated, large format, full colour history of the Target
Doctor Who books.
£19.99 (+ £5.00 UK p&p) Large Format p/b ISBN: 978-1-84583-
021-2

WIPED! DOCTOR WHO'S MISSING EPISODES by RICHARD
MOLESWORTH
The story behind the BBC's missing episodes of *Doctor Who*.
£15.99 (+ £3.00 UK p&p) Standard p/b ISBN: 978-1-84583-037-3

TIMELINK: THE UNOFFICIAL AND UNAUTHORISED GUIDE
TO THE CONTINUITY OF DOCTOR WHO VOLUME 1 by JON
PREDDLE
Discussion and articles about the continuity of *Doctor Who*.
£15.99 (+ £3.00 UK p&p) Standard p/b ISBN: 978-1-84583-004-5

TIMELINK: THE UNOFFICIAL AND UNAUTHORISED GUIDE
TO THE CONTINUITY OF DOCTOR WHO VOLUME 2 by JON
PREDDLE
Timeline of the continuity of *Doctor Who*.
£15.99 (+ £3.00 UK p&p) Standard p/b ISBN: 978-1-84583-005-2

TORCHWOOD

INSIDE THE HUB: THE UNOFFICIAL AND UNAUTHORISED
GUIDE TO TORCHWOOD SERIES ONE by STEPHEN JAMES
WALKER
Complete guide to the 2006 series of *Torchwood*, starring John
Barrowman as Captain Jack Harkness
£12.99 (+ £3.00 UK p&p) Standard p/b ISBN: 978-1-84583-013-7

SOMETHING IN THE DARKNESS: THE UNOFFICIAL AND
UNAUTHORISED GUIDE TO TORCHWOOD SERIES TWO by
STEPHEN JAMES WALKER
Complete guide to the 2008 series of *Torchwood*, starring John
Barrowman as Captain Jack Harkness
£12.99 (+ £3.00 UK p&p) Standard p/b ISBN: 978-1-84583-024-3
£30.00 (+ £3.00 UK p&p) Deluxe signed and numbered h/b ISBN:
978-1-84583-025-0

SURVIVORS

THE END OF THE WORLD?: THE UNOFFICIAL AND
UNAUTHORISED GUIDE TO SURVIVORS by ANDY
PRIESTNER & RICH CROSS
Complete guide to Terry Nation's *Survivors*
£12.99 (+ £3.00 UK p&p) Standard p/b ISBN: 1-84583-001-6

24

A DAY IN THE LIFE: THE UNOFFICIAL AND
UNAUTHORISED GUIDE TO 24 by KEITH TOPPING
Complete episode guide to the first season of the popular TV show.
£9.99 (+ £3.00 p&p) Standard p/b ISBN: 1-903889-53-7

TILL DEATH US DO PART

A FAMILY AT WAR: THE UNOFFICIAL AND UNAUTHORISED
GUIDE TO TILL DEATH US DO PART by MARK WARD
Complete guide to the popular TV show. PUBLISHED
SEPTEMBER 2008
£12.99 (+ £3.00 p&p) Standard p/b ISBN: 978-1-84583-031-1

SPACE:1999

DESTINATION: MOONBASE ALPHA: THE UNOFFICIAL AND UNAUTHORISED GUIDE TO SPACE:1999 by ROBERT E WOOD
Complete guide to the popular TV show.
£15.99 (+ £3.00 p&p) Standard p/b ISBN: 978-1-84583-034-2

SAPPHIRE AND STEEL

ASSIGNED: THE UNOFFICIAL AND UNAUTHORISED GUIDE TO SAPPHIRE AND STEEL by RICHARD CALLAGHAN
Complete guide to the popular TV show.
£12.99 (+ £2.50 p&p) Standard p/b ISBN: 978-1-84583-032-8

THUNDERCATS

HEAR THE ROAR: THE UNOFFICIAL AND UNAUTHORISED GUIDE TO THE HIT 1980S SERIES THUNDERCATS by DAVID CRICHTON
Complete guide to the popular TV show.
£16.99 (+ £3.00 p&p) Standard p/b ISBN: 978-1-84583-038-0

FILMS

BEAUTIFUL MONSTERS: THE UNOFFICIAL AND UNAUTHORISED GUIDE TO THE ALIEN AND PREDATOR FILMS by DAVID McINTEE
A guide to the Alien and Predator Films.
£9.99 (+ £3.00 UK p&p) Standard p/b ISBN: 1-903889-94-4

ZOMBIEMANIA: 80 MOVIES TO DIE FOR by DR ARNOLD T BLUMBERG & ANDREW HERSHBERGER
A guide to 80 classic zombie films, along with an extensive filmography of over 500 additional titles
£17.99 (+ £5.00 UK p&p) Standard p/b ISBN: 1-84583-003-2

SILVER SCREAM: VOLUME 1: 40 CLASSIC HORROR MOVIES by STEVEN WARREN HILL
A guide to 40 classic horror films from 1920 to 1941.
£12.99 (+ £3.00 UK p&p) Standard p/b ISBN: 978-1-84583-026-7

SILVER SCREAM: VOLUME 2: 40 CLASSIC HORROR MOVIES
by STEVEN WARREN HILL
A guide to 40 classic horror films from 1941 to 1951. PUBLISHED
2009.
£14.99 (+ £3.00 UK p&p) Standard p/b ISBN: 978-1-84583-029-8

TABOO BREAKERS: 18 INDEPENDENT FILMS THAT
COURTED CONTROVERSY AND CREATED A LEGEND by
CALUM WADDELL
A guide to 18 films which pushed boundries and broke taboos.
£12.99 (+ £3.00 UK p&p) Standard p/b ISBN: 978-1-84583-030-4

IT LIVES AGAIN! HORROR MOVIES IN THE NEW
MILLENNIUM by AXELLE CAROLYN
A guide to modern horror films. Large format, full colour
throughout.
£16.99 (+ £5.00 UK p&p) h/b ISBN: 978-1-84583-020-5

*The prices shown are correct at time of going to press. However, the
publishers reserve the right to increase prices from those previously
advertised without prior notice.*

TELOS PUBLISHING
c/o Beech House, Chapel Lane, Moulton, Cheshire, CW9 8PQ,
England
Email: orders@telos.co.uk
Web: www.telos.co.uk

To order copies of any Telos books, please visit our website where
there are full details of all titles and facilities for worldwide credit
card online ordering, as well as occasional special offers, or send
a cheque or postal order (UK only) for the appropriate amount
(including postage and packing – note that four or more titles
are post free in the UK), together with details of the book(s) you
require, plus your name and address to the above address. Overseas
readers please send two international reply coupons for details of
prices and postage rates.